kaleidoscope

I0565591

YEAR'S BEST

BEST

YA SPECULATIVE FICTION 2015

EDITED BY
JULIA RIOS &
ALISA KRASNOSTEIN

First published in Australia in August 2016
by Kaleidoscope

www.twelfthplanetpress.com

Typeset in Sabon MT Pro

National Library of Australia Cataloguing-in-Publication entry

Title:	Year's best young adult speculative fiction 2015 edited by Julia Rios, Alisa Krasnostein.
ISBN:	9781922101501 (paperback)
Target Audience:	For young adults.
Subjects:	Speculative fiction.
	Short stories—21st century.
	Anthologies.
Other Creators/Contributors:	
	Rios, Julia, editor.
	Krasnostein, Alisa, editor.
Dewey Number:	A823.408

Table of Contents

Summation: YA in 2015

2015 was yet another very strong year for YA.

At the cinema, dystopian series movies continued with the adaptations of *The Hunger Games: Mockingjay Part 2*, *Maze Runner: The Scorch Trials*, and *Insurgent*, among others. 2015 also saw the first of Disney's live action princess films, *Cinderella*. On television, *The Vampire Diaries* went into its seventh season and the spinoff series, *The Originals*, went into its third, while *Pretty Little Liars* went into its sixth. *The Hunger Games: Mockingjay Part 1*, *The Vampire Diaries*, and *Pretty Little Liars* all won Teen Choice Awards.

In books, dystopian YA continued to be a strong subgenre in 2015, but seemed to be slowing down a little bit. Popular titles included *An Ember in the Ashes* by Sabaa Tahir, *Archivist Wasp* by Nicole Kornher-Stace, and *The Wrath and the Dawn* by Renée Adieh. The trend of royalty continued to grow with *Queen of Shadows* by Sarah J. Maas winning the Goodreads

Choice Award for YA science fiction and fantasy (a popular vote award by members of the Goodreads community). The finalist selection as a whole feature royalty, epic fantasy and supernatural creatures like fairies, dragons, and angels. Royal titles included *The Heir* by Keira Cass (The Selection, Book 2), *Red Queen* by Victoria Aveyard (Red Queen, Book One), *Winter* by Marissa Meyer (The Lunar Chronicles, Book Four) and *The Winner's Crime* by Marie Rutkoski (The Winner's Trilogy, Book 2). Meanwhile, some of the fairy, dragon, and angel finalists were *A Court of Thorns and Roses* by Sarah J. Maas (A Court of Thorns and Roses, Book One), *Uprooted* by Naomi Novik, *The Darkest Part of the Forest* by Holly Black, and *End of Days* by Susan Ee (Penryn and the End of Days, Book 2).

Series remained popular, both just beginning and several volumes in. In addition to all the series books mentioned above, Sean Williams released *Fall* (Book 3 in the Twinmaker Series), Scott Westerfeld, Deborah Biancotti, and Margo Lanagan released *Zeroes* (Book 1 in the Zeroes series), Libba Bray released *Lair of Dreams* (The Diviners, Book 2), Rachel Manija Brown and Sherwood Smith released *Hostage* (Book 2 in the Change quartet), and Ransom Riggs released *Library of Souls* (Miss Peregrine's Peculiar Children, Book 3). 2015 also saw several excellent standalones. Among these were *Seriously Wicked* by Tina Connolly, *Updraft* by Fran Wilde, *Serpentine* by Cindy Pon, *Shadowshaper* by Daniel José Older, *Magonia* by Maria Dahvana Headley, and *Carry On* by Rainbow Rowell.

Updraft had the distinction of being on the shortlist for both the Norton Award (a juried award for best YA speculative fiction book) and Nebula Award (an award for science fiction and fantasy novels selected by members of the Science Fiction and Fantasy Writers of America). Also on the Norton shortlist were *Archivist Wasp, Seriously Wicked, Shadowshaper, Court of Fives* by Kate Eliott, *Cuckoo Song* by Francis Hardinge, *Zero Boxer* by Fonda Lee, *Bone Gap* by Laura Ruby, and *Nimona* by Noelle Stevenson. Naomi Novak's *Uprooted* didn't make the Norton shortlist, but was a Nebula nominee.

Other YA specific awards and honour lists included the ALA Best Books of the Year, Young Adult Library Services (YALSA) list of top ten books for reluctant readers, The Gelett Burgess Awards for books that entertain and teach with an energetic and creative approach, the Children's and Young Adult Bloggers Literary Awards (CYBILS), and The Pura Belpré Awards honouring Latino/a books. The ALA Best Books list included several titles also honoured elsewhere, including *Archivist Wasp, Nimona, The Darkest Part of the Forest, Carry On, A Court of Thorns and Roses,* and *Shadowshaper.* Other honoured books included *Razorhurst* by Justine Larbalestier (2015 in the US, though 2014 in Australia), *The Walls Around Us* by Nova Ren Suma,

Beastkeeper by Cat Hellisen, *A Song for Ella* by David Almond, *Rook* by Sharon Cameron, *Walk on Earth a Stranger* by Rae Carson, *Thirteen Days of Midnight* by Leo Hunt, *The Weight of Feathers* by Anna-Marie McLemore, and *Beastly Bones: A Jackaby Novel* by William Ritter. The YALSA reluctant readers list honoured *Nimona*, *Shadowshaper*, *Zeroboxer*, *Red Queen*, *The Iron Trial* by Holly Black and Cassandra Clare, and *The Silence of Six* by E. C. Myers. On the Gelett Burgess Awards list, *Tales of Arilland* by Alethea Kontis was selected in the Fairy Tales and Fables category, *The Kingdom of the Sun and Moon* by Lowell H. Press won the Fantasy category, and *The Improbable Wonders of Moojie Littleman* by Robin Gregory won the Science Fiction category. On the Pura Belpré honour list was *The Smoking Mirror* by David Bowles, while the CYBILS honoured *Nimona* and *The Walls Around Us*.

This year, speculative fiction had a much larger presence with nine titles on the Rainbow Book List (an ALA list honouring books with Queer/Questioning, Undecided, Intersex, Lesbian, Trans (Transgender/Transsexual), Bisexual, Asexual, Gay (QUILTBAG) content) including some titles from 2014 that were apparently missed last year (when we saw only two speculative books on the list). The speculative rainbow books for 2015 included *The Darkest Part of the Forest* by Holly Black, *Lair of Dreams* by Libba Bray, *Carry On* by Rainbow Rowell, *Wonders of the*

Invisible World by Christopher Barzak, *Stranger* by Rachel Manija Brown and Sherwood Smith (one of the 2014 titles which wasn't honoured last year for some reason), *The Bane Chronicles* by Sandra Rees Brennan, Cassandra Clare and Maureen Johnson (another 2014 release), *Willful Machines* by Tim Floreen, *About a Girl* by Sarah McCarry, and *Lizard Radio* by Pat Schmatz. Barzak's *Wonders of the Invisible World* was also a Stonewall Award honour book.

YA book blogs in 2015 included several devoted to celebrating diversity. *Diversity in YA* (started in 2011 by Malinda Lo and Cindy Pon) was still going strong with lots of news about diverse YA releases and statistical breakdowns of diverse content in books released by major publishing houses. *Rich in Color*, a blog devoted to reviewing books featuring characters of colour, posted a roundup of critically acclaimed books, noting that *Shadowshaper* was honoured on the year's best lists from *School Library Journal* and Barnes and Noble, while *The Weight of Feathers* was honoured by Barnes and Noble. Other favorites of the *Rich in Color* bloggers included *An Ember in the Ashes*, *Serpentine*, *Court of Fives*, *The Girl at Midnight* by Melissa Gray, and *Sorcerer to the Crown* by Zen Cho, which is a fantasy novel released for adults which may have significant YA crossover appeal. *The Book Smugglers*, Ana Grilo and Thea James, also paid attention to diversity in their reading, noting their personal statistics over the course of the year. Ana's best books of the year included *Sorcerer to the Crown*, *Bone Gap*, *Uprooted*, *Archivist Wasp*, *The Lie Tree* by Francis Hardinge, and *Illuminae* by Amie Kaufman and Jay Kristoff (also a Goodreads choice finalist). Thea's included *Illuminae*, and *Uprooted*. *Nimona*, *About a Girl*, *Court of Fives*, and *An Ember in the Ashes* made the *Book Smugglers'* honourable mention list along with several other titles including *Prairie Fire* by E. K. Johnson, *Signal to Noise* by Silvia Moreno Garcia (an adult title with significant YA crossover appeal about magic and music in Mexico City), *A Wicked Thing* by Rhiannon Thomas, *Space Hostages* by Sophia McDougall, *The Scorpion Rules* by Erin Bow, *The Suffering* by Rin Chupeco, and *The Dead Girls of Hysteria Hall* by Katie Alender.

Australia had a healthy crop of YA novels in 2015. In addition to *Zeroes*, which featured a powerhouse of three Australian authors, *Illuminae* was an Aurealis Award nominee in the YA novel category along with *In The Skin of a Monster* by Kathryn Barker, *Lady Helen and the Dark Days Club* by Alison Goodman, *The Fire Sermon* by Francesca Haig, *The Hush* by Skye Melki-Wagner, and *Day Boy* by Trent Jamieson. *In The Skin of a Monster*, *Lady Helen and the Dark Days Club*, and *Day Boy* were also nominated in the Fantasy Novel category alongside *Tower of Thorns* by Juliet Marillier. There was no horror shortlist for 2015, though several YA titles made it into other categories, including *Fall* by Sean Williams in the Science Fiction

Novel category and *Cherry Crow Children* by Deborah Kalin in the Best Collection category with individual entries in short fiction categories. *Illuminae* was also nominated in the Best Science Fiction Novel category.

Popular UK titles included *The Lie Tree*, *Endgame* by C. J. Daugherty (Night School, Book 5), *Half Wild* by Sally Green (Half Bad, Book 2), *The Sin Eater's Daughter* by Melinda Salisbury, *The Mime Order* by Samantha Shannon (The Bone Season, Book 2), and *Half the World* by Joe Abercrombie (Shattered Sea, Book 2).

Meanwhile, Canadian YA had some excellent speculative titles including *The Scorpion Rules*, which was shortlisted for the Canadian Library Association's Young Adult Book Award along with *An Inheritance of Ashes* by Leah Bobet and *Boo* by Neil Smith.

In short fiction, 2015's YA offering was a little lighter than 2014, with most of our selections for the Year's Best coming from general magazines and anthologies. We did find one YA specific anthology of note, which was *Slasher Girls and Monster Boys*. We selected Nova Ren Suma's "The Birds of Azalea Street" for our year's best, but we did feel that the anthology as a whole was strong and well worth reading for horror fans.

On the magazine front, several venues will be recognisable from last year's volume, but a few notable venues from 2015 included *Strange Horizons*, *Asimov's*, *Uncanny Magazine*, and *Visibility Fiction*.

As with last year, our selections come from multiple countries and diverse viewpoints, and the original sources range from large publishing house anthologies to more small-scale productions. We have done our best to include dark and light themes, a mix of science fiction and fantasy, and a variety of story lengths. Our length extremes are not quite so marked as last year with just one flash piece of under a thousand words and one novelette of over 7,500 words. As always, it is our hope that every reader will find something to love within these pages.

Songs in the Key of You

By Sarah Pinsker

Aisha hummed her own soundtrack as she walked into the cafeteria. She had composed the melody herself, an upbeat piece with a hint of swagger. She grabbed a tray from the stack and got in line. Chili day. Her favorite. She kept humming all the way to the cashier, where she used her last credits for the week.

"Do you hear something?" asked a voice behind her.

Aisha turned around, though she already knew who was there. She had heard their soundtracks, recorded to play in perfect harmony whenever they wanted to announce their arrival. It was a gorgeous piece of music, taken as one: three intertwined melodies composed and recorded professionally just for them. All three songs were pretty enough on their own, but the harmonies they created when the Trio walked into a room were gorgeous. She had only heard two parts this time, Dee's brassy melody and Janissa's funky counterpoint. Bryn wasn't with them, so the high part was missing, but it still held together fine. Aisha only dreamed of making music like that.

"Girl thinks she can fool us into thinking she's got a Kurzwailer." That was Dee. The others never spoke until she did. If they were a real musical trio, she'd be the lead vocalist.

"She's faking it. No bracelet." That was Janissa.

"I'm not faking anything," Aisha said, though she knew she should keep quiet. "I was humming."

They all knew it was a lie, or a part lie. She wasn't pretending to have a Kurzwailer on her wrist, but she was obviously singing her own theme song, or what would be it if she could afford the bracelet and the recording.

Aisha turned to walk away, but as she did, somebody's foot shifted to trip her. The chili capsized, hitting the floor and splashing her jeans on the way down. She stared at the bowl and the streaks on her legs, trying to ignore the laughter. She didn't have enough to cover a second bowl. She'd have to go without lunch.

"She's clumsy, too," said Dee. For a moment Aisha had thought maybe it was an accident, but now she doubted it.

The two of them pushed past Aisha, making a show of stepping around the spill. She heard their song playing as they made their way to their table. Most kids had the type with built-in speaker, but the Trio all had the most expensive model Kurzwailer, the one that could override broadcast over any nearby sound system. The ancient cafeteria PA crackled on the low end.

Aisha's stomach grumbled. She walked to her locker to see if she had anything in there to call a snack. She knew she didn't have any other clothes, since it wasn't a gym day.

"Hungry?"

She closed the locker door to find Bryn standing on the other side, holding out a protein bar. Bryn was a boy today, like he was more and more. He somehow made a sweater vest and bowtie look fashionable. All those years running the school with the other two parts of the trio had paid off in residual cool points.

"It's all I've got unless you come back to the cafeteria. I can buy you more chili if you want, but I'm guessing you don't want to go back in there right now."

Aisha shook her head. "I don't need charity."

"I know, but you're probably hungry. Just take this."

Aisha wished she had the pride to refuse, but she was hungry. Hungry and suspicious.

"Why are you being nice to me?"

"I saw what they did. You didn't deserve that. Making fun of someone for a bad song is one thing, but she shouldn't have tripped you."

"My song wasn't bad."

"What?" Bryn looked surprised. "Why does it matter?"

"Because it does. I know I can't afford one of those stupid bracelets, but I'm a good songwriter. I know I am. Y'all make fun of me, but your parents pay people for your silly entrance music. They pay people like me. So how come I'm the one who gets laughed at?"

She folded her arms and scowled at him, trying to will her stomach not to growl loud enough to be heard. She didn't really think the bracelets were stupid. Who didn't want their own theme song to play at the push of a button?

Bryn stared for a moment, then smiled. "Yeah, you're right. It did sound pretty good. Truce?"

He held out the protein bar again, and this time she took it.

"Thanks," she said. Not truce. She didn't trust that. She felt a little bad, but people didn't just go from being mean to being nice. Not that easily. She closed her locker and headed for her next class. She didn't feel much like singing.

That night, somebody posted a picture online of her with chili on her legs. "Accident in the cafeteria," read the caption. Aisha tried not to cry. She'd been teased before. She could handle it. She wouldn't look to see how many times the picture got shared around. Better not to know.

She spent the weekend helping her mother clean offices. She normally didn't mind working with her mother. The office building was quiet and empty, and had great acoustics in its stairwells and bathrooms.

"Sing for me, Aisha," her mother usually said. After Aisha sang, her mother would shake her head and say, "They should never have defunded the school music programs. Someday I'll get you lessons and instruments and everything you deserve."

"It's okay, Mama," Aisha would say. She believed it sometimes. One of the best days of her life was the day her mother brought home a ukulele somebody had put in the trash.

This time, she cleaned separately to avoid having to talk or sing.

On Monday morning, Aisha walked into homeroom behind the bell. When she timed it well, she walked in with a crowd, and nobody noticed she didn't have a Kurz bracelet amid the cacophony of others' entry music. She thought she heard somebody call her "Chili," but she ignored it.

Her homeroom teacher came in with her own music, some bad guy's theme song from a sci-fi movie, and everybody shut up. Ms. Wallace tried really hard to be cool, but it never quite worked. Of course, if she were a student, she'd still be cooler than Aisha for having a Kurz at all, even if she used some tired old movie music instead of paying for something personalized. It was effective, in any case. Everybody shut theirs off once they were in the room, so their bracelets didn't get confiscated. Aisha was the only one not reaching for a button at her wrist. She put her head on her arms and waited for Ms. Wallace to take attendance.

Heading to second period, she saw Bryn at the stairwell. She fumbled for the two dollars she wanted to give him so she didn't owe him for the protein bar. As she walked toward him, she realized he was talking with Dee. She changed directions again immediately, but not before she saw the don't-bother-me looks on their faces. Like she hadn't known better than to approach them. She stuffed the money back in her pocket.

That afternoon she found a note wedged into her locker door's grating. She was almost afraid to open it, but she decided it was better to know.

"This is a hack for your tablet. It overrides the school software lock so you can record on it. There are some good free recording apps once you're unlocked."

She didn't recognize the handwriting, so she stuffed the note in her bag and tried to ignore it. She didn't try the hack that night, or the next. She kept imagining what might go wrong. What if someone was trying to corrupt her tablet? The school paid for the first one, but they charged if you needed a replacement, and her family couldn't afford that. Or what if she did it, and it turned out to be some malicious code that spewed her private stuff all over the web?

But still—a recording app would be cooler than anything. All she had at home was an old four-track recorder she had found at a junk shop. She had taught herself how to record with it, but it was so ancient it took cassette tapes, so even if she managed to find a used Kurzwailer, she had no way to upload her music. She was pretty sure she was the only analog person in the entire school. Possibly the city. Possibly the world.

The thought of a real digital recording app kept nagging at her, until finally all the things that could go wrong didn't seem as bad as going another moment without it. She read the note over and over again while she waited for the bus on Wednesday afternoon. By the time she got home, she had made up her mind. She put her "SSH...RECORDING" sign on the door and barricaded herself inside the closet she shared with her little sister. She made sure the tablet was offline, then followed the note's instructions.

It worked. The note let her behind the school interface that normally blocked out any use but homework and a few approved research sites. Nothing seemed to be going wrong, so she risked a quick visit online to download a free Kurz recorder app. She spent the evening recording her own theme song, singing all the parts herself. It was only a thirty second piece, but she liked the way it sounded with layers. Not that she had a Kurz, but still cool.

She was careful not to let her teachers see she had hacked the tablet when they came by to look at her work, but she had to force herself not to fiddle with the recording app during class.

A video from the chili incident went up that night. It was only a few seconds long, but somebody had dubbed some squeaky off-key song over it, with the caption "Chili thinks she can sing." This time, she looked at the tags to see who had put it up: Janissa.

What had Aisha ever done to her? She stared at the picture, and the dozens of comments.

"What's the matter?" her mother asked her at dinner. "You weren't singing while you set the table."

"I don't feel like it."

"That's why I asked the question. You never don't feel like it."

Her sister Maya giggled, but stopped when she saw the look on Aisha's face. Aisha struggled not to cry. Her mother had enough to worry about. "It's nothing, Mama. Just a tough day at school."

Her mother let her drop the subject and talk about her biology test instead. At least something had gone right.

Even though Maya went to bed an hour before Aisha, she was still up when Aisha came in the room. "Is it that Kurzwailer thing? Is that why you're sad? Because you don't have one? A lot of kids at my school have them now, too."

Aisha sat on the bed's edge and waited a second for her eyes to adjust to the darkness. "Nah. I mean, I still want one, but that's not why I'm sad. Well, it kind of is."

She struggled to explain. "You know the way they bust out with music when you press the button? That's how I feel all the time. Like I'm busting out with music. And they all have it, and they don't even care. They want them to fit in. I want one because the soundtrack in my head is bigger than my head can hold."

"Is that why it leaks out your mouth all the time?"

Aisha poked Maya. "Very funny." It was. Funny and true.

She had planned on going to bed, but now she climbed over her sister's clothes piled in front of the closet and shut the door behind her. She turned on her tablet and navigated back to the video.

In the comments section she wrote, "Chili knows she can sing. Chili Beats charges reasonable rates for your own personalized Kurzwailer songs."

She hit send before she changed her mind.

She didn't have the nerve to look at the video again in the morning. She didn't want to know if people were making fun of her even more now. When she walked into homeroom with the just-before-the-bell noise, she didn't hear anybody laughing at her.

Bryn caught her on her way out of biology. "So I guess you liked that hack?"

"That was you?"

"Yeah." He grinned. "I'm good at code stuff."

"But why?"

Bryn shrugged. "I guess I'm sick of them treating people like garbage for no reason."

"Them?" Aisha put her hands on her hips.

"Us, I guess. You're right. My fault, too." He paused. "But I swear I'm done with it. I've been wanting to go solo. The three-part thing doesn't suit me anymore."

"But that song is perfect. Everybody knows it's you when y'all walk into a room."

Bryn fiddled with his bracelet. "It doesn't sound like me. It sounds like who I used to be. Or who I was trying to be. Anyway, I want a different song. Something made only for me. I don't want to be part of somebody else's melody. It's so high and pretty and it just sounds wrong."

"So get a new one."

"Yeah—only—I can't afford to have a pro write me a new theme and get it recorded. Dee's parents paid for everything for the old song."

"Oh. Plenty of people buy tunes, though."

"Yeah, but I don't want to be made fun of for a bad song. Or a boring one, even."

Aisha waited for a punch line. Bryn spoke again. "Um, would you be willing to write me something? Something just for me?"

"For real?" Aisha's heart beat faster, but she told it to calm down. "You're not setting up to make fun of me?"

"For real."

He looked sincere, but something still bothered her. "But...you said you can't afford a new song. You haven't been nice to me for years. Why should I do it?"

Bryn crossed his arms across his chest. "I don't know. I thought—"

"You thought I was so desperate for y'all to be nice to me that I'd give you something because you smiled at me?"

"I didn't just smile! I gave you that hack. And I stood up for you in the comments on Janissa's video. I even recommended 'Chili Beats' for anybody looking for a new tune."

That shut Aisha up for a second. She hadn't gone back to look, so it might even be true.

Bryn continued. "I can tell a few of my friends, too. Maybe we could work something out on commission? If I bring you ten customers, you help me with mine for free?"

"Fifteen."

He grinned. "Fifteen, then. Maybe if you make enough writing songs, you can buy yourself a Kurz someday. If you want."

"Maybe," Aisha said. "If I still want it."

Bryn held out his hand, and Aisha shook it. Then she turned her back on him and walked away.

Fifteen customers. Fifteen songs. She was going to be a professional musician. She could buy real instruments, and help her mother with bills. Maybe every fifteen customers she'd even throw in a freebie for somebody who couldn't afford one. She'd give Ms. Wallace something to shut up the class for real. No threats of confiscation, just a seriously badass tune. The best part was she wouldn't ever have to be mean to Dee or Janissa to show them up; she'd wait until they came begging her for a new Bryn-less duet. She pictured the whole school walking around with her Chili Beats. It could happen. Maybe.

For the first time in a year, she didn't care if she never got a Kurzwailer. She hummed her own soundtrack as she walked to her next class, making sure everybody heard it.

Blood, Ash, Braids

By Genevieve Valentine

1943

I t didn't take them long to find a name for us; almost
as soon as they knew it was women inside the rickety
biplanes they couldn't catch, the Germans called us
witches.

It was because of the sounds our idling planes made
from the ground, the story went, as if the German
soldiers had spent a lot of time with brooms and knew
what they sounded like, engineless and gliding fifty
feet above them in the dark.

The wires holding the wings in place made the
whistle. The canvas pulled taut around the plywood
made the hush. I still suspect the thing that sounded
supernatural was the whirr of our engines starting up
again, as they realized we had already struck them,
and it was too late to escape the blasts.

The officer who told us had half a smile on his face;
he'd thought of the job as a demotion—most of them
did, at first, to be in a camp full of girls—but if the

Germans were already bleating back and forth about bounties for the heads of the Night Witches, then maybe he had real fighters on his hands.

Popova cracked a laugh when she heard, turned to me with grin that was all teeth. "I like that," she said. "Should we start screeching when we sail through, do you think?"

"I think not," I said. "The best witches know not to give away their position." And she laughed a little louder than she had to, as if she thought it was actually funny.

A couple of the girls glanced over from across the runway. They never took Popova's cue in being kind to me, but they were never cruel, and that might have been all Popova could hope for.

"She'd love being called a witch by the enemy; she might already be one," Popova said after a second, sounding circumspect, sounding a little reverent.

(*She* was Commander Raskova; at some point, she hadn't needed a name any more.)

But Raskova was elsewhere now, with only her shadow cast over us. Bershanskaya was the commander who lined us up and sent us out. She was as steady as they came, and her humor was thin and dry as air.

The first time Bershanskaya heard the name, she raised an eyebrow, and glanced quickly at me before she turned to Popova. Then she nodded, hands behind her, and said, "Let them call us what they like, if it suits them."

"Suits me, too," said Popova.

It suited all of them, I think, even if I was the only witch the 588th ever had.

One of the important things about the 588th was how little it cared where you came from. If you could take the recruiter's withering stare and the doctors' lingering hands and the open loathing of the men who ran you through your paces, and you managed to crawl under the stalled train cars to reach the station from the farthest set of tracks they could find to park your train, by the time you got to the regiment camp they had no doubts about your nerves, and that was all they needed to know about you before they put you in a plane.

I'd come to the 588th out of necessity; my village had reached the end of their patience for someone who seemed always to know when it was going to rain and yet couldn't call it down for you even if you paid her. Easier to go find an open fight than to wait for the one that was brewing back home.

There was no way I could have accommodated village needs. It's too hard to do small magic.

From a one-room farmhouse or a palace in Moscow, anyone you ask will talk to you until their tongues turn blue about all the magic they've seen or heard of, even if they say they don't believe in it. They'll all know how

15

it's being used against them even as they speak, and the hundreds of whispers shared in the depth of the forest by the witches, who gather there for market days and trade in secret spells in a currency of dirty looks.

It's all very well to keep people out of the woods at night, but it's foolish.

There are only three kinds of magic: water, ash, and air. For ash to work, you give blood. For water, you spill tears. For air, you give your breath. They all run out; our gifts are designed to be spent.

The woods will never be a gathering of witches. We don't live long enough.

Our planes were crop dusters, wood frames covered in canvas, held together with metal cords. They were the leftovers of aviation, planes given to people for whom no one had much hope.

But they were so flimsy and so slow that they made a kind of magic—gold out of hay. The German planes couldn't drop down to our speed or they'd stall out and plummet, so when they aimed for us we turned and they hit nothing but air; their anti-aircraft bombs would pop right through our wings and keep going, bursting a hundred feet above us as we banked a turn and the explosion illuminated our path back home.

Raskova courted us with those planes, showed us how to make them spin and make lazy loops in the air like the plaits of a braid, leapt down from the cockpit with her dark eyes glittering behind her goggles, and you could hear her heart pounding even from where you were standing. It was easy to want to go to war, to make Raskova proud.

And once you learned them, those planes were kinder to us than horses, and to sit inside one was to feel strangely invisible, a thrill crawling up the back of your neck like a ghost every time you settled in.

You settled in four, five, eight times a night: the plane couldn't carry more than two bombs at once, and you had work to do.

"You go out at sundown," says Bershanskaya.

Her lips are drawn thin, her hands folded behind her, her buttons marching a straight line to her chin. (She didn't want to lead, when Raskova appointed her. She hated sending us out to die.)

It's a bridge; we all know why it has to disappear— the Germans can't be allowed to move anything else into place. But they've stopped underestimating us, witches or not. They're prepared to throw us a flak circus now, every time they see us coming.

It's rows of guns blooming outward from the ground like flowers made from teeth, and searchlights by the dozens that flood the sky for fifty miles in each direction, and you can't get free of it no matter how you try; when you twist long enough this way and that way like a rabbit, you start to panic for your life.

We lost a team that way, not long back. Their cots are still folded up on the barracks, two thin mattresses for girls who won't be needing any more rest.

"You'll go in three planes at once," says Bershanskaya.

Next to me, the muscles in Popova's jaw shift as she realizes what Bershanskaya means.

Decoys. We'll be drawing fire in our little ghost planes.

We lost our hair to be here.

They made us cut it when we were first preparing for combat; for practicality, the commander said, though I had seen one or two of the training men glare at a line of girls walking off the field those first days, their long glossy braids swinging at their waists, and I always wondered.

I didn't mind, for myself—my hair was the watery brown of old deer hide, and there was no husband or want of a husband to stay my hand from the knife. For me to cut it just meant fewer pins I'd have to scramble for every time the sirens went up. But you can't tell girls for a hundred years that her hair is her crowning glory and then one day tell her to hack it off and not have her pause before the scissors.

We all did it, in the end, every last one of us submitting to the shears, slicing one another's braids off to the jaw.

Recklessly, I offered to burn the hair for any girl that wanted. It was forbidden to leave the base alone—it wasn't safe—but some things go deeper than regulations, and some superstitions aren't worth testing.

You never leave so much hair where anyone can take it from you; petty magic has uses for that, and none of them are good.

I was an odd fit in the barracks, just strange enough that we all knew I was strange, but this superstition was so well-known that not even Petrova looked twice at me as they each thanked me and handed me their braids of brown and black and gold.

As I headed for the woods with three dozen braids draped like pelts across my arms, Bershanskaya saw me. She was standing outside, near the engineers who were patching the planes. Her hands were behind her, and she had the narrow-eyed look of someone who had been watching the sunset longer than was wise.

I held my breath and kept going. If she called out to stop me, I'd keep walking until she shot. Some orders are holy; I had a duty deeper than hers.

She didn't say a word, but she watched me carry the plaits like a sacrifice into the cover of the trees.

In the woods, I built a fire and burned them—one at a time, until there was nothing left. I didn't start

19

a new fire for each plait (we were tied close enough to withstand a little ash), but it was powerful enough that I was careful. I breathed steadily in and out; I thought carefully about nothing at all.

When I came back after dark, stinking of singe, Bershanskaya was standing outside the barracks and scanning the edge of the woods, waiting.

"Commander," I greeted when I was close enough, and waited for whatever she would do to me.

For a long time she looked me in the eye until it felt like I was canvas stretched across a wooden frame, and I could feel the question building on her tongue in the space just behind her front teeth, where people's worst suspicions lived.

If she asks me, I thought, she'll have her answer.

(I could cut myself deep enough to bleed. Blood and tears would summon something, I could hope I had enough willpower to make her forget what I'd done.)

She stepped aside, eyes still on me, and as I passed she said my name low, like she'd checked my name off a very short list; like a spell.

Raskova would have asked me. I don't know if that's better or worse.

In 1938, when I was still in school, Raskova had flown across the country for glory with Polina Denisova

Osipenko and Valentina Grizodubova. When they were recovered after their landing, the news was everywhere: that she and her copilots had broken flight records in the *Rodina*, that it was a marvelous feat of flying, that they were heroes of the nation.

I didn't find out what had really happened until Raskova told me herself. They had overshot in the mist, and when it parted they were suddenly over the Sea of Okhotsk, where the water in winter is the milky flat of a corpse's eye, and they didn't have enough gasoline left for the crossing—they'd flown too high to avoid being shrouded by the fog for a day and a night. They had to turn around and pray for landfall before they dropped out of the sky.

The navigator's seat—a glass bauble at the front of the plane—would be torn to shreds in a crash, and they were hurting for altitude and out of fuel and gathering too much ice to carry.

Raskova marked a map and jumped for it.

Her copilots crashed into the taiga, the bottom of the plane in shreds from the landing, and waited for her. Even after the rescue crew got to them, they refused to budge. They took watch by the plane for two more days, until Raskova staggered out of the woods.

It had been ten days. She'd had no food or water with her, and no compass when she jumped.

(There was no magic in her—not the sort that I had—but you wonder about witch blood in some

21

people, when they manage things that no one should have managed.)

But more amazing to me even than her ten-day journey was the ten-day vigil the other two had kept, sheltering with the plane that had tried to kill them, without enough supplies, without knowing if she would ever come.

Doubt gnawed at me whenever I thought about it, more doubts than I ever had about being shot at, more doubts than I had about my chances of loosing a bomb just where it needed to go.

How long would they have waited beyond ten days? How long would I wait when it was my turn? Would I walk ten days in the wilderness rather than lie down and die?

Osipenko was dead. Wasn't even a strafing run; she'd just been going from one place to another, and her plane had turned on her.

Grizodubova had been sent elsewhere for the war effort. None of us had ever seen her. She was leading a defense and relief outfit near Leningrad, with real bombers and not crop dusters. She was commanding men.

I wondered if she and Raskova ever saw each other, or if they wrote—if it was safe to write. It would be easy to forgive if they had parted ways; it was wartime, and their duty to the nation lay before them.

But sometimes the nights are long and dark, and you feel so alone that you think everyone else must have someone closer than you do, and you think: If they don't still speak, it's because they're both waiting for death, and can't bear to come close and then be parted.

Then you stare up at the leaking roof and wonder, when something wonderful or terrible happened, did one of them sometimes glance over her shoulder to look at the other before she remembered she was alone?

Sebrova volunteers to be one of the three planes against the flak, and Popova volunteers second, and before I can do more than glance at Petrova for her agreement (she's already nodding at me) I'm volunteering, too, because I have few enough friends here. Where Popova is going, I want to go.

It's a foolish thing to do, volunteering to die on a German gun, but I volunteered for that a long time ago. I'm a quick draw on the controls, so I'll be of some use, and anything's better than sitting around waiting, wondering if Popova made it out.

Outside, I smoke a cigarette I won off Meklin at cards and watch the sun going down. I wish I had time to do everything that needs doing.

Popova sits next to me on the fence, lets out a breath at the streaks of gold and pink suspended just above the grass. When she taps me on the shoulder I hand her my cigarette.

She's a marvelous pilot—light and nimble—but you'd never know it from the way she smokes a cigarette, single loud pulls that leave a cylinder of ash that drops wholesale to the ground.

After a little while she hands me a piece of chocolate from inside her pocket, grainy and already melting across my fingertips. I pop it into my mouth and lick my fingers clean, flushing a little at the bad manners, but Popova only winks. I wonder how long she's held on to it, doling out to herself one piece at a time on nights she thinks she's going to die.

"You'll be all right," she says.

"Oh, I'm sure I will," I say. "It's you I worry over."

She casts me a look and half smiles. My lungs are acrid, suddenly. I pinch off the end of my cigarette to preserve the rest.

She shrugs. "We never let them get any sleep," she says, jamming a pin into her cropped hair and wrenching her cap on over it.

(Petrova sometimes reaches behind her to smooth a braid that isn't there. I've never seen Popova do it. I wonder what became of Raskova's dark brown braids, gleaming and pinned to her head as she spoke to us and made us into soldiers.)

Golden hair sticks out just at the edges, half curls below her ears. "I'd hate to see us coming, too. Let's hope they're too tired to aim."

I want to smile or laugh, but I'm staring at my plane and feeling ice down my spine. Why this should be so different I don't know—slightly more impossible than impossible isn't a measurement that has much meaning—but I look at the trees instead, after a moment.

"How did you decide to do this?"

I don't know why I ask. We're all meant to be without a past, and equal. They were carpenters and secretaries and farm girls, but they're pilots now, and it shouldn't matter how they got here.

Popova raises her eyebrows at the setting sun like it's the one who'd asked the rude question. There are only a few minutes left until it's dark enough to load up and set off. I should be going back to barracks and getting my gear.

She says without looking at me, "A plane landed near our house, when I was young."

Young—she's nineteen now, I think, but I don't say anything. Rude to interrupt. Not that it matters; she doesn't elaborate. It's the biography of a masterful pilot who knows better than to waste a gesture.

She glances over. "And you?"

"Oh, I'm a witch," I say. "Flying comes naturally." And she grins as she drops from the fence, snaps her goggles into place.

"Good thing it can be taught," she says and takes off for her plane.

It can't, not really. You can teach the mechanics of a plane, but either you have the flight inside you or you don't.

Her strides kick up puffs of dust in her wake that cover her footsteps; at nightfall she casts no shadow, and for a moment she looks like I'd imagined witches to be, before I knew better.

When she's gone, I unroll the cigarette and scoop up her ashes from the ground with the blade of my knife.

It's a sharp blade; I never even feel the cut I make. When the paper gets wet enough, I use the tip of the knife to mix it and drag a line of blood and ash under the nose of Sebrova's and Popova's planes.

I do it quickly, my eyes stinging, my heart pounding.

Then they're coming from the barracks, and I'm out of ashes and out of time and have to step away and get my gear. We'll need to make sure the altitude gauge is fixed before we're off the ground.

Petrova, my navigator, is already there, frowning underneath the propeller and tapping our windshields. As I haul myself onto the wing, I press one bloody thumbprint into the canvas just behind her seat, where she'll never see.

Blood magic doesn't work as well when you're asking for yourself, but I'll protect who I can, however it comes.

Each of us carries two bombs. It's decided in the last seconds before leaping into our planes that Sebrova will be first, I'll be second, and Popova will make the final drop, after they're already on to us. I don't like it, but I keep my hands on the controls as we enter the flak zone.

The engines sound impossibly loud—three of them, and we don't dare cut them with what we have to do, so there's nothing for it but to go closer and closer, knowing they know we're coming, waiting for the bullets to start.

(I miss the sound of the wind through the wires; it had always sounded to me like an owl on my shoulder, and it was a comfort as you were moving in for the drop.)

The first floodlight is almost a relief—it's something to do, at least, instead of just something to be afraid of—and I wait two seconds longer than my instincts scream to, just enough that the nose of the plane catches the light, that it can almost but not quite follow me when I snap a turn to one side, dropping out of their sight. A spray of bullets arcs behind me, whistling clean and hitting nothing.

I don't look for Popova. It's not safe.

Instead I drop steeply so the searchlights casting at my prior heading can't find me, and pull up at the last second with my heart pounding in my throat and the engine grinding underneath me. I cut through three lights at once, a dead hover for a moment as gravity gets confused, the blinding flashes underneath us reminding me to bank left and out of the line of fire.

I hear a series of dull thunders, then a thudding rip—a wingtip's been struck. Nothing serious, it's a lucky hit for them, that's all, but my lungs go so tight I have to wrestle them for breath as I circle back. There's already ice on my tiny windshield; there's ice in my throat when I breathe.

Then I see Sebrova's plane arcing up to meet us. She's done it; the thunders were her bombs hitting home.

It's my turn.

Petrova gives me the all-clear, and I do a big, lazy loop well out of the scope of the spotlights—I glimpse Popova, barely, practically cartwheeling and vanishing into the dark—and breathe deep through my nose as we sail over the iron garden. Sebrova's been kind enough to mark the way (a fire's already started next to the drop site), but I want to be careful, and only when Petrova gives the sign do I tilt us five degrees closer to the Earth, no more, and let the unfastened bombs slide forward, hurtling toward the ground with a cheerful whistle.

I sweep up and to the left, taking my place on the flank, and the plane shakes for just a second as the payload explodes, a warm burst of orange in the black night. Petrova whoops; I grin for as long as I can stand the wind in my teeth, which isn't long, and then push through the acrid scents of fire and guns and panic toward my secondary position.

Popova's plane drops so fast I think for a second, my grip seizing on the controls, that she's been struck, but it's just the way she handles a plane—I hear the whirr of her engines above the tuneless wind as I cut straight across and through the searchlights, distracting them from her, letting them waste two arcs of ammunition trying to pin me as I drop and spin out lazily, letting the wind pull us the last few inches to the top of the arc.

But it's too bright when I get there, far too bright, and I realize with numb panic that they've got me locked, and the next round of bullets will hit home.

I try for more altitude, already knowing I'm too late, and I wonder wildly if I can point the plane at the ground so hard that Petrova and I die without pain. We have to die—we can't let the Germans take us— but she shouldn't suffer.

Really, the way to go out is a bullet through the heart. The Germans could oblige. It would keep them from wondering where Popova's gone.

Better this than ten days in the wilderness, I think; better this than to wait at the Sea of Okhotsk.

I let out my breath until there's nothing left (blood-ash-air, I think dimly, someplace with no hope left, blood-ash-air), and bank the turn straight into the center of the circling lights.

I die that way, the way Raskova died, with a tailspin and then nightfall—but not on this run. On this run, the spray of bullets never comes, because Popova's plane soars straight in front of me.

The Germans are only tracking two of our planes, and with the interruption they can't tell whether or not they've tricked themselves into a double image with the swinging searchlights, and in the few seconds where the lights freeze in place as they try to decide what to do, I bank as hard as I can and cut down and out and back into the dark, fingers aching, pointed for home.

We're the last to get back. When I climb out of the plane I can barely stand; I don't know where all my blood's gone. Bershanskaya's come to meet us. When she nods, I find it in me to straighten up and nod back.

Popova's leaning against her plane, a few feet back from the mark of my blood and her ashes that she'll never see. There are three bullet holes through one of her wings, like freckles at the tip of someone's nose, but she's there.

She grins around a square of chocolate, calls over, "What kept you?"

I put blood and ashes on every plane that goes out after that.

Once I duck out between the planes and see Bershanskaya watching me, her hands behind her. She doesn't ask what I'm doing there. I never say. It doesn't matter. It's what I've given over, and you can't call it back.

It's on my plane, too, the night I go down, but I never expected that to protect me for long. They all run out; our gifts are designed to be spent.

A little while from now, Popova will go on a raid and get caught in German fire. When she makes it back to the base, there will be more than forty bullet holes in the plane. There are bullet holes in her helmet.

No one will understand how she survived it; no one can imagine what protected her.

Mosquito Boy

By Felix Gilman

Of course we were first introduced to the Mosquito Boy through the medium of the *Weekly World News*. An inauspicious beginning. One feels that the respectable classes of creatures were named in Genesis, or Shakespeare at the latest. There's something bad-mannered about such a late arrival, and something provisional and uncertain and off-balance about the creature itself, as if it came late and in a rush.

Mosquito Boy Escapes From Secret Terror-Weapon Lab, says one early headline, or *Archeologists Discover Hideous "Mosquito Boy" in Ancient Tomb*, or *"He Was Like A Mosquito Boy" Says Violated Blonde*, or who can forget *Mosquito Boy Goes to War* or *Mosquito Boy Weeps At Ground Zero* or... The photographs were unclear. A blur against a jungle backdrop; a slumped figure in shadow at a London bus-stop. More often there were sketches. Between the first story and the last the sketches became more human, somehow, more *relatable*, and not solely because the artists started putting a baseball cap on him. It was something about the mouthparts. Those fragile and pitiable mouthparts. We have not until recently needed a lot of words for describing the aesthetics of mouthparts and my vocabulary is still not up to the job.

The byline on the stories was a fake name, a composite used for many writers, or so the newspaper's offices told me when I called. They wouldn't say who wrote what. I have my suspicions. A few days after *Mosquito Boy Sighting at Disneyland* ran in the paper a Mr. Frank Portis, freelance writer for the *News* and similar publications, was found dead in an Orlando motel room. I can't say whether he was or was not *drained of blood*, as the horror-writers say. The police wouldn't tell me. But there were no more Mosquito Boy stories in the *News* after that.

When writing about the Mosquito Boy, this sort of thing has to pass for research. I don't like it any more than you do.

And then, of course, Oprah.

You can find the episode on the internet, alongside a thousand blurry "sighting" videos. You should take a look, if you've forgotten. Personally I saw the original broadcast, and remember it well. I should say that I wasn't a regular watcher of Ms. Winfrey's show, but at the time I was, as they say, between jobs. On the day she introduced the Mosquito Boy to the world, the better part of a year after *Sighting at Disneyland*, I was at home, flicking through the channels, aimless and also I must admit slightly drunk, on some of the cheap wine my soon-to-ex-wife had left behind during one of her occasional and emotionally exhausting visits to my apartment—in fact I felt flat and disoriented and worn-out, which was very much the proper mood to make the unfortunate creature's acquaintance. Anyway. Look at it yourself.

OK. The theme of the episode is *inspirational persons*. At the beginning of the footage there's a certain amount of televisual fanfare, some wet shining eyes and toothy smiles and clasped hands and audience murmuring. *An extraordinary young man,* Ms. Winfrey promised us, *who has had to overcome so much.* You should skip this part.

Pause as the red curtain backstage parts, as the thing emerges. Two burly fellows in T-shirts flank it, blank-faced, stoic, like one images death-row wardens should be. It wears a hooded sweatshirt, also red, and underneath the hood a baseball cap. Who dressed it, and for God's sake why? It's notoriously difficult to judge their size—they trick one's sense of perspective—but I judge this one to be about four feet tall. Most of that's leg and curved spine. The shoulders are narrow almost to the point of nonexistence. The sweatshirt's not blood-red, precisely, that would be in poor taste; it's more *toylike*. In any case it hides most of the body from sight, and the hood and cap cover the face in a shadow that the harsh television lighting mercifully can't dispel. Perhaps you can make out a glitter of eye, a bulge of black wet hairs, some aspect of the damp sticky machinery of its mouth. Perhaps not. Either way you can unpause now.

Observe a certain awkwardness to the audience's applause, and a flicker of uncertainty in Ms. Winfrey's smile. Watch it shuffle closer. That agonizing slowness, that almost delicate hesitancy. Each individual movement of the legs is snicker-snack quick, but somehow it makes slow progress anyway; it is not fitted for this scale. One leg is longer than the other—you can't tell which, or at least I can't, thanks to the odd swiveling motion of the sweatpanted hips. It's going to take some time for it to reach the couch, during which you may, if you're like me, be reminded of Zeno's famous paradoxes of motion, those perfect figures for the futility and absurdity of existence. Alternatively, you could skip this part.

It sits beside her with its too-long legs drawn up, knees to "chin." Its feet, you may notice, are clad in loose-fitting red rubber boots. Ms. Winfrey smiles fixedly. It's hard to say what she was expecting from it but it certainly doesn't seem inclined to deliver. Yes. It *is* emitting a faint buzz. It's not a defect in the video quality; some of them do that.

Otherwise it's silent, as is the audience. Preposterously Ms. Winfrey informs us that she had discovered the creature in a Eastern European orphanage. Furthermore, she's teaching it English. You should skip this part too.

After a while she hands it a pad of paper, explaining that it doesn't speak—she manages to make it sound as if it's just adorably shy—but is learning to communicate in writing. The Boy is an inspiration, she says. I'm afraid this is true in a way. I am thinking of the young people who react against their parents and indeed their species with what they call the Mosquito lifestyle. The things I saw on the internet while I was looking for this footage! Anyway: look closely as it takes the pad. You will note that, though its "hands" are mostly covered by the sweatshirt, little hairy claws poke out. Also it holds a pen like a stabbing implement. You will, like everyone else, find it almost impossible to read the shaky spattered handwriting, even when, at Ms. Winfrey's coaxing, the creature holds the pad up to the camera. It doesn't look like language at all at first. It looks like smashed things. I remain convinced that it said: *I'm sorry*. But you may disagree. Worth taking a look, anyway; see if you can make sense out of it.

After that she ushers the thing off pretty quickly. The T-shirted men lead it out and bring on a more normal and photogenic orphan, one with cancer or dyslexia or something. And of course we all know what happened to Ms. Winfrey a few weeks later. Anyway.

That was a long time ago now. More appeared in the following years. A couple of them faced arrest and trial for the Winfrey incident, and ultimately solitary confinement, to which by all appearances they were largely indifferent. About a dozen were found in an abandoned hotel in downtown Detroit, and were frequently visited by television reporters, demanding insights and explanations, which they did not and probably could not give. A former Spice Girl was said to have adopted a pair of them, earning herself a brief return to the spotlight. It turned out that there was a sizable population of the Mosquito Boys in Mumbai, and quite a lot in parts of Brazil and in Paris, France, and there had been for decades; they just hadn't previously been written about much in the English-speaking press. The law firm of Milstein & Miller launched a highly public and controversial litigation on behalf of a class of the Mosquito Boys against the Monsanto Corporation, what used to be called British Petroleum, the Army Corps of Engineers, and a number of other defendants. Mr. Miller wept for the cameras on the courthouse steps. He wasn't sure, he said, whether the creatures were human children turned bug-like or bugs forced to suffer human attributes, including self-awareness of their own ugliness, but in either case a wrong had been committed and somebody should pay. His witnesses either didn't show up or were slumped and mute in the stand. The jury could not reach a decision and ultimately no damages were awarded. Around that time and for probably unrelated reasons public interest in the Mosquito Boys began to fade. They were just one more god damn thing one had to put up with.

But their numbers continued to rise. Now there are several thousand in the United States, living more or less openly, slouching in odd corners of run-down neighborhoods in their ill-fitting hand-me-down clothing. It's mostly social workers who dress them. A worthwhile expense of my tax dollars, I think, when you consider the alternative. I say "several thousand" because that's what one hears other people say but I really have no idea of their numbers. Probably nobody does. It's not like they respond to the census or file taxes. Most Americans when surveyed will still say that they've never seen one in the flesh but they must not be looking very hard. Another thing that surveys reveal is a sharp decline in many urban areas of the numbers of birds, dogs and cats. There is a significant inverse relationship between an area's observed population of Mosquito Boys and its homelessness rate. At night they like to hang around in dark areas of town under solitary streetlights, like underemployed hookers, and you can watch them all night through binoculars from your car and never be sure exactly how many of them you are looking at. Afterwards by daylight there's a vague odor of rancid blood, and something else for which there aren't yet words.

They are by no means all child-like in size. Some substantial percentage are as big as a full-grown man or bigger. A few are barely larger than cats. Nobody has yet calculated the percentages precisely. Nobody wants to investigate too closely. After all you never know—the things that happened to the former Spice Girl and to Mr. Miller were said to be accidents but you never know. Speaking of Mr. Miller, he was wrong. I don't believe they're the product of pollution as such. Rather it was the sort of thing that was bound to happen sooner or later. They have been intimately involved with humanity more or less forever and this further step is disconcerting but not surprising. I see them as a symptom of general entropy. I have a few ideas for investigation along these lines.

Some of them have the mouthparts in perfect form and others are more what you might call intermediate. They are so rarely autopsied that one suspects cannibalism. Some of them have a few more limbs than others, not necessarily distributed symmetrically or in even numbers. Their bristling hair (it is not exactly hair) varies widely in length and thickness. Their eyes are identical in their sad awful blankness but occasionally they have a moment of crystalline perfection before a blink rearranges them. Only a very few of them are able to fly, and you can sit out in your car with binoculars for a long long time before you'll see them take wing; but when they do usually a whole group of them goes together, rising into the orange haze over the city and drifting and lurching in ways that look purposeless to me but who knows. Who knows? At moments like that you could grudgingly call them beautiful.

The Rainbow Flame

By Shveta Thakrar

Wiping sweat from her forehead before it could spill into her eyes, Rupali stirred a large iron cauldron over a searing fire. Swirls of silver, shards of sky, and the thorny notes of a forgotten folk melody all danced through the boiling beeswax. It was different every time, like a legend passing from mouth to mouth and changing in the telling. She drew in a breath through cracked, parched lips, and the oppressive air scorched her lungs. Impatience shot through her. Would she always be the one heating the wax, never the one lighting the flame?

She reached for a small jug and poured creamy cow's milk into the mixture. The principles of Ayurveda demanded the milk be heated, but the final ingredient, a honey made from blue lotus pollen, could only be drizzled in once the cauldron had been removed from the flames.

Then there was the matter of the binder, a drop of blood.

She cringed. How much would it cost her this time?

Her mother and grandmother spoke from across the room, startling her. Their voices sounded as though they were melting in the waves of heat from the fire. "She's too young," her mother said as she always did, one hand fanning her face. "She could still be an artist. An architect. A storyteller."

"It's our duty," her grandmother countered. Her white sari clung to her, dark with perspiration stains. "Perhaps some ideas are lost in the process. But this is our art, and Rupali is bound to continue, just as we did in our time."

The familiar cadence of the tired argument comforted Rupali—it might as well be part of the rites—though the words did not. At sixteen, she was the latest blossom in a lush garland that stretched, petal by petal, back to the beginning of their family, the only keepers of the rainbow flame in all Kashi. It was a thing to be proud of, belonging to an old and important lineage, carrying out the ancient ritual. She knew that, yet part of her wondered if playing this role should really make her feel so sick afterward.

The mixture bubbled and spat, calling her back to the moment. With a sharp knife, Rupali pierced her thumb. Though she'd done it many times before, the rush of pain still made her gasp. A single, perfectly round droplet appeared on her skin, thick and red like pomegranate juice, rich with unspoken dreams. Bracing herself to be scalded, she thrust her hand over the cauldron.

The crimson drop hissed as it hit the golden wax, and starbursts bloomed behind Rupali's eyelids. She saw images of indigo palace walls threaded with silver stars, flying sheep with dazzling purple wings, grinning orange puppets manipulating their human masters. They floated before her eyes, vibrant and swaying to an eerie, wordless music.

Something tore free of her spirit and joined the contents of the cauldron.

Blisters were already forming on her exposed skin, but there was no help for it. Rupali grabbed a long wooden pole and used it to hoist the cauldron from the fire. Immediately the wax began to cool. Before it could solidify, she sprinkled in a vial of honey, then tipped the cauldron over a row of molds.

By rights, the cauldron should have been too heavy for her, and the wax should have spilled everywhere, but the magic within the room guided the process. All Rupali had to do was perform the time-honored steps.

With the last of her stamina, she unclenched her fingers from the pole. Then she fainted.

When she woke, the hardened candles had been cut from their molds, and she'd been moved to the cot kept for just this purpose. Her grandmother stroked her hair, and her mother handed her a steaming cup. Rupali carefully sat up and sipped. The hot, spicy dal was just what she needed; she could almost feel her body restoring itself, blood calling to blood, bone to bone. Yet nothing could replace the visions taken from her or soothe the strange, starved ache in her chest.

What had she given up this time? The notes to a ballad of love and loss? A game of seashells and gemstones?

Her grandmother insisted the loss was necessary, that their family was the last one to craft these master spell candles. But Rupali didn't see why the siphoned imagination should allow someone else to dream, to travel, to hold the moon in her palm for as long as the wick burned with rainbow flame.

"May I—?" Rupali paused and cleared her throat. Her tongue was dry despite the dal. "May I try one?"

Her grandmother frowned. "We've talked about this before. Our spell candles are reserved for the Singers."

"Why do they need them so badly?" Rupali burst out. Yes, she thought bitterly, they did seem to have the same argument over and over.

"Child, you know this. The Singers must heal the holes in the star field, the rents in the fabric of our traditions and stories. If even a single thread were to unravel…" Her grandmother raised her chin. "It's a fine thing we do."

Her mother, however, snorted. "Hardly." She brought her face close to Rupali's and whispered, "The Singers get them because they're the only ones with the money to afford that kind of extravagance. Ordinary people have to eat."

Rupali thought about that. She thought about that when her mother and grandmother left with the haul of new-made candles, while she scrubbed off the grime and sweat of the previous night, as she later strolled along the banks of the holy river Ganga, which at night mirrored the changeless stars above, snug in the dark narrative fabric of the sky.

Right now, though, all she could see in its waters was the sun. The sun, and the reflection of a hundred thousand people bustling through the city—a hundred thousand people whose lives were protected by the spell candles and the Singers who used them. Everything was as it had always been each time she walked here.

Rupali's hand tightened around the empty journal and sketchbook she carried. She had never been permitted to record her thoughts, because they might be stripped from her during the candle-making process, and the sacrifice had to be complete. Yet she couldn't stop herself from buying the tools to record things. Nor could she help but ponder what the books' pages might have held. What she might have said.

Her stomach roiled, and to soothe it, she purchased a paper cup of sliced fruit. The sweet-tart mango dribbled cool juices over her eager lips, while the plump cherries burst between her teeth. Rupali imagined consuming a heart, then broke off mid-chew. Would that thought be taken from her, too?

Envy rose up in her, a spiky, soaring thing. It tore at her insides and caught on the place just beneath her breasts.

Clutching her empty cup tightly, she watched children play and laugh and chat together, not a care in the world. They danced, they sang, they sculpted and drew.

She opened the sketchbook and put a stick of charcoal to the page. When forced, the charcoal made rough scratches, but that was all. Nothing in Rupali drove it to turn those scratches into something more.

Her belly aching once more, she closed the book. What would it be like, to retain her own whimsy? To engage it without a second thought?

The Singers, in their isolated diamond-walled palace on the hill, were said to be the guardians of the star-laced stories—and of the people themselves. No one really knew what the Singers did with their spell candles, but rumor had it they went straight to fulfilling personal pleasures. Rupali, though, guessed otherwise; as far as she could tell, the city was thriving.

Yet why should it be at the cost of her own visions? Wasn't she one of the people, too?

She tossed the cup into the river. It floated off, a tiny boat sailing away on adventures she couldn't begin to imagine. If this were a story, a maiden would rise from the waters and offer her three wishes. At the very least, the children would invite her to join their games.

Of course, nothing of the kind happened. Instead, Rupali took one last, longing glance at the city, and then turned to go home.

*

Panting, Rupali finished her latest batch of candles. She could craft candles every day of her life and still not sate her customers' appetites, but the risk of stripping herself bare was too great. Her great-grandmother had done that, pushing harder and harder until she snapped into a schedule that repeated itself perfectly from waking to bed. She would not deviate from it, cycling through the same activities at the same times as the day before, using identical words and intonation to tell the same stories, eating the same foods in exactly the same sequence and proportions, even coughing and sneezing at predictable intervals. When the family tried to intercede, her great-grandmother had shut down completely. Upon waking a day later, she resumed the routine.

With a shudder, Rupali swore now she would never let that happen to her. Even once a month left her drained.

Her mother and grandmother reached for her just as she swooned.

The next thing Rupali knew, an unfamiliar voice called her name. "Wake up, Rupali." A hand shook her.

Rupali moaned and opened bleary eyes. It took a bit of blinking in the dark before she could make out the shape of a girl standing over her. "What—who are you?" she asked, her voice still clothed in sleep.

The girl held a torch up to her face and grinned. "Daya. Pleased to meet you." She rattled the cot. "Now get up."

Too dazed to protest, Rupali let the strange girl pull her upright. "Good," said Daya. "Now you're going to show me where the candles are."

"The—the candles?" Rupali squeezed her eyes shut. Thoughts began to form behind her lids. This girl had come in the middle of the night. She had somehow slipped in past Rupali's mother and grandmother. "Wait, are you here to steal them?"

"Maybe," said Daya. "I haven't decided."

Rupali stared in disbelief. "You haven't decided? How did you even get in here?"

Daya shrugged. "I saw you this afternoon and followed you. Everyone knows who you are, candle girl."

That wasn't the way the story was supposed to go. Rupali was supposed to get a candle of her own, not help a would-be thief take one. She hopped off the cot and snatched up one of the ordinary candles used for light. "I think you should leave now."

"Or what? I know you won't call your family."

Rupali walked toward the door. "Well, you're wrong. That's exactly what I'm going to do."

"Wait!" Daya grabbed Rupali's wrist. Her grip was strong for someone so small. "I don't want to steal anything! I just want to see your candles. Please."

Rupali looked down at the girl studying her anxiously. Daya was actually quite pretty, she realized, with long, thick black hair and large, dark eyes. Her smooth skin, a darker brown than Rupali's own, contrasted nicely with her violet salwaar kameez. But it was the worry in her tone that made Rupali pause. "Why?" she asked warily.

"Because!" Daya dropped Rupali's arm and reached for her hands. "Because I'm not a Singer."

"Well, yes, but—"

"If I hadn't said anything," Daya rushed on, "I would be one of them. If I..."

"If you what?" Rupali asked, intrigued. "What did you say?" She had never been close enough to see a Singer in person, let alone to offend one. "It must have been terrible."

"Never you mind," Daya said, glowering. "Are you going to show me the candles or not?"

Rupali didn't need to think about it. This girl could be anyone, a liar, a swindler. Certainly she had broken into the workroom; there was no arguing with that. "No, and I think you'd better leave now."

"You're just as bad as they are," Daya muttered, "except you don't know what you're doing." She let her gaze roam the cavernous space one more time, taking in every corner, every shadow, as though she could tease out the candles' location. "Next time, then."

"They're not here." Rupali held open the door, fully expecting Daya to resist. Instead, after shooting a final glare, Daya scampered out into the night.

Rupali knew she'd done the right thing, yet as she curled back up on her cot, she could not stop replaying the strange visit in her mind. Why had Daya wanted to see the candles so badly that she would break in for them?

And her final words: *You're just as bad as they are.* A spiteful parting shot, and one that stung. Perhaps, Rupali decided, Daya simply couldn't stand not getting her way. Perhaps that was why the Singers had rejected her.

Either way, it was clear Rupali would have to think more about all this.

Two nights later, on Sarasvati Pooja, the day Kashi honored the Goddess of Speech and Stories with narrative and song, Rupali handed her grandmother the bowl of mushrooms she'd chopped. She'd always loved how they were called "cat's hats" in Gujarati. That had been the product of someone's mischievous imagination.

Yet even the little smile the quaint phrase brought to her face couldn't lessen her guilt at having chased off the intruder girl, nor could she forget Daya's taunt. Imagination, rainbow flames, the Singers. *You don't know what you're doing.*

What if Daya knew something Rupali didn't?

Laughing, her mother rolled out a fenugreek-stuffed theplu. "Dikri, remember how you used to tell Nani and me a story about the clever kittens with their mushroom caps? You changed the ending every time!"

"I did?" Rupali's chest felt hollowed out. Try as she might, she could not recall a single version of the tale, let alone having told it. "What did I say?"

Her mother's mouth turned down. "Never mind."

"Enough!" Her grandmother gestured impatiently. "Let go of what is gone. To do otherwise is to court trouble."

"You're right," Rupali's mother said, her voice distant. "I'm sorry."

Rupali, however, was anything but sorry. The ghost of an image glimmered at the edges of her thoughts, then vanished into the evening sunlight pouring through the kitchen window.

Her grandmother, ever keen, narrowed her eyes. "Is something troubling you, dikri?"

"Yes, Nani," Rupali said. "How does one become a Singer?"

Her mother and grandmother traded glances. "Why do you ask?" her grandmother asked casually. But the vigor with which she stirred the spicy mixture on the stove betrayed her concern.

"Because…because they're our customers," Rupali replied. "If I'm making candles for them, surely I should know more about them."

Her mother nodded. "She has a point, Mataji." To Rupali, she said, "They accept initiates every five years, from every walk of life."

"The idea is that the Singers must never lose touch with the people they represent," her grandmother put in, lifting the lid from the pot of rice. The aroma of cumin and cloves drifted toward Rupali, making her stomach growl.

"But the work they do," she asked, "does it truly serve us?"

Her grandmother paused. "Is it for us to say? Our job is to do as tradition demands. We make the candles as we have been taught, and we sell them to the Singers. That's all you need to worry about."

Rupali lowered her head, though inside, she seethed. Why shouldn't she know the people for whom she sacrificed her imagination, her vision?

But there was nothing to be gained from arguing, so instead she ate quietly, barely tasting the meal. Once her grandmother decided they had eaten enough, Rupali was free to take her leave.

Her mother followed her from the kitchen and all the way to her room. "I've been thinking for some time now that you should try your own candle. It is only right that you know not just the people you're selling your candles to, but also what it is you're creating."

She put her finger to her lips, then reached into the knotted end of her sari and produced a long, waxy cylinder the color of honeycomb. "Think carefully about what you want before you light it. Whatever you ask for will be so for the time it takes the wick to burn all the way down. Even the most powerful sorcerer couldn't ask for more."

Rupali stared at the candle. A smile swept over her face. "Anything?"

"Anything. But," her mother cautioned, "you must not forget the spell will only last as long as the candle burns, so act quickly."

"But how does it actually repair holes in the story star field?"

Her mother pursed her lips.

Rupali let it go. The candle was already an enormous gift, one she'd had no reason to expect. She kissed her mother good night. In return, her mother lay her hand on Rupali's forehead in blessing.

In the solitude of her room, she cleared her desk, set the candle on a glass plate, and struck a match. It flared in the gloom, a spark of life. Unable to suppress a smile, Rupali lit the wick.

She had thought she would ask for a million gold pieces. She had thought she would ask to see inside the Singers' palace. Instead, as she gazed into the undulating flame that, for now, was merely orange, her thoughts jumped to her unexpected visitor from two nights before, who had clearly enjoyed many adventures, likely alongside a coterie of friends. What would that be like?

The flame kindled, then burned red, then green, blue, then purple, yellow, then indigo and orange and red once more, rotating through the spectrum again and again. It was the most beautiful thing she had ever seen.

Still, how could she have been so stupid as to waste the wish? She should have asked to find the Singers!

The candle began to cast off sparks, and Rupali inhaled sharply. The sparks blossomed in the air, scattering bands of light over the bed like the sun through a giant prism. As she stared, the bands merged into something like a window, which expanded until it filled an entire wall.

The portal opened onto a vista of the river at night, thickly salted with the reflection of the stars. Rupali chewed on her cheek, considering. The candle had been lit, the spell cast. She had only the few hours until the wick burned out. If she wanted to see what the candle could do, she needed to try it now.

She clambered through the scintillating frame.

Rupali emerged beneath a moonlit papaya tree near the softly splashing river. The air was perfumed by the fruits' fragrance, and all around, people in fine clothing danced and sang beneath a myriad of colored lanterns. But the leap through the window had stuffed her head with clouds and cotton, and she couldn't make sense of the celebration.

A sweets seller beckoned to her from his brightly decorated stall, which was festooned with a string of tiny lanterns. Rupali thought vaguely that the lanterns might have reminded her of something once, long ago. "Feast days are my best days," the seller announced.

How could she have forgotten? Her family might have stayed home, tending to mundane concerns, but today was a feast day. The proper thing to do would be to purchase milk sweets to give in offering at Sarasvati Devi's temple and tell stories amid the scent of incense.

The seller convinced her to buy a box of round yellow laddoos, diamond-shaped kaju katli topped with silver leaf, and bright pink chumchums. Bemused at having forgotten the date, Rupali didn't even haggle.

A group of five people her mother's age wandered by. One threw back her head and broke into peals of delighted laughter. As Rupali glanced around, she saw everyone was already paired off or in groups. Only she was alone.

Her shoulders slumped. Never mind the temple. All she wanted to do was hide. The papaya tree's branches would be a fine place to wait out the spell…

Rupali, who had never climbed a tree in her life, found herself scampering up the notched bark. There, a large platform sat nestled precariously amidst the branches. She stiffened. Someone had already claimed this tree.

"Who is this little monkey who's come to play?" Daya's voice rang out in pleasure. "Not the candle girl herself?"

Rupali laughed and climbed onto the lantern-strewn platform where Daya nibbled on chevdo. At the sight of the red box Rupali carried, Daya abandoned the savory snack mix. "Ooh, what did you bring me?"

Still slightly cloud-muddled, Rupali opened the box. Per tradition, she plucked out a sugary chumchum and held it up to Daya's lips. Daya's eyes darkened even more, and after a brief hesitation, she opened her mouth.

Rupali deposited the confection there. "The goddess be praised," she recited.

Daya smacked her lips. "Indeed!" She selected a piece of kaju katli from the box. "My turn."

Rupali's cheeks warmed, yet according to age-old custom, she couldn't refuse. She parted her lips, and Daya fed her the sweet, echoing her words: "The goddess be praised." The cashew fudge melted on Rupali's tongue, lush and delicious, making her reckless.

She met Daya's stare squarely, not averting her eyes even when the moment moved from acknowledgement into awkwardness. Daya, who appeared to enjoy a challenge, also stayed put. They sat that way, each breathing the other in, the raucous sounds of celebration beneath them a world away. Rupali could almost...

Then Daya spoke, her words harsh in the silence. "Did you bring my candle?"

Rupali went rigid and responded with a question of her own. "What happened? Why aren't you an initiate?"

"I found out something I wasn't supposed to know, and I paid the price."

"I don't understand," Rupali said. "What are you talking about?"

"Did you bring my candle?" Daya asked again. In the soft light of the lanterns, she seemed more spirit than human. "I want to see the rainbow flame."

Something woke in Rupali at that, something she couldn't name. Her mouth formed words, but her mind had again been ensnared by the strange, compelling eyes of the girl staring back at her. It was oddly difficult to exhale.

Irritated, she tilted her head up at the star field. Above them, the constellations gazed back, steady as ever, their radiance bright against the blue-black cloak of sky. Narrowing her eyes, Rupali tried to make out the patches where they had been mended or any holes awaiting repair. But there was nothing she could see.

Yet her grandmother had been so adamant about the Singers' need to protect the star field. Perhaps they had already done their job with the candles and their song, and that was why she couldn't see any problems?

"Tell me about the Singers," she whispered. The breeze stole her words away, but not before Daya heard her.

"My mother is one."

"*What?*" The space beneath Rupali's ribs constricted. "Then why did you try to steal the candles?"

"I told you, I didn't! I just wanted to see them. My mother may be a Singer, but I'm not." Daya ran a hand through her long hair. "Because I went hunting in the palace archives and found the book that told me how things used to be."

Rupali shook away the phantom feel of her own fingers knotted in those dark, glossy waves. "How they used to be?"

"Yes." Daya pointed to the stars. "See how they never blink?"

Rupali nodded. "Why would they?"

"They should be. It's called 'twinkling.' They're frozen up there, just like we are down here."

"I have no idea what you're trying to tell me," Rupali said, though her stomach knotted tighter with each word Daya spoke. "If you believe you can make up a story to trick me into giving you a candle—"

Daya leaned forward. "That's just it. There *are* no new stories. All we have is the old stories, and we're stuck in them." She took a breath, then added, "That wasn't the first time I broke into your house. Even you and I are starting to get caught in the narrative loop."

If Rupali had thought her thoughts were muzzy before, that was nothing compared to this moment. "What do you mean, you broke in before?"

"This isn't the first time we've had this conversation," Daya said wearily, as if she had repeated this many times before. "The Singers made a mistake. My ancestor thought she could keep us all safe by freezing the star field. And the star field is made up of what?"

"Stories." Rupali fought to think. "So the spell candles don't heal the rifts in the star field?"

"Oh, they do. They keep the field in stasis. The stars are supposed to move, to blink. The narrative flow of the world is meant to move and renew itself. When it doesn't, we freeze, too."

"Prove it," Rupali said. Even if it explained her great-grandmother's last days, how could this possibly be true? "Show me the book."

Daya flinched visibly. "I can't. My mother took it when I confronted her. She...she destroyed it. She won't listen to me. She won't even look at me!"

"A convenient excuse," Rupali said, rolling her eyes even as her hands trembled. Her great-grandmother, lost. "Well done trying to get a candle out of me, but it's hardly my fault you can't get along with your mother."

"But can't you see how everything repeats itself now?" Daya pleaded. "How many times do we have go through this?"

Rupali couldn't stop imagining her great-grandmother trapped inside a single day. Her mouth burned with fear. She couldn't listen anymore. She couldn't.

"I know you know," whispered Daya.

Refusing to look at her, Rupali turned and inched her way back down the tree. It was fiction. It was false. Of course it was.

Yet what if—?

She approached the sweets seller's stall. Again he beckoned to her, his string of lanterns flickering in the same order, and again he greeted her with the same observation on the day's earnings and a box of laddoos, kaju katli topped with silver leaf, and chumchums. Again she felt no urge to haggle.

Again the group of friends strolled by, and again the woman tossed back her head before breaking out in enthusiastic laughter.

Rupali ran, leaving the seller holding the box. She passed Daya, who now stood on the ground, watching her with concern.

"It's going to keep happening, isn't it?" Rupali jabbed a finger at the sweets stall. "Whatever *that* was."

"It already did," Daya said.

"Take me to meet them," Rupali ordered, the words surprising even her. "The Singers. Right now."

Though Daya raised her eyebrows, she took Rupali's hand. "Come, then."

No one gave them a second glance as they rushed through the throng. Tonight, they were just more merrymakers honoring the goddess.

But how many times had Rupali played out this scenario without knowing it? How many times had the people around her? Would they eventually become like her great-grandmother if the spell candles continued to burn?

Rupali and Daya were silent as they climbed the grassy hill, leaving behind the jubilant crowds and festive lights. Rupali traced the moon-silvered river with her eyes. Had her cup sailed away on new adventures, perhaps even located a tiny captain and crew to aid it on its journey?

"Daya," she said, paying no heed to the pounding of her heart. This would be one bit of her imagination no one could take away, not with Daya safekeeping it. "I put a paper cup in the river, and it sailed away, and now I believe it has a crew of miniature sailors. Maybe even pirates."

"All women, of course," Daya said, grinning. She didn't—she couldn't—know the terrible thing Rupali had just done. Her grandmother and her mother would be so disappointed if they knew.

But maybe, she thought, they were the ones who should feel guilty.

Daya abruptly halted. "There," she whispered, pointing. "There's my mother. Mrinalini."

People with elegant hairstyles and glittering, ornate jewelry clustered outside the palace. They wore black silk dotted with silver, a tribute to the constellations above. Tables set with gem-cut jars of blue and green fireflies provided the only other illumination, so it took a moment for Rupali to locate the woman in question. Once she did, however, her heart dropped. The woman was not beautiful, but authority radiated from her like pollen, rich and intoxicating, and the sari pallu covering her head glinted with miniature mirrors that caged the light of the immutable stars.

Not to mention she clutched a spell candle bound up with slivers of Rupali's imagination.

Daya squeezed Rupali's hand hard, too hard, her palm sweaty. Rupali squeezed back.

Mrinalini opened her mouth, and the other Singers followed suit. Eddies of notes tumbled forth, crisp as silver, soft as gold. Rupali could almost see the music in the night air. Some notes flew up into the sky, one by one, and others spiraled around Rupali in an ardent caress of sound. She shivered.

Next to her, Daya sighed.

The candle burst into flame, and stories from the star field began narrating themselves, cascading over Rupali's body, soaking into her bones.

The other Singers held up spell candles, and they, too, were burning, their seven hues shimmering and dancing. As one, the Singers came to a crescendo, and overhead, the stars quaked and tried but failed to shift position before finally resettling themselves. Rupali watched, unable to speak. The story star field!

She could feel how it connected everyone, and how desperately it needed to move. Unable to flow unhindered, it was drowning them.

Then Mrinalini spoke.

"Order must be preserved. Let those who forget the importance of tradition and preservation of the old ways now remember what they mean. We are made of stories, and we must protect them." Her gaze, which had been trained on the stars, now found her daughter.

"No!" cried Daya. "It's not meant to be like this. I know the truth is scary, Mother, but you can't keep denying it. Can you just listen for once?"

"She's right," said Rupali tentatively. When no one spoke, she continued. "I can feel it; the stories belong to everyone. They need to be released."

"You're wrong," Mrinalini said, her voice cold. "We are their guardians. We must protect them from corruption and outside influences."

Though Rupali quailed beneath the force of the Singer's words, she made herself go on. "But it's my imagination burning in that candle right now. I give it all to the candles, and I must never use it myself. Surely I have some say in what's done with it?"

Mrinalini glared at Rupali, her candle flame wagging like a finger. "Enough. I will silence you myself."

Before the spell could be completed, Rupali clasped Daya's hand, then released it. "Run!"

They set off down the hill, legs pumping and sides stinging. When they neared the papaya tree, the window of winding colors appeared in the air, and they vaulted through it, landing in Rupali's bedroom.

The last of the wick burned out then, leaving nothing but a couple drops of singed wax. The window, too, dissolved into darkness. Rupali counted out slow, deliberate breaths. Had the entire evening been just a fantasy brought on by the spell?

Muffled weeping nearby quickly dispelled her doubts. The rainbow flame might have gone out, but the girl it had brought was still there. "Daya? Are you all right?"

"My—my mother tried to cast a spell on us!" Daya sobbed. "I was just trying to save her. To save all of us. How can she not know that?"

Rupali knew her own mother would never attack her like that. How sad Daya must feel, how alone. "Listen," Rupali said, taking her hand, "we're safe. You're here with me. Now explain what exactly is happening."

Daya rubbed her reddened eyes. "My mother knows, but she can't admit it," she said. "It's the candles. The Singers cast spells to keep us wrapped in the old stories. To keep them from changing, so our world never changes, either. That's why I wanted one, to see if perhaps I could break the spells."

Rupali let that information seep in. "Let's set the candles free," she suggested. "If the stories are meant for everyone, then we will give them to everyone."

"If you light them," Daya whispered, "I believe I can sing them free."

In reply, Rupali opened the door and signaled for Daya to follow.

In the shadows of the shop's workroom, Rupali thought of all the spells yet to be cast, all the visions still to be sacrificed in the rainbow flame, and all the stagnation that would cause.

"Tradition is a good thing," she said, "but sometimes we need to make our own." She pressed a vial of honey into Daya's hand and a kiss onto her cheek. "Our first new tradition—demanding recognition for the people!"

Smiling, Daya studied the honey. Rupali had given her the smallest vial she had, one tiny enough to wear on a golden chain about her neck. "What is this for?"

"For binding the imagination to the candle. Honey is sticky, you know."

Daya looked thoughtful. "It is, at that. Shall we gather the candles?"

"Yes, but we have to be silent." Rupali pointed to the doorway. "Wait here."

It was more than risky, it was dangerous. If her grandmother caught them, she would lock Rupali away for years. Worse, they didn't know what the rainbow flames would actually do. But there was only one way to find out. She stuffed the fresh candles into a burlap sack along with a fistful of matches, then grabbed a torch.

Daya, who had been shifting her weight from foot to foot, snatched the bag from Rupali. "Let's go!" she whispered.

With the star field of stories their only witness, they hurried down to the river. Most of the revelers had gone home to sleep, and those who lingered paid the girls no attention. The moon hung low in the sky, ready for its own well-earned slumber. No candle was burning, yet the night felt even more like the work of a magical charm.

"We must hurry," Daya repeated again and again, "or my mother will find us!"

Kneeling on the sand, Rupali lit the spell candles, then placed each glowing pillar in the water. As if weightless, they floated on the river's surface, their multihued flames flickering. She gently nudged them into motion. *Go*, she thought. *Go to those who need you most.*

The individual flames spread, eating through the wax pillars and merging into one conflagration that plunged down in search of more fuel. The water hissed, but rather than dousing the massive pyre, it, too, ignited. Seconds later, the entire Ganga blazed, one enormous, raging sheet of seven-hued fire.

Her thumbnail between her teeth, Rupali backed away as fast as she could. She gaped at the incredible sight of burning water. What had they done?

The shore began to liquefy in the heat. "It's going to burn the whole city down!" Daya shouted over the roar. "We have to put it out!"

"How?" Rupali managed to ask between unsteady giggles. "We can't exactly throw water on it!"

The old world is burning, a story murmured in her brain. *The old world must die, that the new one be born!*

"No," Rupali told it, ignoring her wobbling limbs. That wasn't true. No one should blindly obey the dictates of elders and follow traditions without question, but there was no reason to discard everything all at once. People needed to be able to look up to those who came before. They needed well-worn rituals that linked the past to the present. Power resided in those rituals.

Daya's mother knew that. Her own mother certainly did.

Yes. The heroine. The tempering. The sacrifice, the stories murmured as the fire advanced. *That is how the new world will be born—not in spite of the old but* from *it*.

That Rupali understood. She knelt on the smoldering riverbank. Before she could think through it, she dipped her hand into the firewater.

Her skin shrieked with pain as it sizzled and melted.

Screaming, Daya tried to pull her out, but the rainbow fire had already left the water to leach into Rupali's pores and penetrate her veins. Soon it would reach her heart, devouring, cleansing.

"It's all right," she whispered, just loud enough for Daya to hear. "Just sing."

"Enough!" another voice called, a musical voice. A distant corner of Rupali's mind recognized it as belonging to Daya's mother. The other Singers stood behind her, agape. Mrinalini frantically tore a spell candle from her sari and raced toward Rupali. "This is unacceptable. The order of things must be observed!"

"It's too late, Mother," Daya said softly, stepping back. "There's nothing you can do now." She began to sing, the lyrics about a boat made of a paper cup.

"Stop!" Mrinalini cried. "You have no idea what you're doing!"

Daya kept singing.

The fire, Rupali realized, *it's me. It's my imagination. It's* everyone's *imagination. It's the stuff of stories.* She glanced up, and the constellations shone with the same seven-toned flame. They always had. She just hadn't been able to see it before. But the flame was fixed in place, unable to burn freely. It needed to flow, to incinerate old stories and create new stories from the ashes. *We're the real spell candles.*

As Daya sang, the rainbow flame gushed forth, filling the dark spaces between the now-twinkling stars. The constellations themselves began to spin. How they glowed with starlight and story and song!

All the memories, all the ideas Rupali had ever had and lost flooded back into her, a lava stream of inspiration. She was so hot, she would combust any second now.

The crowd at the water's edge grew as more and more of the city's inhabitants woke, summoned by the fire's call. Rupali spotted her grandmother and mother among them, their eyes wide with fright.

Her song finished, Daya held out her arms to Mrinalini. "Stories change, Mother. Sometimes they die, and new stories are born. They need to, just like us."

"We have new ways now," Rupali added, just before her throat seared shut and her breathing stilled. The fire crackled hungrily in her ears as it claimed every part of her.

Mrinalini waved her unlit candle. "Daya, what foolishness have you wrought? Don't you understand? We *can't make* new stories."

"We have to—"

"You're not my daughter," said Mrinalini, shaking. "My daughter would never shame me like this."

The hope in Daya's face dimmed, a wick spent at long last. Rupali's heart twisted with an ache that had nothing to do with the rainbow fire. Unable to watch, she closed her eyes.

Then, just as abruptly as it had begun, the flames within Rupali ceased to burn her. Now they were hers to command. Just like the Singers.

No, she corrected herself. *Not to command*. That was where the Singers had failed their people. *To guide*.

She opened her eyes. Her skin was whole, untouched, as was the riverbank. But everywhere she looked, from the shadows to the worried faces staring back, she saw the sparks of rainbow fireworks, blossoming, booming. Story was in the people's blood. It was their birthright. It was the signature of the goddess.

The star field arced over them, sparkling, woven through with all the tales that had ever been and would be. Every person in Kashi and beyond was threaded into that magnificent tapestry, and every person could tap into it at will.

They didn't need spell candles or even Singers anymore.

Before her, curious citizens trickled toward the palace, whose diamond doors now stood open to them. Others laid hands on the Singers' shoulders and murmured words of comfort while eyeing Rupali with suspicion. Still others just looked on with bewilderment, her grandmother among them. Her mother, though, beamed with pride.

Mrinalini snapped her candle in half. "Sarasvati Devi only knows what you hope to accomplish here, but I have no need of your imagination any longer."

Drawing strength from her own mother's smile, Rupali stood. "I'm glad to hear that," she told Mrinalini and her Singers. "Today, on Sarasvati's day, the magic goes back to the people entrusted to your care. The stories flow free, to die and change and be reborn. You may have forgotten, but your privilege is to serve them—and us."

Then she walked over to Daya and took her hand. "Would you like to keep me company while I draw the story of what will happen tomorrow?"

With tears still streaking her cheeks, Daya kissed Rupali, and there was only fire.

The Sixth Day

By Sylvia Anna Hivén

'm the corn girl. That's cause I make our corn field grow.

If I take my shoes off and curl my toes deep into the dirt when I walk round the field—although that tears up my feet something bad—I can grow it a quarter inch a day, so long as I make sure to touch all stalks I pass. You'd think that's an amazing talent, especially in a place where them other fields around our farm lie dead. But nobody ain't noticing a lick of what I do—not when my sister can travel to the future and tell us how to keep the stretch away.

Cassie. She ain't no corn girl. Pa, old Jeremiah, the Howell sisters across the corn field—they all just care about what Cassie has to say when she comes back. What will slip away, what knickknacks will vanish: Pa's wagon wheels or Jeremiah's clod-hoppers or the wooden cross under the knotted oak where Ma's buried. Cassie used to be able to tell us what farms the stretch would take, too, but there are just the six of us and our farm left now. So now all that vanishes are things here and there: socks and the scythes in the barn and tiles off the Howell's roof.

Except one day, Cassie ain't telling me what will vanish. She tells me something's coming.

"A man and a boy," she says as she steps out of the mirror. "They got cows. Cows, Jo, can you believe that?"

The mirror shimmers behind her. I catch a glimpse of what all lies beyond—our farm six days from now. I hope to catch sight of cows down the dirt road but all I see's the corn field and the outline of Jeremiah's little shack behind it. Then the mirror goes flat and there's just the reflection of me and Cassie: round and curly-haired and freckled Cassie because she gets away from the stretch sometimes, and me, tall and lanky with sore feet and hair straight as a horse's mane Jo, because I never go nowhere.

"How you know they're cows?" I ask. "You ain't never even seen one."

"They're cows. I just know. At least two dozen of them." Cassie puts the tattered sheet back over the mirror, making a looming ghost out of it in the corner of the room. "You're gonna catch them down at the crossroads and bring them back here."

"At the crossroads?" I shudder. "Why'd I be down at the crossroads?"

The crossroads is where you notice the stretch the most. There ain't nothing out there but empty plains in all directions, and black crows flapping in the wind like a bunch of screeching scabby marks in the sky. Ain't none of us been out by the crossroads since Pa and I went out to put up a sign. We did it in case anybody was still alive out there to need shelter, since we got corn to eat and crows to shoot with Pa's rifle—but that was before the stretch ate his last few bullets, so if someone came now we couldn't feed them, nohow. We ain't been back to the crossroads since.

"You're gonna be down at the crossroads because I tell you to," Cassie says. "You know how it works by now, Jo."

This part is what never makes no sense: how Cassie can see something I haven't gone and done yet—or wouldn't even do to begin with unless she'd seen me and told me to do it. You can go crazy trying to figure it out. But then, the stretch's a weird thing—it groans everything thin until there's nothing left, and screaming at the stretch how it don't make no sense don't make it stretch things any less.

"Guess we'd better tell Pa, then, so he can fix the buggy," I say. "Who knows how far away the crossroads have stretched by now. I sure ain't walking all the way there."

We go outside. We can't see the sun anymore: it's just a tired disc behind corpse-pale clouds too thick for anything to shine through them. Nothing casts shadows in the yard—not the sundial, not the fence with its peeling paint, not Cassie or me. It's as if the thin sunlight goes straight through us, like we're spirits that God forgot to claim.

We find Pa and Jeremiah in the field. They're stomping snake eggs to a slimy crunch beneath their boots. Makes no sense what the snakes be doing in that field, because we don't have no mice or critters in it, but there are always nests popping up all over the place. One time, Cassie saw a snake bite me six days before it happened, and Pa wouldn't let me go into the field for two weeks until he'd checked every corner of it. He said if the stretch hadn't managed to get me in five years, he sure wasn't gonna give me up to no damn snake on something as common as a Wednesday afternoon.

Jeremiah shovels the snake mess over the fence while Cassie tells them about the man with the boy and cows. Sometimes Cassie's words have a way of making the wrinkles smooth out of Pa's face, but today she makes him lick his lips, too.

"Steak," he says, ruffling Cassie's already unruly hair with thin fingers. "Aren't you the bearer of good news."

"I sure didn't think there was anyone else left out there," Jeremiah mumbles, his gray eyes fixed on the horizon yawning wide beneath the twilight. "And with cattle, too."

"You think maybe things are changing, Mister Jeremiah?" I ask. "Maybe the stretch is getting tired and things are pulling themselves together again."

Jeremiah smiles, but it's a rueful smile. "I think the world's too stretched out to ever pull itself back again, Jo. I don't think things are gonna change much, except we might get a few good meals."

"That's change enough," Pa replies. "I think we're all tired of corn."

Mister Jeremiah mumbles something else, about God having given up on us and for Pa to not give us girls false hope, but there's a gleam in his eyes that ain't been there before. He says goodbye and goes off to tell the Howell sisters about the visitors. Cassie and Pa head back home, the corn stalks swooshing around them like brittle ghosts in the evening breeze.

I grow those cornstalks half an inch before I go inside. And wouldn't you know it, nobody notices a lick.

A few days later I ain't walked the fields for more than a few hours when Cassie rustles through the corn. Blotches of red dance high on her cheeks like someone done smacked her round, but her bright eyes are wide in exhilaration.

"Linus *likes* you," she says.

I stop walking—which is nice, because my feet are already burning.

"Who's Linus?"

"The boy with the cattle. He's our age. Maybe a year older. He *likes* you."

The last boy I remember was Jimmy Dixon, a little white stick of a boy with wheat-colored hair. We used to catch silver-bellied fish down in the creek behind the shed where Jeremiah lives now and he had a laughter you could hear for miles. Him and his family vanished with the stretch a few years ago, and I haven't really thought about boys at all since then. Boys, courting, getting married—all of that went away with the stretch. When I done started to bleed and Cassie told me what it was all for, I cried. I'd be going through all that trouble for nothing because there were no boys to make babies with, not in the whole wide world.

But three days from now, there's gonna be a boy at the farm, and he's gonna like me. If Cassie says so, it's gonna happen, because Cassie's never wrong.

"What's he like?" I continue to walk, trying to not sound too excited and trying to concentrate on the field, but my mind's already painting pictures in my head of this boy named Linus.

Cassie follows behind me as I walk. "Tall, like you. Kinda handsome, I guess. He has a rifle with him all the time. Says the crows out there in the stretch are mean and will peck at you in the night."

"The stretch ain't a nice place," I say. "Jeremiah and the Howells always told us it's bad. Much worse than here."

Mister Jeremiah and the Howell sisters came the week Ma died from blood poisoning. By then that weird magic had been eating the plains for three years already, and the town we used to go to for supplies was gone along with all the people in it. Mister Jeremiah wandered off a cotton farm in the next county over, and he done come across the Howell sisters who lost their village and took a wagon and a scrawny old horse and rode out with just the clothes on their back to not go the same way.

Together the three of them came down our dirt road in their wagon, sunburned and bony and rickety as scarecrows, the same morning when we'd put up Ma's cross. Jeremiah claimed he'd smelled the corn cooking from miles away and that's how they'd found our farm.

The Howell sisters weren't really sisters at all but that's what Pa said, anyway. I reckon maybe he thought we'd be shocked at the idea of two old white ladies sleeping in the same bed and touching each other's hands when they thought nobody was looking, but we have weirder things happening around us and it don't bother me any.

So the sisters took the larger shack on the hill and Jeremiah stayed in one of the field sheds. And that's how there are six of us in one little spot, and hardly anyone else in the rest of the world. But soon there's gonna be two more, and a whole bunch of cows.

Cassie tip-toes down the rows behind me, telling me how I'm gonna show Linus the creek and how Pa and Jeremiah will help slaughter a cow and how Cassie herself is gonna be watching it from the porch and gag at how red the blood will be against the bone-white ground. She spends almost all day on the other side, but when she gets back she remembers mostly glimpses like that. Makes me wonder what she remembers of this side when she crosses over to the future. Or maybe this is the past, and we're the ones six days behind. Shoot, I try to not think about it too much.

"They're gonna cook the meat over the fire," Cassie says. "Big slabs of it. I tried some, but I didn't like it. Tastes burnt and wrong. Even worse than crow."

"I won't mind trying," I say, still walking down the field, still brushing the plants with my fingers, teasing the dry stalks to cut me, feeling lightheaded and giddy.

"Jo, stop your damn walking for a second."

Cassie's cussing stops me in my tracks. When I turn around, all the seriousness I'm trying to keep out of my face is aching in Cassie's. There's no shadow cast from the corn stalks to hide the tears in her eyes, neither.

"I think they're gonna ask Pa to let you leave with them," she says. "And you're gonna want to go."

Then my sister begins to sob.

There's an old photo of Ma and Cassie and I on a wood shelf in the kitchen. It's faded a bit round the edges and half of Cassie's face is bleached out. I can see Ma's face just fine, but as terrible as it sounds it's not her face I look at. It the way she's holding me—a tiny bundle with a head shock-full of hair, all snug in her arms like she'd rather die than put me down. I wonder if that's how I'd feel too, if I ever had a baby of my own. Something alive and warm and soft to the touch, instead of a crackle-dry corn field.

Although when I start to think that way I feel my cheeks heat up with embarrassment and I turn back to the stove and the corn stew I'm making.

"It hurts, you know," Cassie says, putting down our chipped blue-rosed china on the dining table behind me with angry, clacking noises.

"What hurts?" I ask, grateful that Pa's still outside because even though I ask, I kinda already know what she means.

"Having a baby. Even making them hurts. Much worse than your bleed."

I blush harder. "How do you know that?"

"The Howell sisters told me. They say men are nothing but trouble. They're probably right."

I turn to my sister, and she meets me with a defiant gaze, clutching the plates in her hand so hard her knuckles turn white. She looks a little scary, even— like she's facing some beast and ain't afraid to go at it, and that beast is me.

"Cassie, you gotta stop," I say. "We don't know what's going to happen for sure when those folks get here. Maybe you ain't seeing things right. Maybe it's all hat and no cattle. And if there's a boy, who says I'll even like him at all."

"I ain't never been wrong," Cassie says. "The only way I'm ever wrong is if we decide to change something before it happens, like when Pa went to kill the snake."

"Well, this ain't no snake," I say, feeling my cheeks burn hotter. "So nothing's gonna need changing, Cassie. We'll just have to see tomorrow, is all."

Pa comes in then, stomping dust off his boots and we don't talk of it anymore. We just eat the corn stew, and drink water from greasy glass cups, and Pa tells me the buggy's oiled and ready for me to take it to the crossroads. He doesn't notice that Cassie's eyes are brimful of tears. But I notice. So after I've done washed up I find her out on the porch. It's chilly out there and it makes my arm prickle like the skin of a plucked chicken. Cassie don't seem to notice the cold.

"He kissed you today," she says. "Behind the corner of the old chicken coop."

My heart beats once, hard. I draw my shawl tighter around my shoulders. My first kiss, just six days away, and tomorrow I'll meet the boy who will give it to me. I want to smile about it, but it feels wrong to smile when my sister looks as though I have betrayed her. So I just stand there, watching the daylight drain out of the glum sky, until she's gone to bed, and Pa's gone to bed, and all's quiet.

For some reason I'd expected the sixth day to look different when I walked outside. Maybe I imagined that would be the day the sun would tear through the cloud cover, or there'd be no crows cawing at me from the barn roof, or there'd be a smell of something new in the air. But there isn't. And that's why I get this creeping feeling that something isn't quite right.

When I see the buggy gone from the barn, and Jeremiah's horse isn't in its paddock, and Pa and Cassie are nowhere to be found, that's when I *know* something isn't right. Not right at all.

My feet burn, as they usually do, but I take off barefoot down the dirt road toward the crossroad anyway.

I don't know how long I run. There's that saying how the road seem to stretch for miles, but in my case, it's actually happening—the road twists and turns across the gray-withered plain, but for each twist and turn there's another one up ahead. I run past field after field of bristly, dead wheat and petrified cotton bushes and all the while my breath scorches my throat almost as much as the gritty road cuts into my feet. The stretch watches me as I go, I just know it. For each step I take I know, just know, *not right* is turning into *terribly wrong*.

Pa's at the crossroads with the buggy. Jeremiah's horse is doing its best to browse on the dried grass on the side of the road, but there ain't much browsing to be had. Pa stares far away, his eyes fixed on some mark beyond the horizon I can't see.

"Pa?" I exhale, too out of breath to sound as angry as I wanna sound. "Why'd you leave without me? You knew I had to come along."

"I know, Jo."

He won't look at me. I follow his gaze. Far away, against the colorless sky, there's a wispy cloud of dust from a wagon.

A wagon that's come, and gone.

"We gotta eat, Jo," Pa says. "You do understand that, don't you?"

At first, I don't understand at all.

Then my knees begin to quiver, and I understand everything.

All night I stare at the mirror, hoping to see something. A glimpse of my sister, maybe, of whatever's happening to her out there in the stretch, or what will come to happen to me. But all I ever see is my own reflection—that lanky girl with tired eyes and bleeding feet.

I wonder all the time if those tears Cassie shed was because she was jealous of the future I was about to have, or because she knew all along she had to rob me of it to save Pa, Jeremiah, and the Howell sisters. Sometimes, when my feet hurt more than usual, I'll just stop in the field and reach out for the corn stalks and listen, hoping they'll whisper the answer to me. But no answer comes.

And I'm the corn girl. So what can I do but keep walking.

For Sale: Fantasy Coffins (Ababuo Need Not Apply)

By Chesya Burke

The sign outside Hello Design Coffin Works read, FOR SALE: FANTASY COFFINS. But the little girl imagined more ominous words floating just below the other letters, *"Ababuo Need Not Apply."*

Many people in Accra bought these beautiful caskets on time, and often took many months and even years to pay off one of their expensive death homes. But no matter, her credit in that city was worthless and Ababuo knew she could never get one. The girl chided herself, but she stopped at the storefront, and stared into the window. Without being able to suppress the urge growing inside of her, she entered the threshold of the tiny building. Fantasy surrounded her within, proudly displayed. Closest to her was a giant, man-sized statue of an eagle. The bird's head was held high, its eyes large and knowing. The bird's body was adorned with feathers, brown and beautiful, its beak and talons yellow and bright. This was a strong bird, proud. That meant that the (more than likely) man who would be folded and stuffed into the narrow opening in the back of the carcass was also strong and proud. Perhaps he was a bird lover or pilot. It didn't matter. Although the coffins often represented people's professions, they just as often represented the wants and desires of the people entombed within them. Across from the wide-eyed bird was a hammer, standing almost twice as tall as she, and more than half as wide around. Its owner would likely have been a carpenter or something. Only a person with a love of tools would want to spend eternity in that thing. Ababuo smirked. It wasn't that the hammer was ugly, per se, but it was not what most people would choose out of admiration or simply a love of the craft—instead, this tool represented honor, skill, pride.

Then she saw it, sitting across the room in a corner as if forgotten. A beautiful, small white elephant. Ababuo made her way over to the coffin, touching it carefully. It was striped like a tiger, with ears too big for its head. But it was lovely. White Elephant was barely large enough for the tiny body that would grace its shell for all eternity, but Ababuo wouldn't mind leaving a limb or two behind to find peace within the belly of this gorgeous creature. She stood for a long moment touching the tiny white tusks and then the thick sturdy legs. The girl patted the elephant's side as if it was real, closing her eyes, imagining that this coffin actually belonged to her. How morbid it was, she knew, to long for nothing more than to choose her death bed. But the truth was that in this room, nothing mattered to Ababuo because nothing was real, nothing was solid, tangible. She wasn't cursed within this room of fantasy coffins—simply because she could never possess one. Perhaps knowing her life was so short caused her fixation with death, her eternity.

"What are you doing here?" Ababuo slowly opened her eyes. She didn't have to turn around to know who had spoken. It was one of the owners of the coffin shop—the son. Too bad; the father was much nicer. "You can't be here. You have to leave." He walked up to her, but didn't touch her. That was the rule.

"I was just looking. No harm in that."

"No point in that either, is there, girl?"

"I can look. I just want to see them. That's all."

"Not here. You're a *Nantew yiye* child. You must go." Then he whispered, "It's dangerous." As a "safe journey" child, Ababuo knew all too well her position. This man did not hate her. In fact, in his own way he probably simply wanted to save her the effort of wanting something she could never have.

Behind her someone spoke. "Dangerous? Pft!" Ababuo recognized the woman speaking as Accra's first lady, the wife of the newly appointed mayor.

The son backed a respectable distance away. "I was just...trying..."

She walked up to him, closing the distance he had set between them, "I know what you were doing. You should be grateful to this child. You're disgraceful."

Most of the world will never know the sadness of an unfulfilled desire to have a fantasy coffin. Most of the world doesn't even know what a fantasy coffin is. And most will not care. Thus is not the case for Ababuo. Her strongest desire in the entire world was to have her tiny body crammed into the frame of one of those monstrous carved wooden boxes and get buried in the earth of her precious Ghana when she died. Well, that wasn't entirely true. Her foremost desire was to never need a fantasy or any other coffin.

But neither of these was the fate for Ababuo. Her soul was not pure enough for burial, and the earth would reject her body, and punish those who had offered her as a gift to it. The last time a Nantew yiye child had been buried in the Ghanaian soil, the clouds had opened up and flooded the land, killing crops and several people in the process. And not dying would leave the people of Ghana without her protection. That couldn't happen. No whole group should suffer for the wants of one person. Ababuo understood this. Her job was to protect the people of Ghana, not harm them.

Either way, her thirteenth was coming and she had to make a decision.

The girl closed her eyes, hoping to clear her head of those thoughts. As if in answer, someone knocked on the door of the home she shared with her caretaker, paused, and then knocked again. Ababuo opened the curtain and looked down at the man from her bedroom on the second floor. The man glanced up at her and looked around as if he didn't want anyone to see him there. Ababuo was sure that she saw shame displayed across his face.

After a moment the man was let in and Ababuo's caretaker tapped on her door, then opened it. "It's for you, child."

The girl sat very still, "This is ten, you know? Only three more."

"We all have a burden, Ababuo. This is yours." The woman sounded harsh, but she did not meet Ababuo's eyes. They would lose each other soon.

Without further discussion, Ababuo sauntered down the stairs, taking one at a time. She was in no hurry to do what was needed of her. At eleven, Ababou shoulders were broad and strong, as if hinting at the woman she would never become, but she was still just skin and bones.

While she followed him, Ababuo let her mind wonder about the girl she had seen just the day before. Ababuo had never met anyone else like her, but this child had been chosen to take over after Ababuo had fulfilled her duty. She was only seven years old, so tiny, so frail looking. So much like Ababuo had been a few short years before. Ababuo hated the thought of what would happen to this little girl when she had fulfilled her own duty to Accra; she felt guilty and ashamed.

The man led her to a path through the woods. Without looking back, he entered the tree line and the dark swallowed him fully. Ababuo hated the woods at night; she always seemed to get bad feelings in there. The trees seemed to whisper to each other and though she felt she knew them, she never fully understood what they were saying, as if there was a big secret that they kept from her. She hesitated at the woods' opening, which seemed to suck all light into a vacuum. The hole looked endless. Nothing but blackness greeted them, despite the moon that shone directly overhead.

This was not good. Ababuo had always gotten feelings about things. She just saw things more deeply than others. It was second sight, her caretaker told her. Ababuo was special. She had been born with a caul covering her face, so that she could always see the way, the old woman had said.

Ababuo knew by experience that this void that she saw now was a sign. One that she couldn't ignore. She looked back, took a deep breath and then followed the man into the darkness.

Half a mile later, the girl could see the light of the moon shining through an opening in the tree tops. Past the tree line at the woods' end and across the railroad tracks it followed the pair, silent as they were. Just as the man reached the railroad tracks he stopped, looked at her. She never really knew how to react when people needed her services, never knew what to do or even what they wanted. She walked closer to him, and he pointed to the tracks. She hesitated for only a moment, and then reached out and touched the cold steel with the tip of her right sandaled toe. Suddenly she was transported into another time, not long before this night, but not completely on the same plane on which she had arrived either.

In this parallel place, there were children. Ababuo counted them. Seven. Four girls and three boys. They had all snuck out of the house to go to the graveyard just across the tracks, though the trees. Ababuo watched the children, simultaneously wishing she could be one of them and fearing what was to come. She would not be there if something terribly tragic hadn't already happened.

"Look," one of the little girls yelled. She was a twin of another child there that night, a little girl. "There it is." The kids loved the way the moon shone on the cold, marble tombstones. The way the beams bounced on the writing made the words look almost as if the names were dancing on the light. And that the dates were the amount of time that they'd been going. It was magical. They loved this place.

The forest was dense, and they'd had to walk single file just to get through the trees. They all had played in these woods since they were able to walk, as had Ababuo, so they weren't in fear of getting lost. But that didn't stop their minds from running wild in this place every single time they ventured here. The night, the trees, the moonlight, the grave stones, the polished train tracks, the dead… It was spooky. But the kids seemed to relish this in a way that Ababuo never had;

she could feel their anticipation growing, while her own fear made her cower.

The distant moon seemed to do nothing for the darkness in these woods and only served to make the surrounding trees look more sinister. As the group entered a clearing, Ababuo looked up at the stars in the sky and closed her eyes. She had been getting increasingly nauseated since entering the woods and now she couldn't ignore the feeling any longer.

Something was wrong. More importantly, something was going to happen. Something she felt down deep. Something bad. She swayed, lost her balance, falling to her knees, reaching out to touch the tracks with her free hand. The world around her swam as if she were trapped in a pool of water, drowning. She began sinking in its unknown depths. She couldn't breathe. Couldn't see. She was in the dark place, though her eyes were open. She had been here before. Exactly nine times before. She would experience it another two times before it was all over. She knew the pain, the fear, the sorrow. But she understood now that this pain was doubled. Two souls would be released tonight, and she was one soul closer to death than she had been only a few moments ago. The total was going to be eleven, not ten as she had expected.

Knowing what to do, Ababuo spasmed and began falling deeper into the dark place, letting it consume her completely until she was there, that night. The world around her spun out of control. To the children, she appeared as if out of nowhere. As she appeared, she saw that the younger of the two twins' legs had gotten stuck on the track and she couldn't move. Her sister worked desperately to get it out, but it just would not budge.

The train approached.

Ababuo could hear it charging forward: a constant chug-chug-chugging coming closer, like the minute hand on a giant clock ticking down to destiny. The other children were screaming, but Ababuo did not focus on them. She could not. She was not here for them. They had survived that night.

With the train chugging nearer, the bright headlight getting brighter, Ababuo grabbed the twins, and pulled them both close to her. A spark of energy went through the group, as if though a live electric wire. Just as the train reached them, she held out her hand to stay it, not letting it demolish these children again. She spoke with words that weren't her own but were honest and sincere.

"Your grandma," Ababuo said to the girls, "misses you. She's waitin' to see you both again. Tonight. Finally." To those around her, Ababuo's voice sounded very much like her own, but to Ababuo her voice sounded like an old woman full of years she had yet to see.

"Who are you?" one of the twin girls asked, as her sister held onto her, not wanting to let go. Ababuo understood why: they had been born together, and they would leave the same way.

"Ababuo, a Nantew yiye child. I came to help you."

"You can't, we do this always. The train." The girl looked on as Ababuo strained to still the locomotive destined to tear through the children. "It's okay. It doesn't hurt much anymore."

Ababuo fell to her knees again, feeling the weight of the heavy train, but not letting it go. Her eyes showed only the whites of time that passed as she spoke, "You must go."

The older girl shook her head, "We don't have anywhere to go."

"Into me. Come into me. I need you as much as you need me."

The train was so heavy now. So very heavy.

The older girl looked to her sister, ever the protector. "Will we breathe again?"

Ababuo smiled. "With your mind, your heart. Never again your lungs. They hurt too much."

Without warning the girl's foot was released, and the two took each other's hand and merged into Ababuo's body, swallowed by her essence. She consumed them fully. They no longer suffered, but they were not extinguished. Instead they breathed, without lungs or the need for air at all.

At that moment Ababuo forgot about the train, letting it go as she relished the girls within her. The steel bullet slammed into her knocking one of her shoes off, throwing her backward twenty feet. She opened her eyes to the girls' father standing over her, holding back tears.

He seemed to want to help, but he was not allowed to touch her. She was considered too pure to touch, but really she just thought that people were afraid of her, and that suited her just fine. She could stand on her own. That was why she had been chosen. She said simply, "They belong to me now. They're free."

The man nodded and walked away, his face downcast. Ababuo stood there a long time after the man left, not really thinking about anything. She didn't really *want* to be thinking about anything, least of which those little girls who were now somewhere beyond their father's reach, the father who would not see them again for many years. The father who had loved them.

The girl made her way home, alone. She could barely walk, as she had taken on the real injury of the memory train and it would take a long time to heal. She died a little more with each of these souls, as she helped to lessen their pain. That was the worst of it, she thought. She suffered for them, she suffered great pain for them, and yet they never even seemed to notice. They never seemed to care. But she didn't want to think about it anymore. She was too tired. Too young, too worn.

Accra, Ghana was Ababuo's first love. She loved it and in its own way, it loved her too. Accra was a part

93

of Africa, like every other city on that continent, but Accra did not represent Africa, speak for it, or call it as one. Just as Ababuo didn't represent the people of Accra, and she only helped and complemented them as any part does its sum.

But if Accra was her first love, then the waterway extending from Lake Volta held her heart within its waves and calm, still surface in a way the land could not. Lake Volta was said to be the largest man made lake in the world, and if you followed it far enough, it emptied out into the Black, White, and Red Volta Rivers. Ababuo had never seen those rivers in person. In fact, she had never been outside of Accra or even seen the whole of Lake Volta in all its glory. This waterway was the closest she had gotten. It was tiny and pathetic; most fish or marine life couldn't survive its shallow depths. But she didn't care; she liked the idea of this underestimated water source flowing silently into the biggest man made river in the world. It was connected to both man and nature in a way that Ababuo herself understood. If no one else in the world did, Ababuo understood.

Behind her, rhythmic song disturbed the silence of the day. She turned to see a group of people leading a procession through the small wooded area beside her precious waterway. Although she realized this was a funeral, she momentarily resented the interruption. Most people didn't come here, as no good fishing could be done from its shallows. But besides the Gulf of Guinea on the other side of the city, this was the closest one could come to a water source. And that was the point, it seemed. The mourners were followed by a group of men who carried a giant, blue-painted, wooden whale on their backs, its tail curved high toward the sky. Ababuo stared as the procession marched its way to the final burial site somewhere beyond her sight. The man stuffed into the whale-shaped box was probably a fisherman, and they had chosen the site near the water to honor him. Although death is a time for mourning in Accra, it is also a time for celebration. People celebrate the life and accomplishments of the dead so as not to forget that they were loved, and a valuable part of the community. This was what they did for this man now. This was what no one would do for her.

After a moment, Ababuo turned to face her water again. She closed her eyes and allowed the calm waves to release her frustrations. There was no point in being angry at anyone, and jealousy was simply unacceptable. What sense did it make to envy a dead man? She who lived every day hoping not to die.

Ababuo didn't realize that someone had walked up behind her until they had been standing there a full minute or longer. She turned and saw the mayor's wife in her colorful attire. The woman had a way of showing up unannounced. "I thought I saw you here, Nantew yiye." The way most people spoke her title was scornful, but on this woman's lips it was lovely, valuable.

"I didn't mean to disturb you. I'm sorry."

"Why should you be sorry? You were here first. I'm Serwa. We weren't properly introduced the other day." The woman looked back toward the festivities. "My son. He was a fisherman." Ababuo nodded. She figured the woman simply needed to talk and it didn't matter who she spoke to. "All we have left of him is his wife and unborn son." A tear fell from the woman's face; she wiped it away quickly. "Why are you here alone?"

"I like the water."

The woman stared at her. "I'm sorry for you, Nantew yiye. I saw you go into the coffin shop the other day...and I was curious. There are so many rumors...about you. The things you can do. But still, I pity you." The woman wasn't being rude. Ababuo had experience worse things than being pitied by her neighbors.

"Have you ever thought about escaping? Leaving all this behind?"

Ababuo didn't answer for a moment. Perhaps Miss Serwa was testing her loyalty to the people of Accra. "Why would I do that?"

"Freedom, dear! Everyone deserves that."

Miss Serwa came for her that evening. Something had gone wrong in the delivery of the mayor's grandson. Perhaps the woman had known something was wrong, or perhaps it was simply a coincidence that the two had met prior to this. Ababuo supposed it didn't matter.

The woman walked into her room without the benefit of a knock, then closed the door before her caretaker could enter. Ababuo stood to her feet and let the woman speak: "I will not take from you without giving." She paused for a moment, was silent as Ababuo had been earlier, lost in thought. "Most people can't offer anything in return, so they suffer without coming to you. But I offer you freedom if you help me tonight. I will take you away, help you escape, if you save my son's son."

The city passed by her automobile window in quick, bright flashes that were almost unrecognizable. When Ababuo reached the house, Miss Serwa took her hand and led her to the room where the doctor stood over the mother, his hands between her bloody legs. "What is she doing here? I told you none of that witchcraft while I'm here."

"And I told you, doctor, that you do not make decisions for me or my grandson."

"Send her away, I warn you." The man was angry. He stared at Ababuo as if he had never hated anyone more in his lifetime than this girl.

But before he could speak again, the pregnant woman screamed and pushed, her face bloating with air, her eyes bulging in pain and fear. After a moment, the baby slid into the doctor's hands, its breathing rushed and rapid. Without a word to inquire about her child, the mother closed her eyes, unable to hold them open any longer. She and her son were in distress; neither would survive. Ababuo could sense it from where she stood in the doorway.

"Send her away," the doctor demanded again.

Ababuo looked up at the mayor's wife, untwined her fingers from within the woman's grip and walked over to the mother and child. All she had to do was save the kid and get whisked away to *freedom*. That word sounded so sweet, so peaceful.

As she reached the other side of the room, the doctor stood and moved out of her way, as if she carried the plague. Ababuo touched the mother's stomach, feeling the blood and energy flow too rapidly from within her. The baby was just as bad. His head was warm and his mind was unfocused, cloudy. Ababuo could sense the life slowly drain out of his body. Ababuo could not save them both.

Thirteen. That was it. That was now many souls she was allowed to save, both dead and alive. She had only two left within her to save. But she had to save one for herself. She had sacrificed enough. She hesitated for a moment. Without giving it another thought, she grabbed the child, placed her mouth over his and sucked all of the illness and cloudy residue in his mind away. She held the child to her, her entire mouth covering his nose and lips. She breathed in, feeling all of the sickness within the child enter her body, fog her soul, overwhelming her senses. He was so tiny in her hands, so cold and scared. Newborns, she had learned, understood little and feared nothing but light diminishing from their too-new souls. When she released him, he began to cry, loud and strong. Miss Serwa smiled and lifted the child from her arms, hugging him. Crying, she laid the baby in his mother's arms and caressed the woman's face. The dying woman did not move, or hear her son screaming within her arms.

"You must go." Miss Serwa kissed Ababuo. "My men will take you to a secluded farm. You can stay there as long as you want. Thank you." She looked back at the screaming child: "I'll take good care of him."

Ababuo walked to the door, stopped, and looked back at the mother still unable to hold her child. Then her eyes fell on the soon to be motherless child. She had lived thirteen years without a mother. A caretaker was no substitute. Before she could regret her decision, she ran to the bed and took both the mother and child into her arms. She placed her mouth over the woman's nose and gave her life away. Death slowly left the woman and entered Ababuo, her body becoming weak. When her knees gave out her body slumped to the floor. She drifted away before knowing whether to regret her decision.

This was her thirteenth. The same number of years she had been allowed to live, only to die and not be buried in Ghanaian soil, but burned, as if a witch in punishment.

The mayor's wife carried Ababuo's body down stairs and laid her on the sofa. The following day she commissioned a fantasy coffin for Ababuo. A sarcophagus: such a lovely, tiny thing, reminiscent of those of Ancient Ghana's kings and queens. Miss Serwa had only one requirement: that the coffin remain buoyant in shallow waters for no less than thirteen days, keeping her promise not to bury Ababuo in the soil of Ghana. The mayor, his wife, and their family celebrated in a private ceremony by setting Ababuo's body to sail on the waters of the small waterway which led into the Volta River, so that when the earth quaked only the depths of the sea life felt it and mourned for this beloved and simultaneously unloved child.

Kia and Gio

By Daniel José Older

I don't know why I can't stop thinking of Giovanni today. I opened the botánica early, even though it's Saturday, because I couldn't go back to sleep, and lying in bed with the sunshine creeping over me just wasn't cutting it. Now that I'm here, it's like there's a tiny Gio hiding behind all the little potion vials and sacred pots on the shelves around me.

Yes, I have homework to do. And Baba Eddie doesn't have any readings till noon, which means he'll waddle in at 11:58, sipping his coffee. But here I am. The sunlight finds its way through the saint statues in the window display, lands on me, and warms my skin. I feel old even though I'm not. Giovanni.

I should probably give up and admit he's dead. Everyone else has. A boy like that, that bright a fire, they figure it's too much to ask to have him around for more than a decade or two. Instead I make up stories about where he ended up: Giovanni in Amsterdam, whoring around gleefully with poets and painters, smoking hash and making fun of American tourists. Giovanni in India, writing plays while riding elephants. Giovanni in Tunisia, fermenting a lusty new remix of the Arab Spring.

When I was ten and he was—what? Sixteen?—I was still plotting how to get him to marry me. I'd done all the math, checked and rechecked it: he would be twenty-three when I made seventeen, the legal age to marry in New York. That seemed doable: seventeen and twenty-three. Shit, Uncle Freddie got married when he was fifteen and Aunt Bea was twenty-eight and they're still going strong. Then again, Uncle Freddie's been known to swallow his own teeth on purpose. Anyway, I scratched the equations out on my little *Powerpuff Girls* notepad and arrived triumphantly at the conclusion that it was doable, mathematically at least. The other concerns—that he obviously had no interest whatsoever in girls and that we're first cousins—those all seemed like secondary problems. Sex was gross anyway, right? Who wanted all that?

I'm gonna be seventeen next week, and Giovanni is…nowhere.

A woman comes in, ignoring the 'Closed' sign on the door. I can't tell if she's white or Puerto Rican or… white and Puerto Rican? She's got loud purple lipstick on and she's almost perfectly round. Maybe she's been here before—Gina? Louisa? Then she opens her mouth. She's definitely Puerto Rican. "Hola, mi niña. Lissen, you have those collares for Babalu I asked about before? It was maybe two weeks ago, yes?"

Oh yeah, she was here before, but it wasn't no two weeks ago. Two months, maybe. "We already sold 'em out, Iya." I use the respectful term for an elder santera, even though I don't know if she's initiated or not. Whatever, one way or the other, she's older than me.

"Ay, mi madre, but I put in the order and everything." A sing-songy whine enters her voice. I want nothing to do with it so I end the conversation quick and she finds her way to the door. And then: Giovanni. Giovanni dressed in a hundred shades of violet, fro unruly. We're on our way home from school. He's rolling his eyes because he got cast as the swan again in the ballet school's version of *Swan Lake*. "Gayest role ever," he said, sipping a cup of milk and sugar with a splash of coffee in it. "So stupid. Why can't we do a ballet based on *Ishigu*?"

I jumped up and down and did little pirouettes around him. "Ishigu! Ishigu!" That's the manga we both loved. Well, I loved it because he loved it, and everything he loved was a holy relic to me. Plus, Ishigu was half-boydemon, half-android, and surrounded by the hottest anime chicks in the Robot City. Gio could be Ishigu and I could be Maiya, who carried a staff with a talking ram head on top that she used to disembowel all the tentacle-bots that came at them from the Red Death Chambers.

103

★

"I'm coming in late," Baba Eddie says when I pick up the landline. I hear him pull on his cigarette. "Something came up."

"I'm so sure." For no reason at all, I'm annoyed.

"Hold things down for me, okay? Why are you there so early anyway?"

"I dunno." I shrug as if he could see it over the phone, but really: it's Baba Eddie, he probably can.

"What's wrong, Kia?" That touch of charismatic condescension he always gets away with because he knows I love him like a father. Uncle. Fatherly uncle. Whatever. I let it slide. Again.

"Nothing."

"Good." He ignores my blatant lie. "See you at one...ish."

"You have a noon reading with Eliades."

"Oh fuck, he's always coming with some bullshit. Keep him entertained till I get there."

"I'm not entertaining."

"Just tell him I'll be a little late."

"But..."

The line goes dead.

Ishigu was a third degree master of Shumanjo Levitating Robot fighting style, but P.S. 143 in

Sunnyside didn't have that as an afterschool option, so Giovanni took Kenpo instead. Gio also was a lead alto in glee club, treasurer of the debate team, assistant-editor at the school newspaper, and president/founding member of the Amiri Baraka Drama Club. Each met on a different day of the week, which I always took to be a special scheduling miracle devised solely to please my overachieving extra-curricular cousin, but it was really just a coincidence.

"Why you still wearing your tutu?" Gio narrowed his eyes at me.

"Because I'm a ballerina," I informed him.

"Ballet is so girly."

I matched his sneer with one of my own. "You do ballet, and you're a boy."

"I'm not *just* a boy." Gio's hands extended to either side, palms out, like Ishigu's do when he's getting ready to levitate. "I'm the baddest boy in town, bitches."

I was laughing, but then I stopped. "Don't call me a bitch." Both my fists found my hips and I frowned, creasing my brow to show I wasn't kidding.

"I didn't mean you." The apology was sincere. "I meant it universally. All the bitches in the universe! Anyway, it's not a bad word if you say it right."

"It's not?" We're walking again, all through the quiet suburbs of eastern Queens. When Gio's with me I can ignore the creeping sensation that I don't belong, I don't belong, no matter where I am I don't belong.

"Shh…we on a mission."

"Where we going?" I'd never been to this neighborhood before. Maybe driven past once or twice with dad, but it was all white folks and the feeling of *don't belong don't belong* hung heavy in the air, like all the molecules wanted me to leave too. But I knew I was safe. Gio'd been studying Kenpo since he was my age; he was a brown belt and not to be trifled with.

"It's a secret mission."

"But where we going?"

"If I tell you it won't be a…" I made the face that I knew gets him, the one that I used to make right before I cried. He caved. "Fine. But don't tell *anyone*." He lowered his voice to such a shrill whisper on the word *anyone* that a little spittle escaped and he had to wipe his mouth. "We're going to see if Jeremy's okay."

I rolled my eyes. For three weeks, all I'd heard about was Jeremy. Would Jeremy like this red leather jacket? Does he read Ishigu too? What kind of cigarettes would Jeremy smoke? If Jeremy was a crayon, what color would he be? (Yes, No, Virginia Slims, and Plain Ol' White, respectively, but who was listening?) The angle of Jeremy's chin: divine architecture; the perfection of his frown when he was thinking about a math problem; the timbre of his voice: angelic. Jeremy the Brave, bringing in articles about oil drilling in Antarctica for Social Studies. Jeremy the Agile, bounding effortlessly across the gym in tights for his solo in *Swan Lake*. Jeremy the Cryptic, explaining in depth his theory of how all six *Star Wars* movies were really one eight-million hour rewrite of the Book Of Job. Or whatever. If the boy had the slightest hint of self-awareness and looked out from the curtains of his thin blond hair once in a while, I'd actually feel like he was a threat to my impending marriage. But as it was, he displayed zero interest in anything more than a platonic friendship with Gio. Which baffled and relieved me at he same time.

So now we were off to see Jeremy the Clueless for some dumb "mission." Great.

Eliades shows up right on time, of course. I'm sipping some bodega tea, no milk, no sugar, staring off into nothing like some asshole in a nursing home when the guy busts in with a loud jingle-jangle from the door chimes. He's always well dressed, but today his green striped tie lies half-undone around his neck like a noose, and the top of his shirt is open, revealing pallid, moist flesh and a hint of chest hair. It's February but he's sweating, like he ran all the way here from his Manhattan office.

"Hey Eliades." I'm grateful for the company; all these memories crowding my head can't be healthy.

Eliades wipes a hand over his thinning hairline. "It's back." No *Hi Kia*, no *How's school?* Just, *It's back*. Okay. I hate small talk, anyway. I don't even wanna know who's back.

"Baba Eddie's running a little late."

"But…"

"You can have a seat and wait for him."

Eliades may be self-absorbed, but he knows me well enough to know not to argue when I use my have-a-seat voice. He makes his way through the aisles, pouting softly, and settles in one of the big easy chairs we got half-price from the vintage spot on Myrtle.

"You wouldn't make much of a spy," Giovanni informed me as we sat in some bushes on a little hill behind Jeremy's house. It's just like all the other ones on this block: three stories, faded off-white shingles, all the decaying decadence of a middle-aged dad in a rumpled suit. "Too much chatter."

It hurt, but with some effort I kept the whine out of my voice. "Well, how am I sposta spy when I don't even know what we're doing here?"

Gio sighed and adjusted his position a little. "Because Jeremy said some strange men had been showing up around his house."

"How do you know he didn't mean *you*?"

"Kia!"

"Keep your voice down, you're gonna give us away."

"What I'm gonna do is take you right home and then come back all by myself."

The idea was so offensive to me I actually squealed a little when I said, "No!" This time, when I made the pre-cry face, it wasn't a ruse.

Gio knew it too and he softened. "Then shut the fuck up, Kia."

"Fine. But don't swear at me."

After a few moments, Giovanni sighed. "He said they were white men and that they would whisper through his window late at night, all kinds of things about how he was destined for greatness and he was the chosen one. All kindsa shit. They wanted him to come with them, but would never say where, and when he'd ask they'd just vanish into the night."

I didn't know what to say. My eyes were open so wide they felt like they were gonna pop out. "And you gonna stop them?"

"I just want to make sure he's alright, is all."

It was getting dark; the bush we were in was already swamped in shadows and the sky turned turquoise through the trees above us. Gio fumbled in his pockets and then produced a black cigarette. I gasped. He rolled his eyes, fumbled again, took out a lighter. The sugary scent of cloves filled the air; it was sweet and perfect, Giovanni's magic pixie powder.

"How you gonna be all mad that I'm loud," I hissed, "and then light a great big beacon of flame and send all that smoke out? You know he gonna see it."

"He's not even home yet—look the lights are out. Anyway, you can't really stake out a house and not smoke. It's like, the rules."

"I guess. If by 'stake out' you mean 'stalk'."

"Shhh!"

I was about to remind him he'd just said no one was home when a light went on. Jeremy appeared, pulling curtains out of the way and then lifting the window. He stuck his head out, smelled the summer breeze (the cloves too probably) and then disappeared back into his room. I elbowed Gio, for no real reason but to indicate that I'd told him so. He nudged me back, but kept smoking.

"You're an asshole," I whispered. It felt good to swear, mature.

"Shh!"

Music swirled out of Jeremy's room. It was trancelike: a gush of strings and then a heavy beat. Jeremy sailed past his window, arms over his head, a perfectly executed grande jeté. He emerged, pirouetting, in the next window just as a pleading, luscious voice came in over the beat.

I tugged on Gio's sleeve. "What's this music?"

"It's Björk."

"What's a *Björk*?"

"Shh!" That was the moment I understood he would never marry me. The boy was entranced. I could see Jeremy dancing in Gio's eyes, the glare from the bedroom lighting up his face, his mouth hanging slightly open. I might not've had the words for it at the time, but inside I knew: it was love. Not that bullshit TV love; not the corny love-song love either. *True love*. The kind that people get themselves killed for.

The kind that makes you do really, really stupid things.

"Gio?"

"Girl, if I have to tell you to shush one more…"

"What are we really doing here?"

The music churned on. Gio kept his gaze fixed on the window.

Something is clogging up the air in the botánica. My eyes are watering, and I can't tell if it's because I'm getting all emo from thinking about Giovanni or if some thickness has settled over the room. No, it's definitely not me. I peek through the aisles, but Eliades is hidden behind a bookshelf. I can't inhale fully; my breath stops at the top of my chest and makes me cough. I'm just thinking how strange it is that there's no actual smoke when the smoke alarm goes off. My heart is in my ears, pounding away, before I can even leap into action. All these saints, all this spiritual power—and yes, let's be honest, some of it is junk, but there's plenty of sacred relics too—I can't be the one that let it all go up in flames. I leap out from behind the counter, scanning the air around me for signs of smoke.

But there's nothing there. No smoke. No flames. I still have to fight to tug oxygen down my trachea though, and my vision is getting foggy. "Eliades!" I yell, but the bleating alarm blots it out. I stand up on a

111

chair and a fiddle with the plastic thing till it shuts up. Then I look around.

It's back. Eliades' words echo through my head over and over again. *It's back.* I didn't even bother asking what—it's not my business and what could I do about it anyway? *It's back.* He elongated the *It* in that way people do when they're talking about something they don't want to speak out loud, like just saying it was a punch in the gut. *It's back.*

"Eliades?"

The room is so quiet now. I don't even hear the traffic outside or the shoppers around the corner on Graham or the bachata that usually streams out of the music store across the street. "Eliades?" I sound like such a little girl—pathetic. I'm standing on this chair, looking like an arch idiot, gazing over a perfectly still room. Awesomely, I left my cell back on the desk. I could call Baba Eddie, but I don't want to move from right here. Somehow I'm positive that if I move, it's all over. So I don't. I wait.

I gasped when I realized we weren't alone in the woods. The men standing around us—they didn't walk there; we would've heard them. They just appeared out of the darkness. There were six of them. They had white, almost greenish skin, broad shoulders, bugged-out eyes, and smirking, deeply lined faces. They hunched over slightly, all of them the same way, but their arms were long, too long. I almost screamed when I noticed them, but I kept it in. They just stood there, staring at Jeremy's entrancing performance much like Gio was. Ever so slowly, I wrapped my little hand around Gio's wrist. He was about to shush me but I squeezed, squeezed so hard he shut up. When he finally saw the men, he let out just the tiniest of gasps. I thought it was too loud, but they didn't look over, just kept those pushed-out eyes squinting straight ahead at Jeremy's house. The air filled with whispers, a dissonant hissing and occasional mumbled words: *come, one, master, breaker, only one, come.*

Then they started walking, all at the same time. They moved through the trees into the backyard. It was a slow, deliberate walk, each step careful and precise, long arms dangling by their sides. I couldn't stop staring at them, but something else was tweaking my attention in the corner of my eye. Something was moving. I looked towards it, but it was so dark, the trees were just shadows against the night. Still, there was movement. The trees—the trees were moving. They were alive somehow, shifting, writhing in the darkness.

No. I stepped closer to look at the nearest one to me. No, it was alive with insects. Shiny-backed cockroaches swarmed over the thing, the big kind. But they weren't the normal dark orange color; they were pale, almost pink.

I opened my mouth to scream and a hand wrapped around it. I was about to start fighting for my life when I smelled that shea butter/BO mix that I knew so well. Giovanni. He lifted me up and turned me around. "Don't say a fucking word," he hissed. "Don't even fucking cry."

I nodded, tears streaming down my face. Giovanni would make everything all right. He always did. Giovanni would get me out of here.

"Listen to me, Kia. Go home." My stomach plummeted. "Go now."

"N…" I started to say, but he shushed me with a look.

"Don't look back. Just go. I'll be home soon."

I shook my head.

"Kia." No debate, no whining. This was not a game. And I had no choices. "Go." He put me down and turned towards where the six men made their slow journey towards Jeremy's house.

The trees all around me crawled with pale roaches. I took a step backwards, but Gio didn't even look to see if I'd gone. He launched down the hill, quiet as a ninja. I saw the light glint over his muscley arm, saw a splotch against it, another roach, just before he swiped it off. I cringed. My whole body wanted to vanish, burst out of the trees and get as far away as I could. But my heart wouldn't let me turn away from my cousin. I stood perfectly still, caught between the two impossible choices, and anyway: useless.

Gio came up behind the first man at a sliding crouch. He anchored one leg in the dirt and flew up into the air, flashing the other leg out in a stunning roundhouse kick. His foot found its mark; the man collapsed with an eerie silence. I think Gio was as stunned as I was: for a solid three seconds he just stood there gaping at the man sprawled on the ground. The others didn't seem to notice, or, if they did, they didn't care; the slow march toward the house continued.

I took a few steps down the hill. I couldn't watch, couldn't stop watching. Gio stepped over the one he'd taken out, but a hand came up from the ground and wrapped around his leg, dropping him to one knee. The man rose up fast, faster than he should've been able to after taking a hit like that. Two of the other men stopped and turned slowly towards the fray. Gio stabilized himself in a sturdy horse-riding stance, so he was ready when the blow came. It was clumsy and slow, like the man couldn't quite get his limbs to do what he wanted them to, but I could tell from the way Gio leaned to the side that there was an unnatural force to it. Gio sidestepped and let the weight of the guy's hit do the work, just like he'd been taught. As the man stumbled forward, Gio brought his elbow down on the back of his head.

The two other men moved in from either side. Gio's hoarse yell cut through the quiet suburban night: "Jeremy! Run!" Even the attackers seemed startled. Jeremy appeared at the window and everyone looked up at him. Gio took advantage of the confusion, kicking in the kneecaps of one man and then spin-smashing the other, another roundhouse. The first was done—I saw him crumple, again with that impossible silence, but the second guy recovered quick and barreled into Gio.

The back door of the house swung open and Jeremy gaped out. "What's going on? Giovanni?" It was like an electric shock went through the three men not busy with Gio. They lurched forward, crowding around Jeremy, blocking the door from closing.

"Get inside!" Gio yelled from the ground. The man closest to him smashed him hard across the face and he fell limp as the rest of them disappeared into the house.

I ran. I ran straight into the center of all that hell. Felt something tickling my arm and swiped at it over and over without bothering to even look at what it was. The man who'd hit Gio was crouching in the dirt with his back to me, and me, I thought of death. No strategy, no caution: just death. Because all my little body could do was surge forward, even as my mind screamed at it to turn back, and the man was only a few steps from me now.

Gio's leg came out of nowhere, swept like a lightening bolt along the ground, and took the guy's legs right out from under him. The guy fell so fast you could actually hear the swoosh of wind. Before I could even yell, the man was on the ground and Gio was over him, and then Gio's foot was smashing down, again and again on the man's face. I heard the squishing destruction of flesh, then a much sharper cracking sound, and then it was just a dull thud, over and over again under Gio's sobbing breaths.

And then something started moving. I saw Gio tense, but it wasn't the man, it was something else. The broken skin of his face writhed to life and the thousand pale cockroaches that had been his skin scattered away. More poured out of his sleeves, from under his collar, swarmed off his hands to reveal shreds of flesh clinging to raggedy bones. Gio and I both stepped back, but the roaches weren't interested in us; they scattered outward in a confused swarm and then flushed as one towards the house. Towards Jeremy.

"No!" Gio yelled. I couldn't even catch my breath before he'd turned and stormed past the roach swarm into the back door.

"Gio!" I yelled. We were still alive. Why couldn't he understand what a miracle that was? A few minutes ago I thought everything was over, and now we were alive: both of us! I hated my cousin almost as much as I loved him right then. The night was so quiet. I heard the gentle evening song of the cicada, a few night birds chirping in the trees above me. Someone was watching TV in a house nearby, a reality show, from the sound of it. Had no one heard us screaming? For a terrible moment, I wondered if any of it had even happened. Then I walked shakily towards the house, barely breathing, barely conscious.

Inside, there was a dim little alcove with winter jackets hung up, and a cubby area full of weathered board games. Something glinted from the short stairwell leading into the kitchen. Not roaches; it was perfectly still: blood. I moved faster, stepping around the wet spots and up into the kitchen; all dark, no one there. From somewhere in the house, Gio was yelling: "Jeremy? Jeremy?" I released a dark little sandbag of weight from my heart. Gio was safe for the moment. If he was looking for Jeremy, he wasn't fighting the crazy cockroach men. If he was looking for Jeremy, he was alive. The thought of ending this with Gio still intact made me want to sit down at the kitchen table and sob, but I kept going, through a windy hallway, past the living room—moderately fancy and very lived-in—and up the stairs.

"I told you to..." Gio mumbled when he saw me. "...I thought I told you to..." His eyes were so wide, the way horses look in movies when they get shot; like, you didn't know they could get so wide, that such noble, magnificent creatures could actually be afraid. "He's gone." Gio fell against the wall and slid down into a crouch, sobbing. "They got him."

"Gio." My little ten-year old voice sounded calm, authoritative, for the first time in my life. And there I was, still in my tutu. I felt ridiculous. "We gotta go, Gio. We gotta go now."

He looked up. I'd broken through to him. He nodded, took the trembling hand I'd reached out to him, and stood.

Kia and Gio | *Daniel José Older*

*

The smoke alarm screams to life again. This time my ears are so close to it that the shock almost knocks me off the chair I'm standing on. Also, the lights have gone out. It's midday, so I'd barely noticed, but yes, a certain glower has fallen over the room now. I turn and wrench the damn smoke alarm right off the wall with a grunt, drop it on the ground. I have to get out of here. I have to go, I have to go now. I step down and nothing comes to kill me, so that's good. The air is so thick, I feel like I'm wading through it. I'm halfway to the door when I hear Eliades groan. I was so anxious to get out I'd blocked him from my mind completely.

Eliades is responsible for this mess. He brought his crap in here, whatever *it* is. I bristle. And Baba Eddie gets half the credit for not being on time, dammit. Either way, it's not my problem. And who am I to get involved? I take another step towards the door, put my hand on the handle, close my eyes.

Inside myself, I know I'm not gonna leave Eliades. I can't. Giovanni is with me, somehow. I know it as clear as I know my name. He's been with me all day, like he was there, whispering the story in my ear all along. I turn. Take a step through the murk towards the back of the store. Make my way down the middle aisle, past the different colored candles and the mason jars full of herbs and tinctures. Eliades is sprawled out in the half-price easy chair, his arms to either side, his

119

mouth hanging open, a little drool trickling out. His breaths come in shallow gasps, his eyes squeezed shut.

Just above him, the air is…it's off. It shudders like those updrafts of heat on a summer day. If I squint, I can just make out a shape—no, two shapes: great heaving forms reaching down towards Eliades, crushing him.

Giovanni is with me. He is my bravery, my strength. I step directly in front of Eliades and look up into the nauseating shimmer of spirit above him.

Baba Eddie says people make too big a deal out of ghosts; they get freaked out and don't know how to handle them, because we so full up with freaky stories about poltergeists and whatnot. He says most ghosts just want something, and usually all you have to do is ask what they want and then give it to them; it's that simple.

I put my hands to either side, not unlike Ishigu right before he takes off, and say "Spirit!" It sounds so cheesy; but still, something shifts in the room. "Spirit," I say again. "What do you want?"

When nothing happens, I feel even sillier, but that's better than the sheer terror. I am, after all, still alive. I exhale, drop my arms. I'm thinking maybe some absurd coincidence happened; Eliades stroked out just as the smoke alarm malfunctioned and the power went out *and* I had an anxiety attack, yes that's it—and then a searing pain erupts in the center of my head. I close my eyes and all the bright color splotches resolve into a pair of diamonds, and then they open, they're eyes. *See me.* It's like a hundred people whispering the same thing at the same time. I hold my breath. *See me.*

"Spirits just want attention," Baba Eddie told me once as he watched a jubilant customer walk out the door. "Like, more than half the time. And they'll do what they gotta to get it. Ignore them, they'll up the ante."

See me. It's not talking to me, this thing. It's talking through me. And I can't really blame it: I volunteered myself. I put my hand on Eliades' contorted face. He's clammy, trembling. "Open your eyes," I say. "Look at it."

Eliades shudders, shakes his head.

"Do it."

Slowly, one at a time, his eyes open. I step back, step away from it all. The heaviness leaks steadily out of the room. I can breathe again. Eliades' face unclenches and tears pool at the edges of his eyes. His chest heaves up and down, silent sobs. The presence is still in the air just above him but it's dissipating. "I'm sorry," Eliades whispers. "Isadora. Lo siento." He's staring up at it, watching it go. "I'm so so sorry."

The night of the roaches wasn't the last time I saw Giovanni, but it might as well have been. In the weeks after Jeremy disappeared, Gio withdrew deeper and deeper into himself until one day he was just gone. His parents had kicked him out years earlier, but my dad loved him like their only son. They wallpapered the neighborhood with flyers, pestered the police about it every day, put search teams together to scour all the back corners and abandoned fields. Nothing. The boy was just gone. It barely got a blurb in the papers of course—a little missing notice in the local crime section of the same issue that had a moving tribute to Jeremy on the front page.

I've made up so many stories. But the practical part of me knew he was just a hurt kid that had been through some fucked up shit he couldn't make any sense of, couldn't even tell anyone about. But then again, so was I. And then he was gone and I was truly alone.

Baba Eddie comes in just as Eliades is leaving.

"You don't want your reading anymore?"

"No, Baba, I'm all set." Eliades wipes his eyes. "I feel…I feel light. I feel like I can go on now. Your student is quite impressive." He whistles as he walks out into the street. The door shuts with a jangle of bells.

Baba Eddie looks at me. "The fuck did you do to him, Kia?"

"I don't wanna talk about it." I keep my eyes on the computer screen. "Just show up on time next time, please." I should tell Baba Eddie all about it, everything. I want to. But I also don't. Because right now, I'm busy saying goodbye. Giovanni has been with me all day, just like Isadora, whoever she was, hung in that cloud over Eliades. Which means Gio's gone. Really gone. Dead and gone, gone. Which means I have to stop pretending, stop making up stories, and finally, finally for real this time, let go.

So I do.

Bucket List Found in the Locker of Maddie Price, Age 14, Written Two Weeks Before the Great Uplifting of All Mankind

By Erica L. Satifka

~~Kiss a girl.~~
~~Fall in love.~~
Get a tattoo, because Dad says that after we all go into the Sing nobody on Earth is going to have a body anymore. I don't care if it hurts.

Smoke a joint.

~~Egg Principal Novak's house.~~

See a solar eclipse. This one time, Sandra's family was going to drive us down to California to see an eclipse, but then her mom called my dad at the last minute and said it was off. I wonder why?

~~Go to the zoo and make fun of the animals.~~

Dye my hair blue. Mom says they'll have to shave our hair to get the electrodes in, the ones that will transmit our minds up to the Sing while our bodies stay behind. So it's kind of my final shot.

Run five miles without stopping.

~~Invite Sandra to the Last Dance. I figure she'll say no, because she's been kind of weird around me ever~~

~~since we kissed behind the bleachers that one time, but I hope she'll say yes.~~

Finish watching every episode of *Star Trek*. I don't know if they have *Star Trek* in the Sing, so I better do it now while I have the chance.

~~Eat sushi.~~

~~Sit at the cool kids' table.~~

Wear that awesome old dress I got at Goodwill to the Last Dance.

Learn to speak French. Mom says that in the Sing there aren't going to be any languages, everyone just thinks at each other all the time. I don't care if it's not useful. I want to learn it anyway.

Help out at a homeless shelter (I don't *really* want to do this, but it feels like something I should say).

~~Learn to ride a skateboard.~~

Take a trip out to the Coast. We were supposed to do that last month, but when Mom started going over the travel plans she just wouldn't stop crying and Dad said no trips anymore. I bet I can get Aunt Alice to take me.

~~Break a bone. (Just a little one, to see how it feels.)~~

Get retweeted by a famous person.

~~Tell Sandra how much I hate her stupid face for standing me up.~~

Go to see the servers where they're transmitting all of us into the Sing. I heard they're like these big needles with bulbs on the end of them, and they roast your body to cinders and beam your mind onto these satellites or something. Dad says this one's impossible because there's so much security around the servers. I guess I'll see them soon enough.

Read *Moby Dick* even though it's probably really boring.

~~See a bald eagle.~~

Write a novel. Although it might have to be a short story now.

Go camping, even if it's only in the backyard. Mom says you can recreate this kind of stuff in the Sing, but I know it can't be the same.

~~Tell Grandma I love her (and mean it).~~

Make up with Sandra and tell her I hope I see her in the Sing.

Get to the highest level on Candy Crush.

~~Take my cat for a walk.~~

~~Paint my fingernails ten different colors.~~

Skype with someone on another continent. Dad thinks this one is silly, because the Sing is kind of like a giant Skype with everyone in the world on it, but I want to do it now. I don't think I'm going to care about the things on this list so much when I get to the Sing. I don't think any of us will.

~~Fly a kite.~~

~~Take my roller blades out of the closet and skate around and around the reservoir, no matter how much it hurts, until the sun goes down.~~

Go one whole day without being scared of anything.

~~Forgive Sandra for not loving me back.~~

Function A:save (target.Dawn)

By Rivqa Rafael

That evening was the last time I ever stepped foot in the White House. Not that I was a regular visitor or anything. Still, my best efforts—being super polite, dressed in my nicest clothes, piercings out or covered, hair braided neatly—weren't enough, after what happened. The fact that Dawn instigated it didn't make any difference.

Dinner hadn't started yet, so we were sprawled on Dawn's bed. Sneaking looks at each other. Carefully not touching. Accidentally touching. She was nervous because she was going to give a speech, and I was doing my best to keep her distracted.

We'd lapsed into silence and she was fidgeting, so I pulled my ace from my pocket. "Dawn, this is for you."

That girl had everything, but her grey-blue eyes still lit up when she saw the game box. "You programmed this yourself, Desi?" She flipped the cube, searching for the button, hair falling in a golden curtain.

I ducked my head. "Yeah. It's just a little sim, and…" My hand closed over hers as I switched on the game box for her, my skin dark against her pale, which never saw the Sun. My train of thought evaporated.

Dawn glanced up. Her lips curved into the smallest of smiles and our eyes met. She opened her mouth.

The soft metallic tapping of a housebot at the door. "Miss Dawn, Miss Desiree. The other guests are arriving."

"We'll be right there," Dawn said. She pressed her mouth against mine for too-brief a moment, stood and held out a hand.

I took it, grinning stupidly, pushing myself up with my other hand. It was habit to be cautious around Dawn, with her condition and all. She lifted her chin and opened her door, still holding my hand. The housebot trailed behind us, its stainless steel tuxedo gleaming bright.

The Family Dining Room of the White House was dazzling, LED chandeliers blazing, carpet springy enough to be a trampoline. The First Lady was the first to notice us. She frowned, and after a second's hesitation Dawn let go of my hand.

"It's OK," I said. "You don't have to…"

"Thank you," Dawn said. She bit her lip, then turned to wave at a woman across the room. "Come on, let me introduce you."

We wandered over. Dawn said, "Lavender, I thought you weren't coming tonight."

The woman was tall, even by gen-modded standards. Her mods were of the delicate, ethereal variety, and her dark, wavy hair was pulled up carelessly into a loose bun. "I shuffled things at the last minute to be here for your speech. Who's your friend?"

Dawn smiled. "Desiree, Doctor Lavender Peters. She heads the research program at FAIRY, well, you know, the research into me." The Foundation for Augmentation and Improvement Research for the Young mainly did gen mods on embryos for the super-rich, but after the attack, they had a whole army of scientists trying to find a cure for Dawn. Fifteen years on, they hadn't had much luck.

I held out my hand. "Nice to meet you."

"Desiree is amazing with tech," Dawn said. "She can code anything, fix anything, and build anything."

"Impressive," Lavender said. She shook my hand with a firm grip. No doubt she noticed my lack of mods—it was obvious close up, from the flaws and all. But she wasn't the sort to surreptitiously look for a neural port, at least.

"Dawn!" I said. My face grew hot.

"Dawn doesn't exaggerate." Lavender pulled out her datapad. "I'll beam you my details. Maybe you can do a summer project with our biomedical engineering department."

I pulled out my pad to take the beam. "I'd...I'd love to."

The housebots began serving food. Dawn was quiet, probably nervous about her speech. She picked at her food with her datapad on her lap. When she eventually stopped swiping through her speech, I reached under the table and squeezed her hand.

After the appetisers, the President welcomed his guests. He was immaculate, as always, in a perfectly tailored suit. His white teeth and glossy hair—a full head of it, of course—shone under the lights. Apart from Lavender, there were some other FAIRY bigwigs and other cronies he mentioned individually by name.

Politicians and businesspeople always made me feel icky, although I never mentioned it to Dawn. Her dad was the most popular U.S. President in centuries, but the way he stiffened up around me and forgot to be President Charming made me wary. My guess was he didn't like that I was a scholarship kid. A reminder of the genetically unenhanced masses who had to resort to neural implants—if they could afford them—to try to keep up with the richer, genetically modified Joneses. Not that we could ever succeed. With so many people around, he just ignored me, his gaze sliding straight past mine.

Suppressing a snort, I turned away and shifted my attention to the First Lady, whose eyes were the same shade as her daughter's, but always held a sad expression. Not everything can be modded or operated out, especially not life experience, and Dawn's condition seemed to affect her more than it did Dawn.

At last the President introduced Dawn. She left her datapad on her chair; speaking without notes was one of her dad's hallmarks.

"People often feel sorry for me," she said, glancing around the room. Her nervousness was no longer evident. "But they shouldn't. Yes, there are limitations on my life because of what a terrorist did to me. Yes, I have regular medical appointments and can't go out in the sun because it would damage my DNA and give me cancer. But I never forget how lucky I am to have received this level of care. With the standard of medicine today, it's easy to forget that some people with conditions similar to mine aren't fortunate enough to have them modded out. And that's why I'd like to remind people that the research FAIRY does on my behalf is not for my benefit alone." She nodded at Lavender and caught my eye for a split second.

"Their work is crucial, not just to increase my chances of ever being able to experience sunshine, but also to improve the lives of hundreds of thousands worldwide. It's incredible that the concept of altering DNA after birth is still revolutionary. FAIRY are at the forefront of this research. Their annual donation drive begins this week, and I urge you all to give generously. You'll be funding the most innovative research on the planet, and you'll be saving lives."

Including hers, but she didn't need to say so. Or that it might mean gen mods for more people. People like me. She slipped into her seat and smiled as everyone applauded. The President beamed at her. If FAIRY's donations jumped that year, I wouldn't be surprised. Lavender was seated close enough for me to ask about FAIRY between bites. Dawn had questions too, but they were about molecular biology instead of engineering like mine, so we kept her pretty busy. Soon they were talking a mile a minute while I struggled to keep up. Dawn studied this stuff in her spare time and was already at college level, despite her own lack of fully functional gen mods. "It's just code, really, Desi, same as the stuff you do," she'd say to me, but molecular biology didn't obey the rules like programming languages did. Epigenetics confused me as much as F++ confused Dawn. So while she and Lavender discussed junk DNA and metabolic cycles, I let myself dream of one day working at FAIRY. Joining Lavender's team, impressing everyone and helping them find a cure for Dawn. Or maybe I would be the one to catch the terrorist Lachlan Cara. Plenty of people thought that finding him would be the key to uncovering data that would lead to Dawn's recovery.

Dawn put her hand on my knee and I jumped back into reality with a fizz of electricity.

"You're not listening, are you?" she accused.

"I, um…"

"You'll need to learn all about this stuff if you want to work at FAIRY."

I glanced at Lavender.

"It's true, DNA is kind of our thing," she said. "But I'm sure you'll get up to speed."

"I'll try," I said.

Dessert was served and before I knew it, Mom had arrived to pick me up. Dawn walked me out and held me close. She didn't kiss me, but I was floating anyway. She'd fast-tracked my career with just a few words to the right person, and everything was settled between us with no words at all.

The next day at school, Dawn wouldn't talk to me at all. I was crushed for a minute, before realising that keeping her distance couldn't have been her own idea. After some manoeuvring I cornered her in the bathroom.

"Did your dad tell you to stop talking to me?"

She stared at her feet. "He says I'm too young to date."

"How did he find out? Your mom wouldn't...the housebot."

"Yeah, I think so. Didn't know they were programmed to snoop."

"So, what? We can't even speak? Or be friends?"

Dawn's eyes met mine. "Can we really be just friends?" Her voice was bitter. "He said, if we sneak around, he'll find out, and he'll be really angry."

I swallowed. "We can be friends. It's better than nothing. Much better."

She swiped a hand past one eye and gave me a quick hug. "Thank you," she said.

The President accepted us being just-friends, probably hoping we'd move on from our 'schoolgirl crushes'. It was unfair, but Dawn had demands on her I'd never have. I wasn't invited back to the White House and she was never allowed to visit me at my apartment, in a part of DC considered 'too dangerous' by most. We only had school, which was covered with enough CCTV to make sure I kept to my word. During lunch breaks, she taught me molecular biology in the library. She could explain it so well. Sure, I could infodump through my implant, but there was no substitute for real learning.

"OK, I get DNA," I said, a few sessions in. "Can you explain what's wrong with yours, now? If you don't mind me asking."

She shook her head. "I don't mind. You know Cara injected me with nanobots at my baby naming, when I was just a few days old. You've watched the vid, right?"

Everyone had seen it. The terrorist used holos to disguise a robot first as a sculpture, then as a person mingling in the crowd. The robot slipped past security and injected baby Dawn with nanobots, right in her mother's arms. Everything happened so fast, it was hard to follow the vid without annotations explaining what was what. And in slow-mo.

"Have you seen it? That would be so weird, watching yourself be attacked."

"Watched it first when I was ten. My parents thought I should have waited, but…" Dawn shrugged. "Anyway, FAIRY still hasn't been able to extract a nanobot from my blood. If they could, they'd know a whole lot more. Their best guess is that the bots do continuous damage to my DNA. That's why I have sun sensitivity and I'm way shorter than my parents. Tumours grow all the time, but they cut them out straight away."

"And Cara could only do that because you had the gen mods from FAIRY in the first place, right?" I fidgeted, tapping at my implant.

"That's right. The bots attack the vectors that FAIRY used to put in the gen mods. He had all the DNA sequences because he used to work there."

"So if your parents hadn't…"

"That's what Cara said. But if he hadn't injected me with nanobots, I'd have been fine too. Just taller and brilliant and gorgeous."

"You *are* brilliant and gorgeous," I said.

Dawn shook her head: in denial or warning I wasn't sure.

We continued like that for the rest of the year, then parted ways on the sidewalk outside school. Any contact between us over summer would be via heavily monitored mails or vid calls.

"It's only a couple of months," Dawn said. "Just keep busy. We'll be back at school before you know it."

My throat caught; I had to swallow before I could speak. "I'm going to study hard. Next year I'll be old enough for the FAIRY summer program."

"You'll get it for sure." She paused. "I still use your game box every night. The whole thing is so pretty, and I keep finding new things in the world you made. You must have spent ages on it."

I ducked my head. "Glad you like it."

Her car drove down to the curb. If we hugged a little longer than just-friends do, if our kisses on the cheek drifted towards the lips, no one noticed in the crush of the last day of school. One last squeeze of my hand, and she was gone.

Molecular biology was my world that summer. Dawn had taught me enough that I could infodump and make sense of most of the material, and questions were always a good excuse to mail her. My own coding study was never as much of a struggle. Not for me. When my head felt like it was exploding, I played video games until my brain could function again. Nothing wiped my worries like putting on a sim helmet and smashing monsters.

First day back at school, I was ready early. I'd never been happier to sit on those concrete steps, surrounded by red brick and prestige. Eyes glued in the direction of the White House, watching the cars stream by.

Hers never came. I called her over and over, not moving when the crowds poured in. There was no answer.

According to my log, I called thirty-seven times before someone answered. The First Lady's face showed on my datapad, her perfectly sculpted nose red from crying. "Oh, Desiree, honey, I'm sorry. We should have let you know."

My stomach clenched, hard as rock. "What's wrong with Dawn?"

"She's really sick, Desi. She had a brain tumour and they just operated. She's in an induced coma now, recovering."

"Is she going to be OK? Can I see her?"

The First Lady shook her head. "We're not sure just yet. No visitors at this point. I'll beam your details from Dawn's pad and call you when there's news, promise."

I thanked her and disconnected, anxious to get away from those sad eyes.

Dragging myself off the steps, I headed to the computer lab. Class was not going to happen; I mailed my homeroom teacher with my excuses. If she was in a good mood, she'd let it slide.

I switched on a terminal and stared at it, thumbing my implant. The President's second term was almost up. Funny how I'd let myself fantasise about curing Dawn, but I'd never thought about what might change next year. The First Family had planned to stay in DC until Dawn finished school, but we'd never discussed what that would mean for us.

Cara must have devised a way to make Dawn sicker, right before the President's retirement. It was too much of a coincidence otherwise; he was surely trying to distract from that and raise the Luddites' profile. They'd adopted him as part of their cause because he opposed gen mods. Never mind that his brand of terrorism messed with nature just as much, if not more, than FAIRY ever did.

Dawn's illness was already all over the news. Socmed was going wild, posts and updates streaming past with conspiracy theories (I *almost* smiled at the one that Dawn was being turned into a mutant superhero), some concern about Dawn, and lots of support for the President, rather than Dawn herself.

My brain was buzzing; I wanted to do something. Contact Lavender? No—she wasn't expecting to hear from me until internship applications opened. And as much as I'd learned about molecular biology, it wasn't my true strength. Instead, I dug around through the junk in my bag, searching for the right cable. I opened a new window, jacked into the terminal with my implant, and started coding.

It took a while to get it right, of course. It always does. My homeroom teacher mailed back, granting me another day of leave; classes were still settling in so I wasn't missing much. I took her up on that and finished my program the next day.

Testing it was the next step. The program worked, with some revisions, but it needed more processing power. So I set up a little website, asking people to donate their spare CPU to my Cara-finding project. I called it Save Dawn and put a plea on socmed on a separate account and behind a proxy, for some anonymity. It would slow down anyone looking for me, rather than stop them, but that was better than nothing.

To my surprise, a journalist from a major news company picked it up and publicised it, so after a few days, I had enough power to try the program out for real. Jacked into my home terminal, my heart thundered as I pushed the script through the orange and grey corridors of the web. This was what I did best, this was where I belonged; riding waves of data, certain I could succeed and—

Something pushed me, or *flicked* me, it felt like, out of the corridor and back into meatspace. Bile rose in my throat. I jacked out and sipped some water. My spam watcher started beeping and I cycled through my browser tabs. The Save Dawn website had been hacked, defaced with graffiti, as if someone had written it by hand on a datapad. All it said was: *Think a child can stop me?* Over the request for help at the end, Cara had pasted a picture of me, one from my personal socmed.

My chair toppled as I stood. "Mom?" I called. "We have to get out of here. Now."

She must have caught my tone, because she ran in. "What happened?"

"I made a really big mistake. We need to go."

She took out her datapad.

I snatched it from her hands. "Better leave it here. I'll explain on the way."

The early evening sky was still streaked with light. We footed it to the police station rather than risk the car's computer being hijacked. Our implants were a risk too, but we could hardly leave them at home, and they were supposed to be immune to hacking. We ran past the crumbling apartment blocks of our decaying neighbourhood. The acrid smell of leaking sewage flooded the narrow streets. People stared as we raced past. I gripped Mom's hand tighter and pulled her along.

Whatever checks the officer ran on us, they made him take us seriously. Despite best efforts, I started crying as I explained what I'd done. "I made things worse, didn't I?"

He shook his head, expression blank. "Can't say, miss. I'm going to get one of our lieutenants. This is more his line. And...we'll need to search your apartment, with your permission, ma'am."

Mom nodded. She gave me a tissue from her purse and tried to hug me.

I pushed her away, sniffing. "I don't deserve any sympathy."

"Oh, honey..."

The officer returned with the lieutenant, who made us go over the whole story again.

"It's true that you were foolish, Desiree," he said. "But you've done the right thing in coming straight to us."

"Please don't tell Dawn's parents," I said.

He patted my shoulder. "This isn't exactly something we can hide from the President. In any case, as a precaution, I'd like to place you in temporary protection. I've taken the liberty..." His voice trailed off as he opened up a comm link.

"Doctor Peters!" I sat up, then put my face in my hands. "I...kind of messed up."

Lavender pressed her lips together. "Desiree, your mistake hasn't done as much damage as you think. Not to Dawn, anyway. And as far as mistakes go, it's pretty impressive."

Startled, I looked up again.

"The fact that you got as far as you did, working from a home terminal, speaks volumes about your potential as a programmer. There's a place for you with our biomedical engineering team, if you would like it. We can keep you as safe as the police can, and get your career moving while we're at it."

"I...what?"

Mom's work gave her leave and FAIRY organised an apartment for us, right near the main research building. A private entrance shielded us from the street, and burly guards seemed to be everywhere. The police quarantined all our data, but they brought our clothes and other stuff to our new place, so it felt almost like home.

Still, I wanted a fresh start. After some coaxing, Mom chopped my hair down into a short 'fro and helped me dye it bright pink. Short enough to show off all the earrings that I sometimes wondered why I'd bothered getting. Tilting my head revealed my neural implant. I felt a million times cooler. Lots of people hid their implants, but not me.

Lavender did a double take when she met me at the gates the next day. "I like it," she said. "The colour is awesome against your skin. You look like a real hacker now...the good kind, of course."

"Thanks." I glanced up at the building. Domed and rounded, it was built to suggest the shape of a curled-up foetus. The current paint job was stark white, but bricklayers and gardeners were working together to scoop away some of the facade and embed vertical gardens. The sterile walls and dirt and greenery were a mess, but it would be pretty when it was done. "FAIRY's getting a makeover too."

She rolled her eyes. "It's taking ages, and there's dirt *everywhere*. Come on, let's get you inside."

Security took a while to go through my bag. "Girl, you need to clean this crap out," one of the guards said to me with a grin. Laughing, I promised to do my best.

Past the automatic doors, Lavender presented me with a swipe card. "This will take you where you're allowed to go. Keep it with you at all times."

She showed me through the labs—some dedicated to Dawn's treatments, some general. They all seemed pretty much alike; bright lights, white benches and lots of complicated machines that scientists used with the confidence I felt when jacking into my terminal.

Then there were training modules to pass. Lab protocols and procedures, OH&S, lots of boring hoops to jump through. They tested me, question after question about anything they could think of. At the end of each day all I wanted was sleep, but I had homework, too; my study was nowhere near enough to keep up with the PhDs, most of whom had gen mods and years of research under their belts. I'd never infodumped so much in one go, and it was a losing battle trying to make sense of it all.

At first I worried about Mom, cooped up in the apartment. But she was determined to treat it as a vacation. She hadn't had a proper one since before I was born, working as hard as she did to pay off our implants. Mom said she was sure she'd get bored of watching vids all day eventually, but it was going to take a while.

While Dawn was under, they filtered her blood to search again for nanobots. They managed to extract a couple this time, a success in terms of research, if not treatment.

"The others must be more deeply embedded in her organs," Lavender said. "But we'll get some good data from these."

I wasn't allowed near them. Frustrated, I offered to help in other ways. Endless, boring data entry and analysis, but at least I knew what was going on—or wasn't. The test results were disappointing. Nanobots were notoriously difficult to study, being so tiny and all, but I'd never expected everyone to be so stumped.

In a lab meeting full of despondent scientists, I raised my hand tentatively. "What if there's more encryption on the bots than we think? It might explain why we're not finding much."

"Can't be," Jerry, one of the biomed engineers, said. "That much data just can't fit in a bot this size."

My shoulders slumped down.

"No, it's worth checking out," Lavender said.

"Just because she's your wunderkid, doesn't mean you need to coddle her," Jerry said.

Lavender raised an eyebrow. "You started here after Cara was fired, didn't you?"

"Yeah, what—"

"So don't assume anything is impossible. He's much smarter than you, and sneakier."

Jerry ducked his head. "Wait, you knew him? What was he like?"

I leaned forward in my chair. A personal opinion on Cara was worth a million infodumps on his shady activities.

"Not much to tell. In retrospect, it's obvious that he was a sociopath. You know he was fired for building nanobots that could be programmed to stop working if the client fell behind on their payments, right? He was always a bit off, but brilliant. Cramming more data into bots than they're meant to fit wouldn't surprise me in the least."

"Is he modded or planted?" Jerry asked.

147

"Modded, definitely. Implanted, possibly also," Lavender replied.

"Isn't that—?"

"Illegal? Yeah, and so's hijacking an infant's gen mods." Lavender pressed her lips together in a thin line.

There was a brief silence. How often had she tortured herself thinking about what FAIRY might have done differently to prevent Cara's bizarre vendetta?

"Right," Lavender said, her expression clearing. "I'd like Desiree to have access to the bot we've been working on. See what she comes up with. If she breaks it, we've still got the spare."

"I'm not going to break it," I said, trying not to scowl. Then I noticed the twinkle in her eyes.

Jerry got over being grumpy and taught me to use the electron microscope. The nanobot was creepy and interesting to see at extreme magnification, but it didn't help me much. What I needed was a way into its data, a way to connect to it somehow. I thumbed my implant as I thought.

"You can't jack into this baby," Jerry said.

"Yeah, I know. But I might be able to interface." I rummaged around in my bag and pulled out a game box, a prototype of the one I'd given Dawn. Its simple wireless capabilities might just do the trick.

Jerry grinned. "With a few over-rides…"

We programmed it quickly, arguing good-naturedly about how best to code it. The first time any of them treated me like a colleague, instead of just a kid. When we were done, I started jacking into the game box.

Jerry shook his head. "Stay in meatspace. Let's test it wirelessly first. We might need a better firewall."

It was true that things hadn't gone so well last time I tried to jack into Cara's domain.

"While we're at it, let's back up before we connect, like good little tech heads," he said. He uploaded the code into the lab's cloud, then severed the link. The game box would connect to the nanobot only, projecting any data it found as a holo, which we would then transcribe. Annoying, but it would keep us, and the data, safe.

Neither of us breathed as we opened the connection. As data began to flow through to the holo display, I read the code aloud into my datapad's recorder.

Jerry spoke softly, so my mic wouldn't pick up his voice. "This is the most sophisticated encryption I've ever seen. Lavender wasn't kidding when—what's that smell?"

The game box was blazing. Jerry ran for the electrical fire extinguisher while I shouted the rest of the data at high speed before it vanished.

"All done?" Jerry asked, waving the extinguisher around.

"Yes, that's everything—that was projected, anyway." When my datapad was safe in my pocket, he put out the fire, so tiny it hadn't even triggered the smoke alarms yet. We opened the windows for good measure.

"Bet you're glad that's not your brain," he said.

I coughed as I inhaled some smoke. "Little bit."

Lavender gripped the edge of her fancy glass desk as we brought her up to speed.

"This section here?" Jerry pointed to the last code fragment we'd recorded. "We're pretty sure it's a transmitter."

"So Cara is still communicating with his bots." Lavender nodded. "We'd thought so."

"He also knows we're onto him," Jerry continued.

"Don't forget the good news," I interrupted.

Jerry frowned at me. "Desiree thinks she can trace his signal back to him in meatspace, find where he's hiding," he said. "But I really don't think she should..." He turned to me. "Remember what that game box looked like."

"But with better firewalls..."

"Jerry, could you step out for a minute, please?" Lavender said.

He left, looking as puzzled as I felt.

Function A.save (target.Dawn) | *Rivqa Rafael*

"In our line of work," Lavender said, "It's important not to let our emotions cloud our judgement. It often leads to poor decisions that don't hold up in front of ethics committees."

"But Dawn—"

"It's obvious how much you care about her. More than just as a friend, right?"

I nodded, blushing at my transparency.

"So, ethics aside, imagine if something happened to you, and I had to tell Dawn that I'd let you do it."

"Lavender, I can do this, I swear. I'll encrypt to my eyeballs, literally. I'll be careful. Just give me the chance."

She shook her head. "We'll find another way. Thanks to the data you've extracted, the biotech team is closer to a cure, or at least a treatment. You've already done enough. Even if you did actually break the nanobot." She smiled, eyes twinkling with what seemed like a mixture of amusement and pity.

I resisted the urge to kick something on my way out.

The biotech team worked around the clock, while my team worked on what they called the delivery system, which was basically a nanobot with as many defences as we could code in. I did my best to make myself useful, even if it meant getting coffee instead of doing real work. No one knew how long Dawn could stay in the induced coma, so everyone was tense. After what seemed like endless testing, Lavender decreed Dawn's treatment ready.

"You should be there when we give it to her," she said to me.

"Her father won't let me."

Lavender put her hand on my shoulder. "They know what you've done for Dawn. Anyway, we need a team there to search for rogue tech. You may as well be on it."

We spent ages scouring the private FAIRY facility where Dawn was being treated. Despite its high security, we found and disabled a few small bots. When we were done, Lavender brought me into Dawn's room.

Dawn's parents sat on either side of her; I returned the President's curt nod and stared at Dawn. Paler and thinner than I remembered, she had wires sticking out everywhere. They connected to a central monitor that displayed all kinds of numbers I didn't understand. Lavender put her arm around my shoulder.

"We'll get her healthy again," the doctor said confidently to the President. He checked Dawn's monitor and, apparently satisfied with the numbers, began preparing a syringe with the treatment.

The monitor's display flickered. Before I had a conscious thought, I was elbowing the doctor out of the way to reach it. With trembling hands I plugged a cable into my implant, hoping the monitor had a standard connector. It did.

A voice emanated from the monitors. "Nothing can stop—"

I ramped up my firewalls and jacked in.

In my daydreams, this moment was carefully planned, with protocols and filters and an arsenal of awesome trojans. Imaginary me would match Cara's stealth, slipping in and out of the dark web until I caught him.

There was no time for anything like that. The data streamed by without any anomalies to guide me. Closer. A small empty space that should have been full. I nudged it and jumped back when it tingled like an electric fence. Firewall. I lobbed a giant, overly obvious trojan at it. While the wall consumed it, I used a tiny one to cut through. I jumped through just in time; the hole was reabsorbed in microseconds. The buzzing reverberated through me, then faded. No way back now.

Cara's corner of the web was dark, darker than the shadiest hackers' corner. A slender strip of grey light directed me to where he was likely to be jacked in. I pressed on as fast as I dared, doing my best to hide behind data as it moved through.

The centre of his domain suggested a shadowy castle. Someone had delusions of grandeur. Back in

153

meatspace, my guts clenched. I reminded myself that none of this was real, that all that mattered was Cara's avatar. The entrance was unguarded apart from some easily dodged turrets; his defences would be inside.

Further in, a second firewall presented itself. I threw another trojan. The time for subtlety was over. It crumbled easily—more warning system than real defence.

The terrorist stood facing away from me, his flickering, shadowy avatar camouflaging him and making it hard to see particular features. He turned quickly. "Ah, the baby hacker...the young lover. Come to save your princess again?"

I reached for another trojan, but my stash was empty. Knocking together another would take time. I angled my avatar away from him. "I've already done better this time." I hoped I sounded braver than I felt. "Haven't I?" Grabbing a fistful of data, I began twisting it to my needs.

"Undeniably," he said, "but you will still fail, and the Luddites will rise!"

My hand stilled for a second. "Luddites? Everyone knows you're just out for revenge against FAIRY for firing you. In the stupidest way possible. All you've done is given them more research opportunities." I resumed working as fast as I could. Almost done.

He bared his teeth, too pointy to be human. "Their cure will never work. I'll always be one step ahead. Always!" His form began to shift.

Function A.save (target.Dawn) | *Rivqa Rafael*

I jumped back as his avatar changed into a giant dragon. A convincing illusion, even though part of me couldn't believe he was this cheesy. The smell of burning plastic enveloped me as I dodged flames. Yellow eyes glowed in purple-black scales. A lashing tail was another hazard to avoid.

He's still just a man, I told myself, and twisted one more strand of data. Long hours of gaming had trained me to stay away from extremities and find the weak spot, usually the belly. One hand on my implant—I'd only have one shot—I threw the trojan and jacked free as everything exploded.

"Desiree!" Lavender and Dawn's mother called in unison.

"Is Dawn OK?" I leaned on the monitor for support.

"Stable," the doctor said. "After you jacked in, I thought I'd better proceed with the injection just yet…"

"I put a trace in my trojan, Lavender. You should be able to track it in meatspace." My breathing was almost normal now as I beamed the details to her.

She nodded and made the call, stepping outside to speak to the police.

"Sit down, Desi." The First Lady gestured to the bed. Dawn didn't take up much space in it. She was propped up into an almost-sitting position.

It was awkward, but my knees were shaking and there were no free chairs. I sat at the First Lady's side. Opposite, the President smiled at me for the first time ever, and the doctor injected the treatment into Dawn's arm.

We waited. Dawn flinched. Without thinking, I took her hand. She was holding something. "What...?"

The First Lady smiled. "Dawn brought that game box into surgery with her and she's had it ever since. We thought it was best to let her keep it."

Dawn opened her eyes. Her parents hugged her gently but I was in her line of sight. "Desi?" Her voice was croaky, and the doctor held out water for her to sip. She kissed her parents' cheeks in turn.

My hand tightened around hers. "Dawn."

The door clicked as Lavender came back in. "The helicopters are out. They should have him any minute—hey, did I miss everything?"

"Hi Lavender," Dawn said. She let the game box drop and clutched my hand. "So, am I better now?"

"Thanks to Lavender and Desiree and the rest at FAIRY, we hope so," the President said.

"You really did it. I knew you would." Dawn said. I thought she was talking to Lavender, but she was looking at me. She leaned forward and pressed her lips against mine.

Noah No-one and the Infinity Machine

By Sean Williams

The Machine was out of bounds, but still Noah had to dust it. That was his punishment for changing every picture of Billy Samuelson on the school website into one of an ape. Billy *was* an ape, and a bully. He had been whispering *Noah No-one Noah No-one* behind Noah's back for weeks now, but nobody ever did anything about it.

It was Saturday. Mum was at a science conference and she expected the house to be clean from top to bottom when she got home. Then and only then would Noah be allowed to do anything fun.

"Shoo!" He brushed his cat out of the way so he could get at the cables around the back of the Machine. Quicksilver wasn't helping. He thought the duster was a giant mouse and jumped on it whenever Noah swished it most vigorously.

"You missed a bit," called Eli through the open doorway to mum's study. Noah ignored his older sister. She was even more irritating than the cat.

Stupid Eli. Stupid Quicksilver. Stupid chores. Stupid Billy—

Click.

A particularly furious dusting had brought the Machine to life. Strings of lights coursed up and down its white plastic sides, forming an arc around the door at the front. The lights were red at first, but changed one by one to green. Noah stepped back and looked up in amazement, his eyes growing wide. The Machine had been a permanent fixture in his home for weeks, but he had never once seen it switched on. It was a booth two and a half metres high and one and a half meters square around the bottom. His mum called it the Mark Five, but everyone else just called it the Machine.

Noah had overheard enough dinner party conversation to know what it was supposed to do. When the Machine worked, a person could get inside it and be turned into data. That data could then be sent by wires somewhere else, where the person could be turned back into matter exactly as they had been. If the cost would only come down, mum was always saying, the Machine would change the world. Noah didn't know about that, but he knew what he would do if he had one of his own. He would escape.

Quicksilver stood at his feet, watching the spinning lights. Noah glanced anxiously over his shoulder into mum's study. Eli was silent. She hadn't heard the faint hum the Machine made when it switched on. This, if he dared, was his chance.

With fingers that shook only a little, Noah reached out and touched the door. Something inside the booth clicked and the door slid open, wrapping around the outside to reveal a spacious, mirrored interior. Noah leaned forward and sniffed experimentally. The air issuing from the Machine smelled like their electric car on a hot day, which wasn't unfriendly. On particularly hot days, they went to the beach. Noah liked the beach. Maybe the Machine could take him there as well.

He warily stepped one foot through the door, and then, when nothing terrible happened, followed it with the rest of him. Inside, he stood with his arms at his sides and looked around in amazement. The walls were entirely mirrors. Floors and ceiling, too. Reflections of Noah stretched to infinity, all with Quicksilver standing at his feet, tail swishing. The cat had followed Noah inside, not wanting to miss out on this curious new development.

They both turned as the door began to slide shut.

Noah felt a flutter of fear in his belly, although he was *sure* the Mark Five had been tested. Mum wouldn't allow it in their home if it was unsafe, would she? Maybe she used it to get to and from work, when he and Eli were asleep. She was a workaholic. That's what dad had yelled at her before he left.

Maybe the Machine could take him to Africa, Noah thought, where his dad lived now. He told himself to think about that.

But the Machine didn't ask him for any instructions, and there wasn't a keyboard for him to type into. He looked around for some other means of telling the machine what to do when the lights in the corners grew brighter, the air seemed to thin, all the hairs on his body stood on end, and then—

Snap.

—the lights dimmed, the air became normal again, Quicksilver shook himself as his fur settled back down, and it was over.

Noah checked his hands. Still there, with the correct number of fingers, although maybe they were shaking a little more, now. The Machine had done its thing and he looked the same as he always did in the mirror. Wherever he was, he appeared to have arrived in one piece.

The door slid smoothly open. Noah peered out in nervous anticipation…and sagged on seeing the familiar contents of his mum's study. He and Quicksilver hadn't gone anywhere at all. Maybe, Noah thought as he stepped through the door, he had knocked one of the cables out at the back while he was cleaning…

"No *way*," said a voice he recognized although he had never heard it from the outside before. Beside him, Quicksilver crouched low on his forelegs and hissed.

Coming around from the back of the Machine was another Noah and another silver cat who looked exactly like Quicksilver.

They gaped at each other for a moment, utter amazement stopping all thoughts.

"W-where did you come from?" Noah eventually managed to ask.

"Out of the Machine," the other Noah said. "I was around here checking the cables when the door opened again and out you came."

They looked at the Machine, and then back at each other.

"It copied me?" said Noah.

"*I'm* not a copy," the other Noah hissed.

"Well, *I'm* not either. We must both be real."

They looked down at the two Quicksilvers, who had stopped circling each other and were now touching noses, making tentative friends.

"The Machine turns people into data," said Noah slowly, testing this strange new reality one piece at a time, "and data can be duplicated. Maybe mum was testing if it could do that."

The other Noah snapped his fingers. "Roast chicken!"

"Of course!" Roast chicken was their favourite dinner. At least it had been. They normally had it once a month, when mum took a day off. This week, though, they had had it every night, even though their mum had gone nowhere near the kitchen. They had had it so many times Noah was starting to get sick of it.

"What's going on in there?" called Eli from the lounge room. "I don't hear any dusting."

"Get off my back!" the two Noahs shouted at exactly the same time.

They leaned in close to whisper.

"Mum cheated."

"She must have cooked one roast, put it in the Machine, and created a copy every night."

"So it must be safe!"

They grinned at each other, relieved that if they had survived the last week they weren't going to drop dead now. The chicken, however, wasn't so lucky.

"I've just thought of something."

"Me too!"

Grinning even wider, they went back into the Machine and cycled through a second time. When they stepped out, the booth closed behind them and then opened a minute later, revealing two more Noahs, amazed and excited like the others.

"Brilliant!" They executed a clumsy high-five, fumbling only slightly as the tails of four Quicksilvers tangled around their ankles.

"We'll get the chores done in no time at all, now."

"And then what?"

Noah was still getting used to the idea of having an identical twin, three times over. He hadn't thought any further ahead than that.

One possibility came instantly to mind.

"Go visit Billy the Bully?"

"Yeah! When he sees us he won't call us Noah No-one anymore!"

"Maybe we need more of us. He's huge."

"There's one way to fix that…"

This time the booth was a bit of a squeeze, with four of them inside it. And then there were eight Noahs in the study, and the thought came to all of them: why stop at eight? With a machine like this they could create an army of Noahs, enough to take on every bully on the planet.

The noise of their excited whispering was too much to conceal.

"What do you think you're…oh my god!"

Their sister's voice put an end to their merriment. Eli was standing in the doorway with her mouth open and her hands slipping from her hips, where they had been perched in an imitation of their mum's best telling-off pose.

"Cool, isn't it?" said all eight Noahs, even though they knew she wouldn't agree.

"Mum will freak!"

"Why? We can do more around the house, and it won't cost anything to feed us, now she can copy everything."

Eli smacked one Noah on the top of the head. "Where are you going to sleep? You've only got one bed."

"We can copy that, too."

"Yeah, but you've only got one room to fit all of you in. Did you think about that? And what about school? Mum will have to pay eight times the fees."

The Noahs' faces fell equally.

"Can't we just copy some money?"

"Yeah, and the police would just *love* that. After

they've finished working out what to call you, they'll throw you all in jail forever. How would that be?"

Their excitement ebbed even further. Eli was such a buzz-kill. But she was right.

"We have to put you back," Eli said, "before mum finds out and grounds you forever."

"How are we going to do that?"

"I don't know. We can't just erase seven of you, much as I'd like to. Maybe..."

Eli opened a hatch in the side of the Machine that Noah hadn't seen before and fiddled with what lay within. The eight Noahs jostled to peer over her shoulder, hoping she knew what she was doing. It was hard to get a good view with so many heads all trying to look at once.

The eight Noahs pushed and shoved, worried about what Eli had in mind. The word *erase* had spooked every one of them. None of them could tell who the original Noah was anymore.

"Okay," she said. "I think I've worked it out. Mum had it on the *replicate* setting, which obviously works just fine. There's another called *merge*. We should try that."

The Noahs shifted on their feet. "What happens to our memories?"

"I don't know," she said. "You're about to find out."

"But—"

"Get in. You should have worried about this before you did it."

Grumbling, Noah squeezed himself into the booth with the seven other Noahs, stuck under one of his own armpits. The door slid shut, and he closed his eyes. At least when the merge was finished he would be able to breathe…

Snap.

He gasped, feeling no less suffocated than before, but in an entirely different way. There was only one of him, and the booth appeared to have shrunk around him. He could barely turn in its coffin-like space to squeeze through the door.

"No, no, no!" Eli was saying. "That only made things worse!"

He realized what she meant when he wriggled free of the Machine and banged his head on the ceiling. The Machine had merged all of the Noahs into one super-Noah, as big as eight of him combined. Eli looked like a doll next to him.

He raised his hands and clenched them into fists. If only Billy the Bully could see him now!

Then a pang of hunger stabbed through him, making him double up. He was nearly always hungry these days, but he had never felt anything like this before. Sick of them or not, he could eat a dozen roast chickens just for a snack! His giant body was burning energy too fast.

Eli shoved his left thigh, trying to get him to move. It was like shoving a mountain.

"Get back in," she said. "I think I can fix this. There's a *reduce* setting I'm sure will work."

Reluctantly he did as he was told. If he stayed like this he'd be starving all the time, and they'd need to build a new house for him to live in. He would be even worse off than he had been before.

Careful not to step on any of the Quicksilvers, he folded himself back into the tiny space and waited with his breath held tight and hot in his chest.

Being physically enormous wasn't the weirdest thing. He could feel all eight sets of memories in his head, each slightly different than the others. They had all started off as the same person, and they had been doing pretty much the same things since being copied, but what would have happened if one of them had gone off and had their own adventures, then returned to be merged with the others?

An experiment for another time, he thought. If he survived this one...

Snap.

This time when he stepped out he was his normal size—perhaps slightly taller than before—and his sister hugged him in relief.

"Oh, Noah, you idiot. I'm glad you're back."

He squirmed free. "What about Quicksilver?"

The cats were everywhere, playing with papers, chasing each other around the desk, snoozing on the warm cables. It took Eli and Noah ages to herd them all into the booth, and even as the door slid shut Noah wasn't entirely sure that there were actually eight in there.

"Wait," he said, grabbing Eli's hand as she leaned over the Machine's insides. "Not *merge*. We don't want a giant cat jumping around here." A *hungry* one too, he thought.

"Yeah, you're right. Hmmm. There's *normalise*. Maybe that will work."

She made the change and the booth hummed for a long time. Noah didn't like the worried look on her face. What if Quicksilver died in there? That would be all his fault for playing with the Machine when he shouldn't have. They would have to tell mum and then he would really be in trouble…

The Machine's hum began to ebb. Noah and Eli ran to the front.

Through the opening door stepped a tall man with silver hair, wearing a fur coat over a smart grey suit.

"Perfect," he said, performing a graceful pirouette in front of them. "Or should I say *purr*-fect?"

"Quicksilver!" Noah gasped. "Is that you?"

"None other." He bowed. "I've seen from the school boundary how Billy torments you. In return for many years of tinned mackerel and belly rubs, I will make him feel like a mouse in cat's paws…" At this, he grinned widely, revealing teeth that were very slightly pointed. His slitted eyes gleamed. "And then I will consider my debt repaid."

Before Noah or Eli could do anything, he swept from the room. The front door slammed, and when Noah went to go after him, Eli held him by the arm.

"Leave him," she said. "He seems to know what he's doing."

"But how will we explain it to mum?"

"I don't know. That he got tired of living with a brat and ran away?"

That rang at least partly true. Noah felt glum until something rubbed against his ankle. He looked down in surprised relief. Quicksilver! They *had* missed one of them. Or one had deliberately stayed hidden. Quicksilver had a mischievous look in his eye. Maybe he had known all along what the booth would do. Maybe he had seen their mum use it on herself…

Noah felt a wave of dizziness and put a hand to his forehead. This was all too much. There had been eight of him, and now there was one. There had been eight Quicksilvers too, and now seven of them were loose in the body of a person. Everything had changed.

"Nothing's changed," said Eli. She must have been thinking similar thoughts but coming to the opposite conclusion, as she always did. "This room is a mess. Mum's going to be home in an hour. Get cleaning, or I need to tell her what you've done."

"You wouldn't!"

She grinned and pointed at the feather duster.

*

The next day Billy gave Noah a new nickname. Noah just grinned and called him Billy the Baboon in return. Maybe it was because Noah was taller (exactly one centimetre) or maybe it was because of Quicksilver. Or maybe it was because for a brief time there had been eight of him. Either way, "No-Nonsense Noah" seemed a vast improvement on being No-one. Not even the thought of another chicken dinner could take that away from him.

Forgiveness

Leah Cypess

The day Michael came back to school, I was still wearing long sleeves.

Not because of the bruises. That's what everyone thought, but the truth was, the bruises had faded weeks before. I didn't know why I was wearing them myself, until Michael slunk through the front doors, and everyone stopped what they were doing and turned to stare at him.

Once, he would have laughed and strode through them, meeting their eyes and daring them to say something. Instead, he focused on the yellow-speckled white tiles as he walked down the hallway.

My heart lodged in my throat. He had always been so fierce, so vital, with so much life in him that it spilled out around the edges and infected everyone close to him. Now his steps were slow and heavy, and when Nandini stepped ostentatiously away from him, he flinched.

I did that to him.

I took a deep breath, stepped out of the classroom

where I had been hiding, and walked across the tiles to meet him.

Aim #1 accomplished: No one was looking at him anymore. Everyone was looking at me.

Everyone but Michael.

He saw me, but wouldn't look me in the face. His blue eyes flicked to my sleeves, and I waited for him to ask if the bruises were still there.

That was why I had been wearing long sleeves. Waiting for this moment.

His eyes finally met mine, his expression a mute plea, and my heart thudded dully. Somehow, just by walking over, I had hurt him. Again.

Walk away. How many times had Nandini urged me to do just that?

Only this time, I did.

As soon as I slammed the stall door shut, I heard someone else walk into the girls' bathroom. No question who it was.

"Go away," I said. I hadn't started crying yet, but my voice was quivering.

"It's Nandini."

Like it could be anyone else. Nandini had been playing concerned-best-friend to the hilt the past month. And though she eighty percent meant it, I was still really, really sick of hearing it from her.

"Go *away*," I said again, with a viciousness Nandini claimed I learned from Michael. She doesn't know me as well as she thinks.

A pause, and then the bathroom door closed again.

I wondered if Michael blamed me. Probably. Ms. Thompson said he could still feel anger, he just couldn't act on it. But she didn't know Michael as well as she thought. Acting on his feelings was the way he felt them.

Nobody knew Michael, not really. Ever since he agreed to get a chip—and people only agreed to chips to avoid jail time—everyone talked about him like he was a monster. Like his mistakes were all he was. Like *they* had no flaws, nothing ugly deep inside them.

The way they looked at him. As if he was a zoo exhibit. A monster in a cage. The way his head stayed down, as if he had been forced to agree with them.

Oh, Michael. I blame myself too.

Of *course*, I had to have an extra therapy session that afternoon, to help me deal with him being back. Ms. Thompson, leaning over her desk with her blond hair swinging around her chin, wanted to know how it made me *feel*.

"It made me feel happy," I said. I had been behaving for weeks now, playing my part. But just being in the same building as Michael made me defiant. The way he once would have been. "I missed him."

Result: an extra therapy session the next week. Clearly, that "Feelings Can't be Wrong" sign on the office wall was a blatant lie.

I spent the next week scheming to talk to Michael alone. Going to his house was, of course, out of the question—his parents hated me, and I didn't blame them. School was equally problematic. Nandini stuck to me like lichen, warding off everyone else with protective looks, steering me clear of the more obnoxious girls. As if I couldn't handle their questions.

More likely, she was afraid of what I would answer.

In the end, Michael found me. The way he always did. I was on my way to extra-cred bio when he stepped into the hall in front of me, gave me the crooked grin I had missed so much, and disappeared into an empty classroom.

He didn't say anything. He didn't have to. I slammed the door behind me and flung myself into his arms. At that moment, it didn't even occur to me that he might push me away.

He didn't push me away.

Maybe twenty minutes later, I finally untangled myself from his arms. My lips were puffy, my skin was on fire, and I was so happy. I hadn't realized how unhappy I was.

"I love you," Michael said. He was breathing hard, almost desperately, his dark hair a mass of damp tangles. "Anna. I missed you so much. The treatment was awful, but not being able to see you was the worst part of it."

I burst into tears.

"Don't." He grabbed my hand and drew me close. "Don't cry. It will be all right. We're together again."

And we were. Just like that.

I should have known it was inevitable.

Not that it would be easy. My parents would never accept my decision. Just thinking about how they would react made me want to crawl into a hole and hide. They couldn't know. No one could know.

"How are we going to manage that?" I said. "We go to the same *school*."

"We'll manage," Michael said, with the easy confidence I remembered. He had never, ever been afraid of a challenge.

And when I was with him, neither was I.

I was hurrying out of the cafeteria—if I ate quickly, I could steal ten minutes with Michael before lunch ended—when someone stepped in front of me. I almost collided with a silver sports jersey.

"Oh, sorry—" I began.

"No, my fault," Darryl said quickly. "I, um. I wanted to ask you something."

I blinked up at him. In retrospect, it was stupid that I had no idea what was coming. Darryl was a jock, not one of my and Michael's usual crowd, but I had been in a study group with him when Michael was arrested. He had been concerned and sympathetic, just like everyone, and I hadn't really noticed his existence, just like with everyone.

"The spring dance," Darryl said, and ran a hand over his short curly hair. It was unusual to see a guy that good-looking get nervous. If his skin was lighter, he definitely would have been blushing. "Would you— do you think you would want to come with me?"

I froze.

That night, I thought of a dozen good reasons for saying no. *It's too soon. I need to be on my own. I'm going with Nandini, a girls-only sort of pact.* Anything.

Instead, I said the worst possible thing. I said, "I can't do that to Michael."

Darryl's jaw tensed, but his voice went gentle. "Anna. You don't have to be afraid of him anymore."

I wanted to slap him across the face and fill that patronizing mouth with blood. For a moment, I understood exactly how Michael used to feel.

Still feels, I guess. Though he can't slap anyone, not anymore.

As if the only thing between me and Michael was fear. As if Michael's temper erased his brilliance, and his courage, and his sly sense of humor, and his love for me.

Back when he *could* hurt me, it was all true. His temper, his need for control, overshadowed everything else. For a long time, his fists mattered more than anything. I proved that when I reported him. It was the hardest thing I ever did, but I did it, because I knew I couldn't be with someone who was hurting me.

But he couldn't hurt me anymore, and that changed everything. Why did nobody get that?

"It doesn't matter how angry he gets," Darryl said. "The chip removes his ability to engage in violent behavior. He can't hit you."

"Thank you, Darryl. I know how it works." I crossed my arms over my chest. "And weren't you on the anti-chip side of the debate team? I remember your speech. Human freedom, moral responsibility, blah blah blah. What happened to all that?"

"What happened," Darryl said tightly, "was that I saw your bruises."

Like it was my fault he had to let go of his holier-than-thou beliefs.

I stepped back, and his eyes widened. He said, "You don't have to be afraid of *me*. Even without a chip, *I'd* never hurt you."

He looked over my shoulder when he said *I*. I turned around. Michael was leaning against the wall, watching us.

I knew I didn't have to be afraid, but I couldn't help it. I was.

I waited for the inevitable consequences. But nothing happened.

Nothing happened for five days. Michael didn't come over to me, didn't talk to me, didn't meet me at any of the places we had been meeting. We weren't in the same classes anymore—his had all been switched—so I didn't get to see him at all.

Was that what he was going to do now, when he was mad? Just *ignore* me?

It was almost worse than the alternative. I didn't know when the silent treatment was going to end. I didn't know *if* it was going to end.

And that scared me worse than waiting for the blow-up used to. At least then, I knew that when it was over, everything would go back to normal.

On the sixth day, I did something I never would have dared do before. I went to Michael and forced the confrontation myself. Told him he was being an idiot, Darryl was only asking, I hadn't said yes. I loved him and would never cheat on him and he had to trust me.

He was furious, his eyes sparking, but he had to listen to me. There was nothing else he could do.

We had a month together—a blissful, joyous month—before my parents found out. That went about as well as could be expected.

"I'm seventeen," I shouted, after they had been going at me for an hour. "I'm old enough to know my own feelings and make my own choices. I love him. I need you to trust me."

"*Trust* you?" My dad was doing all the talking by now, since my mother was sobbing hysterically. "Do you understand how hard last year was for us? Forget us—for *you*. We don't even know everything he did to you. How can you possibly—"

"You're being irrational." I was doing my best not to cry, but I was fighting a losing battle. "Michael won't hurt me ever again. He *can't*. If you look at it logically, I'm safer with him than with anyone else in the world."

"It's not that simple! He's a monster—"

"He is *not*! He had one flaw, and *it is fixed*. So what's your problem?"

"He's not fixed," my father said. "He's controlled. Muzzled."

That did it. I whirled on my heel.

"I just don't understand," my mother gasped, through her tears. "I don't understand, Anna."

"I know you don't," I snapped. "But I'm the one who was hurt, and I forgive him. Why can't you?"

To be fair: I had to meet Darryl, to get the assignments I missed during the new extra-extra therapy sessions requested by my parents.

179

To be honest: I didn't have to laugh quite so hard at his imitation of Mr. Purcell, and I definitely didn't have to brush his arm with my hand when I said thank you.

"You're testing," Ms. Thompson said, when I brought it up. "Making sure you're really safe with Michael, even when you do things that used to lead to his...outbursts."

By now, the fact that I was back with Michael was public news. But Ms. Thompson, unlike my so-called friends, still had to talk to me.

She didn't know me that well, though, which was why she was giving me the benefit of the doubt. I knew better. I wasn't testing. I was goading.

But I didn't know *why*. I loved Michael, I didn't want to upset him...or didn't I? Maybe I wanted a little bit of revenge. Maybe anyone would, in my position.

That answer made sense, just like Ms. Thompson's. But it didn't feel any more true.

Michael was practically crying when he confronted me. He said it proved what he knew all along, that I was a stupid slut who couldn't be faithful unless I was afraid. His fist clenched and his arm bulged, and I almost backed away, but he was so clearly...helpless. He couldn't touch me.

I *was* safe.

I stood my ground, and he was the one who left, storming away with his fists clenched at his sides.

★

He gave me the silent treatment for a week, this time, but in the end he couldn't resist me. He never could. And it wasn't like anyone else would talk to him.

Or me. Nandini's interactions with me had been reduced to sending me article links (the last one: "Chips: How Safe Are They? Are There Workarounds—and Are Criminals Figuring Them Out?") Darryl and I still hung out, because we were in almost all the same classes, and he was surprisingly smart for a jock.

A part of me felt guilty for hanging out with him—guilty with a lining of fear. But that was just old habits, and I had to overcome them. Things were different now. I could be with Michael and still have a life. I *should* be able to have another friend, even a cute guy friend, without feeling like everything would come crashing down on me.

I wasn't doing anything wrong. Not being with Michael, not hanging out with Darryl. This was what a normal life felt like.

This was the way things were supposed to be.

Then, during one of our fights (about Darryl, they were always about Darryl), Michael grabbed my wrist.

Just for a second, and then he winced and let go. But I didn't think he could have done that a few weeks ago.

Did chips weaken? Could they weaken if someone was fighting them *all the time*? They're not supposed to—they're supposed to last forever—but even though I never read Nandini's articles, even though they were all by crackpots, they had planted a seed of doubt.

And I hadn't deleted them.

I read them until three in the morning, and read the comments, too, which of course was a terrible mistake. A lot of people were convinced the chips could be fought. That the human brain could find ways to work around them, to gradually weaken them by sheer persistence. There was no proof. But there *were* a lot of anecdotes from random strangers on the internet. People, I reminded myself, who I didn't know and had no reason to trust.

By the time I clicked the computer shut, I was scared again, and I didn't like it. I had forgotten how it felt.

The next week, Michael grabbed my wrist and squeezed. Long and hard enough to hurt.

I had also forgotten how it felt to be hurt. There was so much *pain*. That was obvious—should have been—but everyone had talked to me so much about the other parts of it: the helplessness, the guilt, the loneliness. I had almost started to think the pain was unimportant.

It wasn't.

Fear spiked through me, and memory came flooding back: of being hurt, and hurt, and hurt. I didn't want that. I had never wanted it. What I had wanted, always, was Michael. A Michael who didn't hurt me.

And now I had that. So why was I doing this? Why was I spending time with Darryl, pushing Michael harder and harder?

I said, in a low whisper, "I won't talk to him again. I promise."

Michael let go of my arm and leaned in to kiss me as if nothing had happened.

After he left, I sat for a long time holding my phone. I could call my parents—or Ms. Thompson, or the police—and tell them. The chip had been part of Michael's plea bargain. It wasn't an agreement he could back out of. If I told, he would be taken back to the clinic, and the doctors would find out what was wrong. They would implant a new chip, a stronger one, and monitor him more closely afterward. I would be safe with him again.

Why wasn't I dialing? Was there a part of me that *wanted* to be hurt?

Was it my fault, the way I used to think it was?

Michael was really sweet the next day. Like he used to be. During lunch, we lay together on the lawn, and talked so long we both forgot to eat. He told me he wasn't making any college choices until I decided where I was going. My heart turned over and flooded me with hope.

It wasn't like he had left bruises on my wrist. It wasn't like he even grabbed that hard. I was overreacting.

"I love you," he whispered. "I tried to stop loving you, when I was in treatment, and especially after the operation. I tried so hard. Then I saw you, that first day back, and in one second it was all over."

I floated through the weekend in a haze of happiness.

Darryl cornered me after study hall on Thursday. I tried to squeeze past him, and he grabbed my wrist, exactly where Michael had. I yelped, and he let go instantly.

"What's going on?" he said.

"Nothing," I lied. "I'm not trying to avoid you. Michael and I are spending a lot of time together, that's all. Deciding on colleges."

He stared down at me, chest heaving, and I waited for his accusation. I hadn't been fair to him, and I knew it. I wished I had done things differently. But in the end, he was just a random guy, and he'd find someone else to flirt with. Michael was the one who mattered.

"*Why?*" Darryl said. "Why are you with him? I don't get it."

"I love him," I said. "I never stopped loving him."

Darryl's face tightened. He shook his head, and then, finally, turned and walked away.

Not quite fast enough. I caught Michael's steel-blue eyes across the room, recognized the familiar set of his mouth, the fury building in him.

Ms. Thompson's office was down the hall. Nandini's number was the first speed-dial on my phone. My parents' was the second. I could have called any of them.

I didn't, even when he started toward me.

I didn't know why until I saw him coming up my front steps, a bouquet of flowers in his hand. Blue and lavender—my favorite colors—so large the petals almost obscured his face. And then I understood.

My upper arm throbbed beneath my long sleeve, and my stomach felt tight and bruised. It hadn't been his worst rage, not by a long shot. He had been sufficiently in control to avoid my face. My parents hadn't noticed the careful way I was moving. Nobody knew anything. Nobody would.

I picked up the phone and dialed.

He was on his tenth knock by the time I got to the door. After only a moment's hesitation, I opened it. I knew his pattern. There was nothing to be afraid of, not right now.

I took the flowers without speaking. His face was drawn, stark hollows beneath his eyes. He looked at me, then away.

"Anna," he whispered. "I'm sorry. I don't—I can't—I love you so much, and I hate that I—I'm just so, so sorry."

"I know," I said.

He looked up, a faint, fearful hope dawning on his face. "Can you forgive me?"

"Yes," I said.

He smiled at me, radiant, the smile of pure joy that had drawn me to him the first time I saw him. It filled my heart, to know I had caused that joy in him. It eased the fading pain in my arm and back.

But when he stepped forward, I stepped back.

"Anna?" he said, hesitant.

And then he heard the sirens.

He could have run, but he didn't. He stood there, the brightness draining out of his face, staring at me.

"*Why?*" he whispered.

Anger came to my aid, at last. "Are you joking?" I yanked up my sleeve. The bruise was purple-yellow, still darkening.

He flinched. "But then—why not yesterday? Why now, when I came to *apologize?*"

As if his apology should have made everything better.

But I had also thought it would. It was what I had wanted, what I had never gotten, while he was chipped.

He hadn't been able to hurt me anymore, but he also hadn't been sorry that he had.

This was why I flirted with Darryl. This was why I hadn't told. It wasn't that I wanted to be hurt.

I wanted him to be *sorry*.

I had thought that once he was, we could be together again. I took another step back, hoping I wouldn't cry.

A new chip, hopefully, would fix him. But it wouldn't fix *us*.

"You don't have to do this," Michael said.

"I do," I said. "I have to do exactly this."

He stared at me blankly. Behind him, a police car pulled onto the curb, red and blue lights flashing.

I went inside, through the kitchen and into the family room. I put the flowers carefully into a crystal vase and filled it halfway with water, and by the time I was done, I had my tears under control. I yanked my sleeve down over my arm and went outside to give my statement.

Probably Definitely

By Heather Morris

Savannah Sullivan is dead.

Savannah Sullivan is dead and Tommie isn't taking it well at all.

For starters, the news came from HoHo, Tommie's hideous little brother. If the universe were kind he would have been playing a stupid prank, but the universe is not kind.

Second, Tommie's been holding on to a Revolutions ticket since *November*. Tommie's never seen the band live before, never seen Savannah Sullivan strut across a stage close enough to reach out and touch. It was supposed to be the show that changed everything, Tommie's first concert. And it was supposed to be tonight.

Third, even though the most important person in Tommie's whole life is gone, burnt out somewhere on the Long Island Expressway, Tommie has to go to school.

Mami was nice, brushed back Tommie's hair and said *I'm sorry, baby, I'm so, so sorry*, but she wasn't sorry enough to let Tommie take the day to hide under the covers, was she?

So it shouldn't surprise anyone that it all becomes too much. It's hot for May, and Tommie has spent the day feeling hungry and nauseous all at once. The atmosphere of grief around school is a living thing, a tight hand around the throat. Tommie muddles through biology, stumbles through phys-ed, and then, crossing the field towards third period, the world is suddenly too bright and too big, and Tommie hits the ground. Just turns off like a lamp.

Tommie's first memory, or the first one that matters: five years old, a Saturday night at Abuelo's house, HoHo screaming in the background and Tommie's bare knees digging into the short pile carpet, while Tommie stares at the thing on TV. One of those music competition shows, or an awards show or something— Tommie never has been sure which. Could look it up in a second, but that would break the magic of it, turn it into a video clip and a nasty comments section, erase the itch of the carpet, the smell of ginger ale and lime.

There is a redhead on TV. Five-year-old Tommie thinks *grown-up lady*, but she can't be more than seventeen. She is all alone on a huge stage with a microphone stand and a screeching guitar, and she is wailing a song about someone called Billie Jean like it is the most desperate song in the universe.

"Ay," Abuela *tsks*. "Is that a girl or a boy?"

"Of course it's a girl. Look at those *tetas*." This from Abuelo, appreciative enough that he gets a smack on the arm for his trouble.

"What is she singing that song for, then? That's a man's song, listen."

Tommie doesn't know what to listen for. The song feels like a hole in the chest, and Tommie even looks down to make sure that hot blood isn't dripping onto the carpet.

"Is it a rule, now? Songs only for girls, songs only for boys?"

"It's *indecent*. Why would she want to sound like a man? It's not right."

And Tommie thinks: *why not?*

This was long before Revolutions, long before Savannah Sullivan transformed from an almost-forgotten pop-star to rock royalty. Long before she and Nick White became famous for writing each other's songs, adopting each other's perspectives and persona. Savannah Sullivan didn't have the slightest bit of butch about her, not then and not ever, but still her femininity always seemed like a costume that she wore, and for Tommie, with one song, that opened a whole world.

*

A two-finger flick against the forehead, a disinterested thrum against a bass string, brings Tommie back to life. "Hey. Hey you. Thomasina. Wake up."

A flash of dull, dirty sky, a dark smear of something red. No one's used *Thomasina* since the first day of kindergarten.

"Tommie." It's a tires-on-gravel crunch in the throat.

"Oh. Sorry. I didn't get nicknames."

Something is so, so familiar about that voice. Tommie rockets upward, blood rushing to the head. Kneeling in the grass in artfully ripped jeans and an over-large grey t-shirt is Savannah Sullivan.

"No," Tommie says. Absolutely, no.

"Yeah," Savannah Sullivan says. Like she's sorry.

"You. You're. This isn't real. You died."

"Figuring that out, thanks." She looks around, head flicking in random directions like a tiny bird.

"Did *I* die?"

"Ah, no. Definitely not. Probably definitely not."

Tommie blinks, expecting the hallucination to disappear. It does not.

"This doesn't make any sense."

Savannah Sullivan's head keeps flicking, her attention zipping from one thing to the next. It's making Tommie dizzy. "You're telling me. I grew up Catholic, but I wasn't a very *good* one. Still, I don't remember learning about this. Did you know everyone has to do it?"

Do what? Tommie is having trouble concentrating. That flicking has got to stop.

Tommie crawls over, starts snapping fingers. "Hey. Hey. What are you doing?"

Savannah closes her eyes, takes a deep, dark breath. "Sorry. I'm kind of in a lot of places right now. It's hard to focus."

"A lot of—?"

"It works like this. *Apparently*." Her eyes roll up to the sky in annoyance. "Turns out I was important to a whole lot of people. Which is flattering, don't get me wrong. But I was more important than I thought to a whole lot of you. More important than some stupid songs. So, anyway, one minute I'm bopping along in my own life, and then the next minute I *die*, which, let me tell you, I'm not overly thrilled about this development, and *then* I find out that I have to get messages to all those people like you, and hey presto, I get to be your Jacob Marley."

Tommie stares, lost in the rapid-fire stream of words. Manages to bite down a dumb question about Rastafarians. That's the wrong Marley. Probably definitely.

"Your Clarence?" Savannah ventures, when no validation is forthcoming. Still nothing. "Guardian angel thing? Never mind."

"What message?" Tommie asks. Something canned and corny from an after-school special, undoubtedly. *It gets better.* What a load of bull.

"Well. Uh. Here's where it gets fun. Nobody told me."

Tommie struggles to stand, wondering where everyone is. Why no one, not even a teacher, could bother to help a student passed out on the ground.

"Wow. Even my delusional fantasies are completely useless."

The ghost—if she's a ghost and not a stroke or something—crosses her arms. "*One*, I am not a delusional fantasy, and *two*, you are not completely useless. Or in any way useless. Thoughts like that are poison, so get it right out of your head."

"But I am standing here talking to a dead person that no one else can see, right?"

"You...may be standing here talking to a dead person that no one else can see."

Fantastic. Another Weird Tommie Aguilar story to add to the school's lore.

On that note, Tommie fidgets. "Where is everyone?"

Savannah shrugs. "Class? I made them not see you, so we could have a private minute. Weird ghost powers."

Well that's unsettling. "What do we do?" Tommie asks.

"I think I get to follow you around until I figure everything out. High school. Joy of joys. Do you know, I am at four hundred and thirteen high schools right now? I'm so glad I skipped it. High school, I mean."

The imaginary-friend/possible-ghost version of Savannah Sullivan, Tommie is rapidly learning, can't shut up for more than two seconds at a time.

Savannah natters on through four more classes, while Tommie's patience thins. Tommie gets through the day in a daze. Skirts the cliques in the hall. Everyone wants to talk about the crash, or huddle in knots around their phones to watch Revolutions videos, but no one wants to talk to Tommie and that is more than fine.

It's almost the same as any other day, except for the hallucination of a famous dead woman offering color commentary on Tommie's every move.

At home HoHo, practicing being mean, throws a basketball at Tommie's face, calling "Heads up, Big Tits." They both know it was not an accident, but there's no point in confronting him. He's been like this for a while, ever since Tommie stopped being his big sister and started being something else. Mami says he'll come around. Tommie's not so sure.

"Wow," Savannah says drily, as Tommie dribbles the ball back. "Your brother is a dick."

"He's thirteen."

"I remember my brother when he was thirteen. He wasn't a sociopath."

"He's not," Tommie says, unsure why HoHo is even worth sticking up for. "We…we don't get along." Pretty much the understatement of the century.

The ghost drifts into Tommie's bedroom. This is different than her being at school. It's Tommie's *bedroom*. Mortified, Tommie kicks a pile of dirty underwear under the bed. Savannah doesn't seem to notice.

"Want me to scare the pants off him? I could, you know. Mercilessly and publically."

"Yes. No." Tommie slumps onto the bed, exhausted. "Can you get to the inspiring already? I don't know how much more of this I can take."

"Ouch. Guess we're done with the hero-worship portion of this haunting."

"It's not that. It's just—do you always talk so much?"

It's supposed to be a joke, but Savannah takes it seriously. She sits next to Tommie, weightless on the comforter. "I'm trying not to fall apart, okay? Being dead is really, really scary."

"You don't sound scared."

"I'm in two thousand, seven hundred and eighty four places right now, and none of them are with my kids. I'm terrified."

Tommie is embarrassed to have not even thought of Savannah's kids. They're just toddlers, they won't have any idea of what is going on.

"Your husband—"

"I think he died with me. Right?"

Tommie nods.

Savannah's voice turns hollow. "I can't find him. I can't find him *anywhere*. And I can't find the kids and I don't know what to do."

"I'm sorry," Tommie says, so inadequately.

"Not your fault." Savannah flexes her fingers, buries the grief she'd let through under her snappy, get-down-to-business tone.

"Well, let's do this. Tell me. What kind of girl is Tommie Aguilar?"

Tommie winces. "Don't call me a girl."

"What?"

"I'm not a girl, okay?"

The ghost of Savannah Sullivan ogles Tommie's breasts. Tommie blushes and wants to disappear. This day just keeps getting weirder and weirder.

"Okay," is all she says, which is already way better than Mami or Papi. "Not a girl."

Of course, that's the *easy* part to explain. The *not a boy, either* part is harder.

"What kind of *person* is Tommie Aguilar? What are your goals?"

Tommie shrugs.

"Come on. Work with me, here."

"I don't know. I'm fifteen. Do I have to have goals?"

"When I was fifteen, I already had a career."

"Yeah, well, I'm definitely not you."

"Ah, that must be the answer. Make you an international superstar so I can move on to the Great Beyond."

Unexpectedly, Tommie laughs. "Know what my goal was? To see your show tonight. I was going to be in the front row, and you were going to play 'The Modern Prometheus' and I was going to sing and dance. That's the only goal I had."

Savannah's eyes spark with interest. "We haven't played that in ages. I don't think it's made the setlist in two tours."

Unexpectedly, ridiculously, Tommie's heart sinks. "It's my favorite."

"Where's your music? Records, CDs?"

Tommie points. Computer.

Savannah scoffs at Tommie's laptop and cheap speakers, scrolling through Tommie's music collection. "Digital files are worthless on this thing. You have got to get a real sound system. And listen to more than four artists. Grab a pen and I'll give you a list. That is definitely what I'm here for."

"Are you insulting my taste in music? Mostly I listen to you."

"Exactly." Her tongue sticks out a bit as she concentrates on shuffling songs into a setlist. Eventually, she crows in triumph. "Okay, Tommie, I'll give you your show. I can't quite get it right without the boys, but I'll do my best."

And then she is singing over a recording of her own voice singing Tommie's favorite song. It is impossible to be sad in the face of that. Soon, Tommie is singing too, awful and loud, and dancing. They go through song after song after song, much longer than a real concert would last, and for just a moment, even if Tommie is going insane, everything is perfect.

Tommie wakes to a ghost's face, hanging over the bed and grinning wide. She still exists. She's still here.

"Any big weekend plans?"

"Um. No?"

She rolls her eyes. "You're seriously going to hide out in this room for two days?"

"As much as humanly possible."

"Unacceptable. Get dressed. We're going out."

The force of her personality is just as staggering this morning as it was yesterday. Tommie rolls out of bed, shoves on jeans and a wrinkled t-shirt, grabs keys and a banana, and walks with Savannah out into the neighborhood.

"I've been thinking. About you not being a girl."

Here it comes. Tommie sighs. "Yeah?"

"Well, what would you say you are?"

Tommie shrugs. "I'm not good at labels."

"I don't know what I'm supposed to do with you, kid. I feel like this is the thing I'm supposed to help you with, but there's not anything that's actually wrong."

They walk without further discussion while the subdivision starts to wake up. Tommie thinks about categories. Usually, it's easier to be nothing at all than to think about *male* and *female* and where to fit on that spectrum. If you are nothing, then nothing can hurt you. But now all the insecurities Tommie thought had been vanquished are back, crowding Tommie's brain.

The ghost seems to have drifted to other thoughts. They are walking through the dog park behind the subdivision when she stops, puts out a hand, jars Tommie to full awareness.

"I got it. Her."

She points to a girl sitting on a bench, hunched over a sketchbook. Tommie knows her by sight. Lanie, or Laurie, or something.

"'Her' what?"

"You should be friends with her."

"How do you know that?"

"Look, I don't know for sure. I'm making this up as I go along. But you, and no offense here, but I mean it, you *really* need a friend. And I think she'd be good."

"Why?" Tommie's voice quivers with distrust.

"Call it intuition."

"Call it a guess?"

"Okay, fine. If you insist. But don't forget, it's like a magical mystery tour in my brain right now. I have access to all kinds of stuff you can't even imagine." She wiggles her fingers in front of Tommie's eyes, makes a spooky ghost noise that sounds cartoonish and silly.

Tommie's not friends with girls. Not like there are a ton of guys lining up, either, but still. Girls. They never were easy, they always had sharp edges, but at least there used to be rules, used to be a code. Share your plastic ponies, swap cookies at lunch time, say the right words and sing along to the right boy bands and you get to be BFFs for the school year, or during church camp. Now girls cultivate viciousness, and the rules are out the window. Tommie used to have a best friend. Zoe Fischer. They shared a heart-shaped necklace that split in two, and passed folded notes to each other in the hall even though they shared every other class. And then one day, out of the clear blue sky, Zoe Fischer called Tommie a cuntlicker in front of half the school and never spoke to Tommie again.

So maybe Tommie does need a friend. Maybe. But why this girl, aside from the fact of her proximity?

"You just want to be done with me, don't you? I'm that bad."

Savannah rolls her eyes "You're not *bad*. Whatever your hang-up, kid, you need to relax. Stop hiding from people all the time."

"I don't like people."

"Then you just haven't met the right ones yet."

Bright anger flairs inside Tommie. "You think it's so easy. I'm *not you*." Not beautiful or smart, or charismatic, or brave. Especially not brave.

"I'm not asking you to be me. It's a little thing. Just

walk over there and say hello."

But it's not a little thing. Even *hello* seems insurmountable.

"I can't."

"Go talk to her," Savannah persists. "Take a look at what she's drawing. Ask her favorite song. Maybe you guys won't hit it off. Maybe you will. But you have to make a leap, Tommie. Please."

Tommie shuts down. "I *can't*. I really can't. Go on, go to the light or whatever. Whatever your mission is with me, just forget it."

"Not gonna happen. Don't you know how stubborn I am?"

"What are you going to do? Haunt me for the rest of my life?"

"Maybe. I told you, I don't know how this works."

Tommie takes a deep breath. Maybe it's time to talk to Mami about this, go to the doctor and bury this whole mess under some kind of drug. But what if it's real?

Tommie takes one step forward. Two. Lanie/Laurie looks up, not at Tommie but *through*. Then she bends her head back to her work. Tommie stops.

It's too much. Savannah shouldn't ask for this. It's too much.

Tommie runs home, not daring to look back. Spends the rest of the day safe in the bedroom, headphones on. The ghost reappears at some point, but if she says a word of reproach, Tommie never hears it. The music is too loud.

*

Sunday morning, instead of a bright, shiny face Tommie wakes to the sound of crying. Savannah sits curled up in a corner, t-shirt stretched over her knees, face hidden in her curls.

"What's wrong?" Tommie asks, forgetting the anger and humiliation of the day before. The ghost sniffles.

"I'm fading. I'm starting to finish. I've only got two hundred and twelve people left, and then I'll be gone for good, and I still can't get to the kids." Her breath hitches on a sob.

"Do you know where they are?"

"With their grandpa on Long Island. That's where we were going when…well."

"But you can't just…" Tommie makes an ineffectual gesture "…get there?"

"I don't know how."

Tommie takes a deep breath. There are ferries, there are buses. This is something that can actually be done.

"If I went, could you go with me?"

Savannah's eyes widen. "You would do that? Why?"

"Maybe that's why you're here. Not so that you can help me, but so that I can help you."

The ghost stares at Tommie like Tommie has sprouted three heads. "You can't just knock on the door."

"So I won't. But I can get you close. Maybe it will be enough."

"Tommie Aguilar, I think I love you."

Tommie blushes. This is both the worst idea ever, and the right thing to do. Savannah should be able to see her kids, say goodbye to them. If Tommie's the only person who can make that happen, well, so be it.

A fake stomachache gets Tommie out of church. There's some money saved up from birthdays and Christmas, rolled into a sock in the bureau. It should be enough. It has to be enough. Tommie leaves a vague note on the refrigerator and runs away with a ghost.

By afternoon they have made it to a quiet suburb, which doesn't look like it would be home to anyone famous, or even famous-adjacent. But the crowd of news vans and posturing reporters gives it away. Tommie loiters on the edge of the block with a few other voyeurs, hoping not to look too conspicuous.

"This is crazy. Who are all these people?"

"Welcome to fame, honey. I suppose it's flattering, in a morbid kind of way. But if they're upsetting my kids I'll have to go poltergeist on their asses."

"Your funeral isn't even until tomorrow. You'd think they'd have better places to be."

"How do you know when my funeral is?"

"Does the magical mystery tour in your brain not include the internet? Stop stalling. Go. It's not like they can see you."

"You'll be okay?"

"Yes."

"I don't think I'll be long, but I don't know. Please don't—"

"*Go.* I'll be here as long as you need me."

Savannah looks uncharacteristically nervous, but heads into the fray. Tommie waits for hours, sitting on the sidewalk staring at the house and ignoring tons of phone calls from first Papi and then Abuela, then texts from HoHo that start out obnoxious but gradually start to show actual concern. There's a lot of time to think, about hurt, and loss, and whether it's better to feel pain or feel nothing at all. It's always been safer to be nothing, to try to feel nothing. But maybe safe isn't everything.

When Savannah reappears, she seems more solid than before. She's crying and smiling, and when she reaches out to touch Tommie's hand, Tommie can actually feel it.

On the ride home, the ghost chatters about her kids, her brother, her friends. Tommie doesn't mind, could listen to that voice say anything. Savannah gives Tommie her list of essential albums, and tells funny stories about the night she met Nick, about pranks she played on the rest of the band, about wardrobe malfunctions and long days on the tour bus. Tommie falls asleep somewhere before home. When the driver shakes Tommie awake, Tommie is alone.

*

On the last day of school, Tommie sees Lanie or Laurie sitting on a retaining wall, one leg dangling, the other balancing her sketchpad, scribbling furiously. *Lily*, a voice whispers into Tommie's ear. The little hairs on Tommie's neck prickle.

Maybe it's time to be a little bit brave.

The girl is drawing Revolutions in manga style, copying the poses from a promo picture but turning them into something all her own. Lu's hair defies gravity. Noah's glasses are razor-sharp rectangles that seem to glint even though they are only pencil on paper. Savannah and Nick are mirror images of each other, shoulder to shoulder, their mouths sardonic slashes slanting in opposite directions.

"That is amazing," Tommie says.

The girl, Lily, shrugs. She doesn't seem bothered by Tommie's presence, but she doesn't react to the praise, either. "I've done better. Want to see?"

Tommie hoists up onto the wall next to her. "Sure. Hey, what's your favorite song?"

"The Modern Prometheus," Lily says instantly, without hesitation.

The heels of Tommie's sneakers kick a percussive beat against the brick wall. Tommie smiles. Pretending this is easy almost makes it so. "Really? Mine, too."

I'm Only Going Over

By Cat Hellisen

There are a million of them, flicking between worlds faster than grasshoppers, the whine of their wings cicada summers, white scythes sighing.

I caught one, once. Or it caught me.

We are at a party. Teen drama of stupid petty fights that happen under electric light, in sterilized bathrooms and modern kitchens, stealing vodka from a liquor cabinet, topping up the bottles with water. Cheap crackling wine bought from under the counter at the local corner shop. She's watching us and talking to no one. Lonely, maybe. I thought she was just some friend of a friend of a friend's. No one gatecrashes lame parties like this. Louise had thrown it—telling her mom she's inviting a few friends 'round, and she's so big-eyed and neat and she'd never be like that, oh no, and of course her parents believe her.

So here we all are, half drunk on watered-down spirits and being seventeen. Some best of Pandora station is playing and it is bland as shit. I've been watching the girl from the other room, kinda falling in *not-love but hey, I wanna know your name and chase your smile through the dark.*

She reminds me of my childhood, when the nothings would come sit with me when I hid in the little alleyway on the side of the apartment, and tell me that it would get better. It had for them, they said. I just had to wait until the time was right. And then I grew up, and I stopped inventing imaginary saviors. Now I look for the other people who don't fit in, and we have a five-minute connection. Or a one-minute, or whatever. At least they're real, and we both know no one's ever going to save us.

She's one of us, dragged here to a stranger's house by someone who has already deserted her. We could be soul mates.

Russell is well on his way to falling-down drunk, making out with some girl he'll mock in the morning. Tracy, looks like. He hates Tracy. He's just doing this to make Janine jealous. It's all so bloody pathetic. I look away from the bodies on the couches, from the middle-class floor lamps with their middle-class fringes, back to the girl on her own. I walk over, proud that I don't stumble or trip. I am completely cool.

The friend of a friend of a friend is sitting on the kitchen counter, black hair falling over her face, head bowed, feet swinging. She's wearing a long scarlet coat in some fluttery material that drapes and flows as she moves. She's got a cigarette thin as a matchstick in one hand, but I never see her smoke it. It doesn't smell right. Not like weed either, too dry and clean. The smoke veils her hand, twisting about itself, dragons chasing their own tails.

"Hey," I say, because I am suave as fuck. I am drunk on Lethe water and running away. I have bruises across my ribs and a black mark on my heart. This gives me courage. The friend of a friend of a friend could say anything and it wouldn't hurt. "You know Louise?"

She looks up, unsmiling, confused. "Louise—oh, right." She glances over to where our merry hostess is trying to clean up the mess as it's made, panic starting to eat into her eyes. "Not her, no. I'm not here for her."

"Oh?" I settle, leaning back against the kitchen island so that I'm almost facing her. "Someone else, then?"

"Yes." She digs in the pocket of her red coat, and I hear a skittery rustling like insects crawling over each other in the dark. She pulls out a folded piece of paper, thick and torn at the edges. "Janine."

Odd thing to do. "Yeah, I know her—"

"Russell," she continues, "Tracy, Benjamin." She folds the paper up again, sets it back in her pocket. "I'm a little early," she says with a shrug. "It happens. The department isn't exactly run by geniuses."

I take another sip from my coke. It's rum-sweet, and it's the only way this conversation will make sense. "Ben," I tell her. "No one calls me Benjamin."

The girl's face changes. Where before she looked

bored, a little out of place, now she looks completely other. It passes in a millisecond, just a flash where for a moment she wasn't sulky and young, but ageless, her skin like drying fish scales, hair made of knotted darkness. "Dammit," she says. "I thought you were—never mind. That shouldn't happen. Not today. You can't be on two lists, though it explains why you can see me."

"Can't I?" I finish my coke. The room is swimmy and strange, and I have to focus, to keep her at the center of my world. Of course I can see her, it's the only way the universe stays in place. "What's your name?"

"Jordan," she says. "Like the river."

"Yeah? Your parents all crazy religious?" Mine are, so I know how that story goes. I need another drink, but I don't want to leave Jordan, half-convinced that if I turn my back on her she'll slip away. I scan the counters—someone's left a half-finished beer and I take it, checking first that they haven't used it as an ashtray.

"I forget," Jordan says. She finally takes a drag of her cigarette, and when she does, it's like she becomes more real. More there. "Maybe."

Now there's an opening to a conversation if ever I saw one, but I'm not stupid enough to take it. You gotta be careful with those kind of statements. I make them myself. I open the door wide enough to see who will walk forward before I slam it in their face. "So what two lists am I on?"

"Dead and Deader," she says, and sticks out her tongue. "Forget it. You can only be on one."

"You're crazy," I tell her, like she hasn't noticed. "It's a good crazy. Manic pixie dream girl goes Goth"

"Deader," she says. "I'm putting you on deader. That's for insulting me."

"I was trying to chat you up, not insult you." The beer tastes awful, like something died in it. I grimace and push myself away from her so I can go pour the rest down the drain. I need to sober up, anyway. Gotta get home. Russell's lifting me and if I get back to the house smelling like alcohol, and obviously drunk, I'll be asking for it. "Where do you think they keep the coffee?"

"There." Jordan points to a corner cupboard with the remains of her cigarette. It's almost out. "And the mugs are in that one." She points to another cupboard. "Milk is in the fridge." Flicks the stompie vaguely in the direction of the bin. I don't see it land.

"Milk I could have worked out for myself." But I'm grinning. I like her. I select two cups—one black and one white, both with cartoon red hearts on them. Tacky shit. "How do you take yours?"

"I don't—" She glances up at the clock that looks like a giant Marie biscuit stuck to the wall. "Oh, what the hells, it's not like I'm in a hurry. Lots of milk, three sugars."

We drink our opposite-world coffees, looking at each other and saying nothing. She doesn't smile, and I like that. I like how she looks unfriendly and spiky and full of hate all while drinking something sweeter than melted ice cream and milkier than baby porridge. I like how the kitchen lights make her look like she's crowned in stars, and the shadows splay around her like vulture feathers. I like how she reminds me of falling.

"Don't get in the car," she says, and puts down her empty cup. "I'll give you time to say goodbye."

She comes back for me. After the crash.

"Deader, remember?" Jordan takes my hand and she's not cold, or warm, or anything. It's like holding smoke. "We always need replacements. Deaths get lost all the time. It's a long stretch between here and there, and some of us go missing in the dark."

"I—what?"

"You saw me." She's serious, brow pinched. "No one sees the Deaths, unless they've been put on the shortlist. Or, you know, just after." She looks away, and her hands are strong as claws, there's no escaping her. "It won't be so bad. It's not like dying."

"Really." It's all I can say. My throat is tight, it feels like it does after I've been choked. This is not how things were meant to go. I was going to leave home, put myself through university, get a decent job. "How's that?" When I move, my skin sounds like the sawing of cicadas, the shriek of a million locusts.

"Oh, dying always ends," she says. "It's Death that takes forever."

The Ways of Walls and Words

By Sabrina Vourvoulias

Solitreo

"If it were not for Thee, what would become of me?"

She's not speaking to me when she says this. Her poetry nests behind a prison's walls. I am an unknown noise on the other side of her door—the only spot where sound enters or exits her world—a sweep of bristle against wood, some transitory trace of life that has nothing to do with her.

She and her people are in cells lined along a corridor in the deepest reaches of the convent. On occasion the mentally disturbed have been kept here, tended to and made safe by walls so thick they are more than an arm's length. These people, however, are all one family: a mother; an adult son; four older daughters; and this one, who has spent nearly half her life in here.

That was all the information the Dominican Brothers shared with me the day I started. Except that I must not attempt to speak to the girl or her family through their doors. The Brothers made me swear this before I swept even one stone.

In the language I share with jailer and jailed, my name is Bienvenida, though my Nahuatl name is different. By the Brothers' reckoning, it has been 1,562 years since the death of God.

As I sweep in front of the locked doors, I don't really think of who is behind them, or why. I think of my traps and whether they are filled or empty of food. I think of the lessons my mother teaches me, because I am the eldest and must care for my siblings if something happens to her. I think of how many chambers are left for me to clean before I can get back to the turquoise and emerald of our world. A world filled with living gods, not dead ones.

Though that, like everything else, is changing.

But if the timing is just right, if I'm by the door as the girl recites her poems, I wonder about her then.

Is she like me, alive for words? Someone who believes in offers of beauty? Who trusts that a perfect couplet will prompt the gods to fulfill its meaning?

I sweep. I wonder. I think about the ways of walls and words.

This Day, For It Is Your Day

I say the names aloud, so I won't forget, and so the walls know who we are: Francisca, Luis, Isabel, Leonor, Catalina, Mariana, and Anica.

The Ways of Walls and Words | *Sabrina Vourvoulias*

My name is Anica but I bear others too: one from the land my forebears claim as home; one for our hidden heart; one for the many times that heart has been betrayed.

I was born where the water shapes the coast of New Spain, the only one of us natural to this New World. Eight generations of our family lived along a different coastline—the Iberian one my mother still talks about—so the sea is part of us. I learned young to mix salted water into dough and knead it with a rhythm that pulls and crests.

When we moved inland to the greatest city in New Spain, my mother shed enough tears to harden the crusts of many loaves.

It was a shift from the domain of one element to another. This city is guarded by mountains that open their mouths to spew fire. After she wiped away her tears, my mother taught me to consign a piece of dough to the flame before baking. Though it might seem so, it is not a concession to our new home nor its governing element.

What my mother teaches is deeper than element or place.

We are behind these walls because we sweep the house clean on Fridays. Because we light two new candles before sunset, and bless our wine and bread at the table. Because, when we are done, we hide what none but family may see behind locked wardrobe doors.

When we say Dyó, we mean one, not three.

Someone took our tale to the Holy Office. That is what my mother thinks. My brother believes it was not a story but success that betrayed us, and my sisters accuse each other's husbands. In Old World or New, the outcome of attention from Inquisitors is the same. In a plaza full of people, we were ordered into captivity. To renounce and reconcile.

Conversos. New Christians. Judaizers. Marranos. Anusim. There are many names for us. I hardly know myself what name to use. Except family.

At first I tried to do as the priests commanded. But I cannot go days on end without saying prayers the way I was taught, and I do not believe my mother would go even one. On the first anniversary of our imprisonment, after hours on the rack, my eldest sister Isabel confessed what everyone already knew: forced conversion is not faith. What resides where no human hand can touch it cannot be forsworn.

I look out my window now and, instead of an empty sky caged by bars, I imagine the leaves of our fig, pomegranate, and lemon trees fluttering there. My mother bought them dear, right off one of the Spanish ships, then planted them in our courtyard so that they would rub lovingly against one another when the wind blew. None had yet given fruit when we were taken from our home, but I picture globes of brilliant red, ovals of green, and sweet, dark teardrops hiding among their leaves. I pretend I am swallowing the sparkling, rubied seeds of the first, and reaching for the scion of the last amid its fragrant greenery.

And for a moment, by the power of memory and imagining, the sun pours down on my shoulders as it does on those of the free.

There are many hours in a day. When my imaginings turn sour, I fill the emptiness with the cantigas my mother and sisters and I used to sing together, for these are made for women's voices and women's work—the work of keeping things alive. When evening falls, the songs turn into to my brother's words: prayers once celebrated in literary societies, praised for their clarity. "Las palavras klaras, el Dyó las bendize," we say, and I hope it is true.

Let the harsh chains be smashed;
this day, for it is your day,
has to be the day of forgiving.

Only I change the last word. Instead of *forgiving* I say *escaping*, and in my mind, I grow wings.

We Unwind the Jewels

The slab and block with which the Spanish have hidden our ancestral city is full of fault: it does not fit together without seams. The gaps between the stones of the cells are sealed with a paste that cures hard, but begins to crumble with time.

The mortar between the stones near the girl's cell door needs a bit of coaxing. I work at it with my broom until I clear a small gap. I squat to look through, then whistle to get her attention.

217

"Aquí," I say. *Here*. The edict that the Spanish should learn Nahuatl still stands in the city, but the reality is that most of them won't. There is power in words, and they want that power to be shaped to their speech, not ours.

The girl gets up from her bedding, follows her ears.

She is my age, or perhaps a bit older, but not too many years after first blood. Her hair is curly, even around the mats. She is no beauty by Nahua standards, but the Spanish seem to admire skin like hers—lustrous like the inner chamber of a shell. Her garments are filthy, but except for her hair everything else about her is tidy. It must take her a long time to scrub clean with the water the Dominicans provide for drink.

She drops down so her eye meets mine through the hole.

"Your poems are beautiful," I say.

"They are prayers," she answers.

"Of course. Our Nahua poems are too," I say. "Would you like to hear one?" I recite it in Nahuatl, then translate it: "We take, we unwind the jewels, the blue flowers are woven over the yellow ones, that we may give them to the children."

In the quiet that follows, I hear her hitched breathing. All of them breathe that way. *Breath caught between walls* is what my mother calls it when the Nahua who work in the city's mills come to her for treatment. She can't cure it, only lessen it with anacahuite.

"I miss the moonflower and morning glory vines

my mother planted so they twined all around our courtyard," the girl says. "Are there many flowers where you live?"

"No," I say. "But sometimes the trees fill with blue and yellow butterflies, and then it is as if they are in bloom."

She closes her eyes to picture it behind her lids.

"How is it you speak Castilian so well?" she asks when she looks at me again.

"My mother says I was blessed with a quick mind just to torment her."

"My mother says that to me too." Then, "Used to say it."

"She is in the cell next to yours," I say, motioning at the wall to her right. "If she is taken to be questioned you will be able to see her pass by through this hole I've made."

Her face twists. "I must hope never to see her, then."

"How is it you are here?" she asks after a time.

"I was recently considered converted enough to clean for the Brothers."

"Are you?"

"The Dominicans are mostly concerned that we repeat exactly what they say in exactly the way they say it. My mother tells me I sound like a parrot." When the girl doesn't smile, I add, "My real words come from her."

I can tell my answer troubles the girl because she turns her face away from the gap and says something under her breath. Not in Castilian.

When she turns back, her face is hard. "If you come again and recite more of your poems for me, you must not include mention of any pagan gods. Are we agreed?"

I nod even though I suspect she knows a poem doesn't have to mention the gods to be meant for them. "You liked my poem then?" I say.

"I like that it brought the outside in with it." Then, "You know what I miss even more than flowers and trees?"

"What?"

"My mother used to spend an hour running a comb through my hair every night before I went to sleep."

"I have something you can use," I say. I take the small comb from where I stick it in my nest of braids and push it through the gap.

"Thank you," she says, "but that's not really what I meant."

"Take it anyway," I say.

"It is so small and my hair is so snarled. It'll probably break."

"No, it won't," I say, getting to my feet so I can start my work again. "The turtles around here are tough, and so are the combs I make from their shells. Still, if you want, I can give you a charm to say so your hair untangles as easy as water pours from a gourd."

I hear her nervous laughter. "No. No magic."

I want to tell her it's all right. That magic, like poetry, is a gift from the gods. But then I remember where I'm standing. Neither gods nor gifts abide between these walls.

With the Keys of Abraham

Bienvenida's daily visits have become everything to me.

She brings more than just the images that form in my mind when she recites her poetry. Despite the meals the silent priests bring twice a day, I am always hungry, so she secrets morsels of food in the folds of the sash under her tunic. She passes the day's tidbit through the gap between the stones with such reverence, I bite my lip to stop myself from laughing at her odd ways.

"Food can be as strong a magic as poems," she tells me, when she notices my facial contortions.

I nod, even though magic, as we know it, is the province of men. My mother cannot leap from bread-making to alchemy, nor from siddur to kabbalah, though she is accounted nearly as wise as my father was.

What Bienvenida brings with her is strange fare: Grasshoppers roasted crisp and dusted with a salty, spicy ash; cactus fruit with lurid flesh; even a small, greenish steamed pudding made of corn, pumpkin, and honey, wrapped in a leaf. I turn down the chunks of dark turtle meat she brings me though.

When I push the unclean meat back at her, she takes it, pops the chunk into her mouth and starts chewing it loudly. It occurs to me that this isn't just an expedient way to get rid of it. She's really hungry.

"Of course I am," she says when I ask her. "After the encomendero takes our tribute, there isn't much, and some days my traps are empty. I have three siblings."

Before I can say anything, she adds, "Plus, turtle meat is like no other. Yesterday Fray Antonio said I had left dirt pushed into the corners of the refectory so he grabbed a stick but, because I had eaten turtle meat the day before, his blows rained off my back as if from a shell."

At my snort, she gives me an obstinate, hard look. I've learned that when she gets angry she doesn't raise her voice or huff away, as I would. Instead, she goes quiet and everything about her seems to turn darker. She scares me a bit.

The silence between us draws out until I ask about her progress in creating gaps in the other cell walls. She hadn't intended to create any, but I've asked her to. Because these are the thoughts I worry most between her visits: if my family is alive; if they stand; if they are still themselves.

"A small hole in the wall to your mother's cell," she answers. "And an even smaller opening in another, which houses one of your sisters. The other walls are too freshly sealed."

"Which sister?"

"The one they say has eyes like water."

"Mariana," I say. "Have you been feeding her and my mother as well?"

"No. Are you asking me to?"

I remember the hungry look when she gobbled down the turtle meat and still I say yes. She is my friend and, some days, all that keeps me from despair—but that is no bond compared to the one among family.

"I have to go back to work," she says after a moment, and gets to her feet.

She's told me that along with sweeping the hallway of cells, she's responsible for cleaning the Brothers' whole convent, from top to bottom. Except for the chapel. She says she's fortunate it is only a convent and not a full priory or her cleaning would burn all the hours of sunlight.

"What does your mother owe that she would agree to let you be worked this hard?" I say. It's half query, half sympathy.

Bienvenida shakes her head as if she doesn't understand. "We owe everyone. We're a rope of people, all woven together. Even the Brothers are part of the rope now."

After a moment, she continues. "My mother's knowing is a debt owed to the gods. She cannot turn her back on those who come to her—sometimes on their knees—begging a cure. And when Fray Bernardino comes to her to learn herb lore, that teaching is owed too."

"But she could still do what she does elsewhere, and more happily if she were farther from the priests. Couldn't she?" I ask after a moment. Maybe in saying this I'm really wondering why my brother and mother chose for us to stay here, even after my father died and his brother asked us to join him in Nuevo León, far from the threat of Inquisitors.

"I already walk a long way to get to my work here," she says. "More than an hour according to Fray Bernardino, though maybe his long legs make it shorter for him than for me."

"I meant even farther away," I say. "Days and days away from here."

"Tonalxochitl. Cuachachalate. Tlachichinole," Bienvenida recites. It sounds like her first poem, the one she had to translate for me.

"Those are only some of the plants that root my family where we are," she says. "We would never abandon them."

"Things of the earth," I scoff. "They're created for us, not us for them."

The look she returns is full of disdain. She takes some steps down the hall, out of my sight line, then I hear her stop.

"The rest of you are like mosquitoes swarming over our mother's earthen skin. But we are her blood, Anica. Without us, she dies. Without her, we die."

The steps resume, then fade away.

I wish Bienvenida back, wish it as if it were a prayer. I have told her a bit about our customs—mostly to better control the sort of food she brings me—but what I want her to understand now goes beyond custom. I want her to know that we are not like the others either. We, too, cannot be parted from what we love best. We carry it with us in law and ritual and cantilation. Without us, it dies; without it, we die.

Hours later, as the sun ducks beneath my barred window, I hear Bienvenida at our gap. "Put your hand under the hole," she says after I kneel to the spot.

She rolls three black berries into my palm. "Don't eat those," she says. "Smash one between pebbles that have fallen from the walls. Use this to write with." She pushes a single bristle of her broom through to me.

"I have nothing to write on," I say. "And what am I supposed to write?"

"Your mother will not take food from me," she says. "If you tell her that you trust me, she might be easier about it. Write on this." She drops a pale bean through the hole.

Small, curved surface; flexing stylus; clumpy ink—has there been a greater test of will? I manage to trace one Hebrew letter.

As soon as I pass the bean through to Bienvenida, she disappears with it. When she comes back, she instructs me to put my palm up to the gap and a seed tumbles onto it. I turn it over on my palm. It carries the word "strength" in tiny, perfect solitreo.

"Your mother only took half a morsel," Bienvenida says. She shakes a loosely clenched hand in front of the gap, and I hear the sound of crunchy things rattling against each other. Grasshoppers. My stomach grumbles and she pokes several of them through the opening to me.

"Next time she'll eat more," I say after I've finished chewing. "What about Mariana?"

She shakes her head. "The unseen harries her. She circles her cell, and the spirits compel her to scratch at her face and draw blood. She did not even hear me whistle for her attention."

"Do something," I say. I haven't cried since Bienvenida started visiting me, but now I feel my eyes fill.

"I'll ask my mother," she says, then she gets up. I hear the bristles of her broom scrape at the door.

"What are you doing? You already swept."

"It is Friday," she says. "I am doing this now in your name. Our gods accept such substitutions. Perhaps yours will as well."

I don't know whether to be moved by her action or infuriated. She continues to speak openly of her terrible, false gods, and perhaps that should be the worst part but it isn't. I have told her enough about our rituals that she knows the Sabbath's prayers are special. It is the meter and cadence of poetry she is hoping for. Doing this for. Loyal to.

Not friendship. Not me.

Something rises in me, sharp and jagged, and I do not recite anything before she finishes and leaves.

The next Friday she does the same, and the Friday after that. I lose count of how many times it happens before I get over my anger. What does it matter if she's here for me or my words, as long as she's here?

Still, the prayer I recite for her is not truly to be said

at sunset, only a childhood favorite recited every night after my mother laid down the comb but before she extinguished the light in my bedroom:

I have closed my doors
with the keys of Abraham;
the pious will come in,
the evil ones will leave;
the angels of the Lord are here with me.

"Magic," she says a moment after I finish reciting. "Do you hear?"

Before I can answer, a loud bellow sounds clear through my door. Bienvenida moves away from our gap and I hear her running.

After that, the stifling silence of my imprisonment falls again.

But no. There it is. Like hope where there was none before. The sound of wings.

We Are Loaned to One Another

When I arrive home—after a long detour to check my turtle traps in the waters off the causeway nearest the Tree of the Sad Night—Fray Bernardino is with my mother, waiting for me. It is unusual for him to venture out of the city except for his herb lessons, and those are done long before darkness falls.

The Brothers at the convent have told him about catching me with Anica. Unlike most of the Dominicans, the tall, red-faced Franciscan speaks to us in Nahuatl, and as if he believes us of more than

227

usual intelligence. He has told my mother that if she were a Spanish man she would have made an excellent physick, and might even own a book like the little leather tome in which he records the appearances and properties of the plants she identifies for him.

She smiles whenever he says it and doesn't tell him about the amatl bark books she hides under her mat. Women have always had to hide their wisdom from men, and the Brothers are men, if strange ones.

"I vouched for you," Fray Bernardino says to me. "The Brothers have agreed to let you continue cleaning the convent, so your family will not lose that prestige. The lower cells, however, are off-limits. I have sworn that you will not be caught there again."

"Who will clean that hallway?"

"Perhaps they'll purchase one of the slaves newly brought to city," he says dismissively. Then he stoops so he can look me in the face. "What do you speak about with that girl, Bienvenida?" He chose my Christian name for me, and I am thankful it is a nice one that means welcome. Some of the Nahua girls got names that mean loneliness or pain.

"I recite the flower songs to her," I answer. I know better than to tell him about Anica's recitations. His face creases anyway.

Fray Bernardino shakes his head as he gets up, then looks at my mother. "There is talk. About witchcraft in word and deed. And about the demonic nature of the pipiltzintzintli plant. You understand?"

My mother nods. "A peyotero, a midwife, and a sobadora have been taken from the people already."

"But they have not been subjected to an auto da fé," he says. There is something out of place in his voice, and I am struck by the thought that he craves my mother's forgiveness.

My mother hears it too, but is not one for words dipped in honey. "Your people have completed the quemadero," she says. "My people may not be the first to burn, but we will burn."

After a moment, Fray Bernardino turns his face from hers and walks out. She follows him with her eyes.

"Tell," she says without looking at me.

"The ones that need your help are women. One is sick with fright and haunted by unseens," I say. "And one…my friend…she must fly away or her spirit will die."

My mother doesn't say anything.

"They need you," I say.

She turns to look at me. "One day you will *be* me."

She is short and wide, like a tepozán tree. Her hands are too big for her arms, and her feet are broad and horned with calluses. Nested deep in the wrinkles are eyes the color of silt, eyes that see everything. She is beautiful to me, as I will be beautiful to my daughter, and she to hers.

"Come, then," my mother says as she sweeps by me. "While we can."

Put on me a necklace of varied flowers.

The next morning, I leave our house with a garland on the outside of my tunic and one on the inside. The visible one is made of many-petaled white flowers woven in a perfect round; the invisible one has pieces of root, insect, bud, and bone strung unevenly on sinew. I arrive earlier than usual at the convent and search among the Dominicans for Fray Antonio.

He scratches the flaky skin around his tonsure when he sees me. "Are you here to be shriven?"

I take the garland from my neck and hold it out to him. "We made this. For the chapel."

There is a moment when I think he might foil our plan by giving the flowers to the novice who cleans the sacred space. But after some consideration he takes them. They aren't spectacular blossoms, but they have a pleasant fragrance that stays long on the skin. My mother has people rub them between their hands because the warmer the oil, the faster the sleep.

Fray Antonio motions for me to follow him, and as he walks over to the chapel he strokes the petals, then sniffs his fingers and wipes them on his habit. As soon as his fingers leave the fabric they're back at the petals, and the whole process starts again, without the Brother noticing he's doing it. He unlocks the church, then moves to the side where a small statue stands alone.

"Are you devoted to Our Lady?" he asks me.

This statue is not the Tonantzin the Brothers

named Guadalupe. This one has a pale, delicate face surrounded by reddish-gold ringlets and a demure look that makes me doubtful she would ever understand our Nahua needs and delights. Still, the Dominicans bring her offerings like the ones we take to our own mother at Tepeyac.

Fray Antonio returns the garland to me. "Are you tall enough to crown her with it?"

"I think so," I say.

"Good. I'll go pray while you do," he says.

All the gods favor beauty, so I take my time with the crowning. When I'm done, the priest is dozing in the pew. I drop an extra blossom in his hand on my way out.

When I arrive at the cells, Anica is crying.

"Last night I saw my mother," she tells me, wiping her nose with the back of her hand as she walks over to our gap. She doesn't need to say more. The only time the prisoners go anywhere it is to the room where they are stretched until the right words pop out of their mouths.

I pull the necklace from under my tunic and release three pieces of root. "These kill pain," I say. I push one of the pieces through the gap. "Write on it that she must chew it to paste, then smear that over the worst of her hurts. Also, that she must swallow the juice that comes from the chewing. It is bitter but it will take away the pain."

"She is used to bitter," Anica says, then does what she's told. When she passes the root back through to me, I move to the gap in her mother's cell wall.

"Doña Francisca," I call. The old woman lifts her head from the bedding, then fights to get up. It takes her a long time to cross to me.

"Anica sends these," I say. I push through the first piece of root, the one with the writing. She squints to read it, then catches the other two pieces I pass through.

"I've lost most of my teeth," she says. "I doubt I'll be able to chew them."

"Hold them in your mouth. Let them soften in the water that collects and swallow that. It will help."

She nods, then, "I cannot write a seed message for Anica today. Tell her: She is the darling of her mother." She starts her slow shuffle back to the bedding, the roots clenched tightly in her hand.

Anica's jaw sets in hard lines when I tell her, and there is a silence so long I have to break it for fear it will outlast Fray Antonio's nap.

"We must find a way to draw your sister to the gap in her wall, so I can give her this," I show Anica the bud strung on my necklace. "Its spirit is so strong it will overcome the unseens that assail her."

She settles on the pet name they had for Mariana, something to remind her of happier days and the bond between sisters. Still, when I say it, there is no break in the older girl's pacing. I try explaining what I have, what it does, how she will find relief. When there is no response, I return to Anica.

"Why didn't you just leave it?" she asks. "If she goes to find it later, there will be nothing there."

"If anyone finds it, they will know it is my doing," I say. "I am not allowed here anymore, not even to clean."

"You're here now," Anica says. When I keep silent, I see realization dawning on her face, followed by a pinched, lonely look.

We are loaned to one another.

"Sister," I say. As if she were an elder sibling. As a sign of respect even beyond friendship. "This is my mother's deepest, most secret magic. One day, when I am old enough to have mastered it myself, I will use it to come find you."

I take the hollow bone from my necklace, and the beetles shimmer blue to orange as I untie them. I pass them through one by one and tell her what she must do with them, and how it must be done.

I see her mouth twist as the beetles' barbed legs move a bit on her palm. They are still very sluggish from their pipiltzintzintli meal.

"Must they be alive?" she says.

"Recently killed when you do it."

"Tell me again why I should."

"Because it will set you free."

I have nothing left to give her, but I put my fingers to the gap anyway. Her slender, strong index finger hooks itself on mine. We sit for a few minutes like that, linked and silent.

Then I get up and leave.

Go, Find Another Love

The beetles crawl under my bedding. I shove the bone in after them.

I lay down. Hours pass.

The jailer brings bread and cheese, cold water. He takes away the slop bucket.

There are no words but mine to break the silence. Night falls.

Day comes again. The same silent priest appears and brings the same dry, hard meal.

Then another day.

I know the strength of whatever Bienvenida's mother fed the beetles must be waning. Like food steeped in brine or alcohol loses its flavor after a while. Or does the long wait make it sharper, more concentrated? I no longer remember. Either way, I do nothing.

One day after many, the priest who brings my meal is a different one, with a brown cassock instead of the usual white. "Tomorrow, before midday, you will be taken out to the quemadero," he whispers as he grabs the slop bucket. His face flushes a deep red. "God have mercy."

I have thought often about dying. With fear, and sometimes with longing. Especially in these lonely days without Bienvenida. Yet now that I know the hour of my death, I do not want it.

As soon as the priest leaves, I tear my bedding apart. I find the bone and one of the beetles. There is no trace of the other, and I think maybe the living one ate it.

My hands shake as I get the chips of stone on which I crushed the ink berries. The beetle crunches and I keep grinding until its wet innards are so thoroughly mixed with bits of stone and carapace that the mixture turns dry and grainy.

When beetle grit is as fine as it's going to get, I fit the smaller end of the bone into one nostril as Bienvenida instructed, hold the wider end over the dirty-looking little pile and snort it up.

Pain shoots into my head; my nostril stings and my eyes start watering. I move the bone to the other nostril and inhale what remains.

If it were not for Thee, what would become of me?
And who, except Thee, would free me from myself?

I sit back on my heels and put my head in my hands. The spiky grit keeps cutting as my breath pulls it deeper. The pain intensifies, then spreads across my shoulders. They can no longer bear the weight of my arms and my hands fall, leaden, to the floor. Spine, hips, legs. Wherever the pain hits, the muscle recoils and tries to tear itself from the bone and tissue next to it.

I have not been tortured as my brother and sister and mother have, but I wonder if this is how it feels to be put on the rack. I wonder if they screamed as I am screaming, full-throated and from the center of my being.

Then, as the pain stretches me in all directions at once, I hear a pop and it all stops—the pulling, the pain, the screams. My body flops forward and my forehead cracks on the floor.

235

But I rise.

The girl beneath me crawls to her bedding, stretches out on it, eyes open. Blood seeps from the spot where her head connected with stone.

The wings that bear me aloft catch a draft through the window. I coast up to the deep sill, then scrabble onto it with tiny, sharp claws. I tuck my wings to my body, and with the waddling gait of a creature that finds grace only in the air, squeeze through the bars.

The Convent of San Diego is set on high ground, and the back end, where my window gives, looks not onto the splendid, sprawling city but to the far reaches of the lake over which the urban hub was built. The water pools dark turquoise in some spots, murky emerald in others, under the multiple causeways that span it. And on every surface that isn't road or water, I see small trees covered with blue and yellow butterflies—opening and closing their wings in time to my memory.

I don't know how far I range on the wings I've long dreamed of possessing—far enough for the bright air to warm me like I haven't been warm in years. But I am more than just wings and the freedom they grant. If training brings the falcon back to the hand of the one who hunts with him, how much stronger are the jesses that tether the dove to her people?

I return and light on the window of my mother's cell. She is stretched prone on the floor, where the afternoon sun falls brightest, holding a seed in one hand and a broom bristle in the other. She dips it in berry pulp, then touches it to the surface of the seed.

She looks up as I swoop down. There are dozens of seeds with words of perdurance and inspiration scattered around her.

"Hello, beauty," she says as I land beside her.

I open my mouth. The words I intend come out as trills and coos. She reaches. I hop closer and rub my head along her hand.

I stay until the sun starts its downward arc, then I peck at the seeds and carry one out in my beak. The next window I fly into is my brother's. I drop the seed into his hand and fly away to retrieve another from my mother's cell. She watches me come and go.

I drop her seed messages in each of my sisters' hands as I fly into their cells and see them for the first time in years. Even Mariana stops her raving to receive what is given. Their faces are pallid and grim, but when the word drops, each flares with love.

I fly into my cell, nudge a seed into the limp hand of the girl who was me. When I wished for freedom, I imagined it to be different than this. Can it be sustained: a body yoked, a soul unfettered?

I return to my mother's cell and mark each word as she prays, then, as she falls asleep, I doze too. When I wake at dawn she is already standing, washed and ready for what will come. She will go to the quemadero as Doña Francisca Nuñez de Carvajal, with all the meanings her names carry.

237

When she hears the rustle of my wings, she holds out her hand and I land on it.

"Adyó. Adyó, kerida." She sings the cantiga that was my favorite once—in another place, another time. An enchanted time of perfumed dusks sitting in a courtyard filled with flowers gleaming like the moon, embroidery hoops forgotten in our laps as our voices joined in a tale of departure and heartbreak.

"No quero la vida. Va, buscate otro amor, aharva otras puertas…"

Goodbye,
goodbye, beloved.
I do not want to live.
Go, find another love,
knock on other doors…

A key turns in the lock. My mother draws me close to her lips, kisses the top of my head. "Adyó, kerida Anica," she says.

I don't have time to think of how she knows it is me before she flings my small bird body off her hand and toward the window.

I don't want to fly away from her, but I do.

Where Is My Home?

It is December 9 by the Dominicans' calendar. Smoke hangs black across the valley. The first burnings at the quemadero took place yesterday, a year and a day after I first met Anica. My mother and I are out behind our house—a tremendous distance from the plaza where the crowds had gathered to watch the spectacle—and still we breathe in what happened.

Our work of the past days has been uprooting the plants the Holy Office has declared demonic, to replant them where the Brothers will not find them. Remote, wild places that will sustain magic.

I cannot stop thinking about Anica. From Fray Bernardino's recounting when he came for his lesson late yesterday, I know she and Mariana were spared—one for her youth, the other for her derangement—and that the Dominicans hope more years in detention will ultimately reconcile them to the God of the Cross.

But it is not my friend who is still behind those walls.

The real Anica is an immigrant spirit, feathered and winged. She crosses waters, crests mountains, rides the scorching air of the desert to a remote and wild place where she might thrive until I set out to find her.

I want to believe this is a triumph, only I am never going to forget how loneliness looks on her face.

"Pay attention," my mother chides as I clip the root of a pipiltzintzintli I'm digging.

I tell my mother what I am thinking: how the gods make cages of our lives, lock us in them, and only occasionally let us find the key.

My mother puts down her digging tool. "Come," she says, and starts walking. I trail her all the way back to the water near the Tree of the Sad Night.

"Pull your trap out," she says.

I yank on the rope, bring up the cage. A small

turtle slips back into the water through the slats. A big turtle—an old rope scar across its neck—stays caught.

"The gods don't make cages," my mother says. "We do. We choose to lock or unlock. Word, beetle, bud, and leaf—sometimes they are keys, sometimes not. There is only one thing that is always a key."

She waits for me to say something and when I don't, she stomps on the trap with one leathery foot. Slats splinter and break on top and bottom. The turtle slides its bulk into the water and swims away.

"That was tonight's meal," I complain.

My mother smiles at me, but there is sadness in it. "You know this isn't the only trap. Nor the only creature caught by one."

"I am just a girl," I say when I work out that my mother's imperfect couplet demands fulfillment.

"Yes," she says. "But it is owed anyway. Today. Tomorrow. The days after that."

As we start back to the stand of sacred plants waiting to be moved, I wonder why poems and gods and magic alone aren't enough. I wonder why it all depends on us, a rope of people that so often leaves a scar.

Where shall my soul dwell?
Where is my home?
Where shall be my house?

I think I hear wings. When I look up, the sun has broken through the smoky overlay but there is only a small clear patch of sky.

It is empty with waiting.

Reflections

By Tamlyn Dreaver

The reflection on the water looked like blood as it trickled between the grey dust and boulders of the moon. Hana Kato McRory curled on an overhanging rock and refused to look up at the brilliant, too-clear sky. The beautiful green and blue of the earth hung as a perfect picture; if she looked she could have seen South America embraced by pearly wisps of cloud.

The moon's atmosphere was failing. As the first attempt at terraforming on a large scale, the failure was expected—but it had lasted longer than any anticipated. The flora died early: the graceful, sweeping trees, fronds floating free in the low gravity, and the hardy blue-green grass, a species of *Festuca*, almost sharp enough to cut. Hana's mothers had planted a rose bush in the community garden bordering the habitat, but the fragile perennial had been among the first to die. Hana always thought the roses smelt like lemon; she was certain Earth roses did not smell like lemon. Or perhaps moon lemons smelt like roses. She knew all the plants on the moon—it was her home—but she didn't know Earth's.

The introduced insects and arachnids and presumably the microbes had also died early. Man had been the largest animal.

The streams remained, speckled with dust and, today at least, the illusion of blood. They limped into the vast connecting seas, a shadow of their former selves, their islands multiplied and mountain ranges rearing teeth that the largest tides never before exposed. The habitat was situated near to Lake Atlas, but this Atlas could not bear the world, unlike its namesake. Hana stretched out her bare foot and dipped it in the warm flow of water. Her toes tingled unpleasantly, and she yanked her foot free. Breathing outside the habitat was becoming harder: she inhaled deeply, and it felt like a shallow rasp. The levels of oxygen had plummeted. The air now smelt like a laboratory.

Hana stood, then staggered as her vision blurred. She held still long enough for the grey landscape to stop dancing, thankful no one could see her. Jacinda McRory hated Hana leaving the habitat; Reiko Kato allowed it, but even she would ban the excursions if she saw how hard Hana fought simply to move sometimes. Hana leapt from her hanging rock and landed as light as the dust that puffed around her. If the researchers had managed to create moon-wide artificial gravity, she wouldn't be moving at all.

She took a meandering path between grey stones toward the habitat. She tried not to remember when the colour had been accented by a pretty, hardy vine with large pink and white leaves. She frowned a second before she remembered the species: a mutation of *Actinidia kolomikta*, though the moon's version never fruited. The path had been compacted earth, but the wild winds in the early days of failure had stripped the moon to bare rock. She soon reached paved pathways; no matter what fell, those would last.

The dull grey habitat blended into the moon's surface. The primary dome, connected to smaller ones, and the entrance shaft never changed; it had been built before first settlement, before funding for terraforming was assured. Seeing it, Hana could almost pretend nothing at all had changed. She loved her home, even while it died. She didn't want to leave—didn't want to abandon it like everyone else, even though to stay would be to die herself.

Hana carefully pulled herself into the first decontamination chamber of the entry shaft and winced at the return of weight. The habitat's gravity was kept on similar levels to Earth's to ensure easier travel back and forth; the expense meant that didn't happen often. Hana wiped the dust from her feet and pulled on her shoes before her mothers saw—and berated—her; then she headed into the residential dome. The layout was that of a traditional town with streets and individual buildings, but the view from the clear ceiling panels

243

was of Earth. Hana couldn't get used to the echoing silence of the dome; her memory filled it with bustling residents, mostly the researchers and their families, but some others who also made the moon their home.

"Hana, Jacinda was looking for you," one of the few remaining residents called from his front porch as she passed. The elderly general, once a hero, now forgotten, rested on a carved deckchair in front of his single window as if he was on the Earth and not staring at it. Despite having spent more time there than on the moon, he showed no inclination to leave. Hana suspected he'd stay till the end. Her mothers talked when they supposed she couldn't hear. They figured her too young for the oddest things, yet old enough to act an adult about the moon's death. The idea that General Pozharsky would rather die on the moon than haul himself up for another painful sling around the galaxy to die somewhere else was obviously considered too much for Hana's delicate, youthful mind to handle.

"Hello, General. Do you know what for?" she asked with edgy wariness.

He shook his head, but it was a silly question anyway.

Hana stayed long enough to make sure he didn't need anything, an ingrained habit; then she sighed and shuffled along the pathway to her home.

The family had technically been assigned a house in the residential dome, but they were never there. The research lab had bedrooms and a kitchen. Jacinda and

Reiko took possession of them from their first day on the moon, and Hana's birth had changed nothing. Hana passed the garage on the way; it held on to the illusion of normality. Most of the machinery was too unwieldy to waste money transporting offworld. The greenhouse had only a few plants left for study. Hana spotted Reiko's slim form moving behind the frosted glass but didn't bother turning down that way. Instead she palmed open the lab door and braced her shoulders to face her other mother.

"Don't, Hana," Jacinda said as soon as Hana walked in. The weariness in her voice swept away all the arguments Hana had composed for why she should be allowed outside the habitat right up until they left. She knew a total ban would come as soon as the environment became more inhospitable.

Jacinda bent over a microscope at the counter, and a low, steady beep filled the sterile room. She always brought her less delicate research into the main lab so she could be near her family. She was tall and heavy where her wife was tiny, blunt where Reiko was subtle and evasive. Hana inherited a mix of both: tall but skinny no matter what she ate or did, and she couldn't put on any muscle. She thought it might have been nice to look a little less like an emaciated spike tree—*Spica katinus*. Reiko had bioengineered them, and Hana knew them inside out, but it didn't make the resemblance any better. They were all dead too, despite being the best adapted for the moon.

Hana chewed her lip and watched the lines on Jacinda's face, the exhausted droop to her mouth. "Do we have to go?" she finally whispered and hated how much she sounded like a child.

Jacinda's hand paused on the microscope's focus. Her sigh was almost imperceptible. "You know we do, sweetie. I'm sorry. You know why we've stayed this long and, well, we can monitor just as well from the station."

Hana hung her head and swallowed her words. Yes, she knew. Jacinda and Reiko stayed to study the failure, to analyse the way the atmosphere broke down, and test what survived the longest. They'd then be able to apply the terraforming to Mars, the hope for the future, where the moon had been an experiment. Hana stayed because she was their daughter.

"Hana."

She scuffed her foot along the dull grey floor.

"Look at me, Hana."

Hana held off long enough to make sure Jacinda knew she really didn't want to—as if that wasn't obvious—then peeked through her dark fringe. Guilt twisted her stomach at the deep weariness in Jacinda's pale blue eyes. Hana knew they'd tried their best to not only study the breakdown but forestall it. She knew they'd succeeded in tiny amounts, but it wasn't on file and never would be because it hadn't been enough.

"Please don't make this harder than it already is. We don't want to leave either," Jacinda said softly.

"I know, Mum," Hana said and slipped from the lab before the guilt could twist further.

Despite it, she headed back outside. She should be packing; that was the one good thing about being last to leave. There was room to take their belongings instead of leaving them as a dust-gathering cemetery. The habitat would remain, empty and decaying, with minor repairs carried out by robots until a random meteorite barrage hit it or the terraforming collapse flung another bout of wild weather across the moon and destroyed every trace of humans. It didn't matter because Hana wouldn't be there to see it. *Or there to die*, she tried to remind herself. It was as hard to imagine living elsewhere as it was to imagine dying.

Hana had always lived on the moon. She had always run its dusty paths and round lakes with trickling streams, sailed its seas, and marked her days by the turning of the Earth. She had strung hammocks between spike trees and built hideouts in rock piles. She knew everyone left home eventually, and her mothers thought she acted normally. Most people's leaving home didn't involve an entire planet dying. And the moon was a planet, not a dead hunk of hitchhiking rock, no matter what Yolanda, the last teenager besides Hana left on the base, said. Where the others born on the moon had been excited to leave, Hana held on with everything she had. Jacinda and Reiko tried suggesting all the good things that would come from leaving: Hana could see more of the solar system; she'd get to spend real time, not time-delayed screen time, with her grandparents; she'd go on to a proper college instead of the piecemeal online studies she currently did. Finally her mothers gave up trying to deal with Hana's sulkiness as well as their own regret. Knowing she wasn't being fair didn't make Hana feel any better.

She let her feet take a familiar path without thinking about it. Grey dust coated them by the time she reached the shore of Lake Atlas. The waters were murky grey, the corpse of the life-giving algae a slimy coating on the crater bowl. Hana curled her toes, and the cold slime squelched unpleasantly between them. She was far from the current waterline, but even if she could navigate the exposed and fracture-ridden lake bed, she wouldn't. The acidity of the water burnt as much as the bloodied streams. Hana didn't know why it reflected red. Perhaps the moon wept blood.

She squatted and traced a finger through the film of slime. She wrote her name in looping old world letters, wrote the year, her family's names, all small things. She added a few chemical equations she knew represented the various imbalances in the atmosphere, though she didn't understand them. She could remember anything, but to her mothers' disappointment, she'd never been good at the hard sciences—mathematics and physics especially. Hana bit her lip and wiped the graffiti clean, then clenched her slimy hand into a tight fist. If she had been good at those, if she'd followed Jacinda's path into chemistry or Reiko's into bioengineering, perhaps she could have returned. The moon would be studied again. It wasn't needed anymore: the rest of the system had been thoroughly probed, and gazes turned outward as possibility caught up to dreams. Mining was better elsewhere, and there were better candidates for the improved terraforming. But for tourists, for history, perhaps the moon could be saved.

It wouldn't be by Hana, whose lack of interest was due to lack of skill, despite her mothers' confused belief she could do anything.

She stood again, tilted her head back, and tasted the stale air on her tongue and lips. She closed her eyes to feel the sun, its perfect warmth mocking the historic temperatures it strived to reach once more. She yawned and made to return to the habitat; she wouldn't sulk so far as to kill herself. She ran back towards the lake rim, then along the dusty path, and a sudden sharp pain sliced through the fogginess in her head. She yelped and stumbled to a halt. She'd been out too long. Reiko would yell. *At least she can't ground me for another month*, Hana thought sourly. That would ground her forever.

Hopping wildly about, Hana grabbed her foot in one hand and tried to peer at its underside. She finally had the sense to sit. A thin cut bled from the pad of her toe; the trickle of blood mingled with the grey dust and splashed indifferently across the rocks. Hana swore and, grumbling, bent to patch herself up. Even the moon turned against her. Perhaps everyone else was right, and she should look upon it as an adventure, a chance to see new places.

Hana didn't think she was such a bad person for not caring about exploring new planets.

She sighed and her fingers paused on the slip of antibacterial plaster. Her wandering gaze fell on a small hint of grey-green in the crack of two rocks. She blinked. She frowned. Then her eyes widened, and she scrambled across the bumpy ground. She fell down on her knees next to the rocks. *A leaf? A weed?*

Regardless, it was alive. Where everything died, it lived, and it didn't matter what it was. Hana reached out a hesitant hand but froze before she touched it. What if it was an illusion? What if it was poisonous or delicate, and she broke every rule she knew about unfamiliar plant life by touching it? She chewed her ragged lip. It was a fuzzy grey-green wisp of a plant, a fat stem lying along the ground and terminating in a round phyllode. Her hesitation seemed to last a week; finally, with a huff of breath that made her head spin, she jabbed it with a rough finger.

Its surface was sticky despite the fuzz. It didn't disintegrate under her nervous enthusiasm, and she didn't promptly keel over. Hana ran through her mental database of plant genera in the area. It didn't quite fit anything she knew. *Of course it doesn't, it's alive—it's surviving.* Her eyes widened. It had to be a mutation—perhaps of that invasive ground creeper accidentally introduced a decade ago. She leapt to her feet and bolted in the direction of the habitat.

It took only twenty metres for her to slow again. Her head pounded, and she drooped. It wouldn't make a difference. She crouched in a ball and buried her face in her hands and didn't cry. She never cried. A faint breeze whispered around and stirred the dust. The weather systems on the moon had always been temperate, by chance as much as design, until the beginning of the end. The lone, tiny plant probably wouldn't survive much longer. The breeze cooled Hana's flushed skin. Now that she wasn't moving, she was able to think.

The plant had to make a difference. Maybe not now and not here. Hana still had to leave, and so did her mothers. But its presence meant others would return. They surely couldn't ignore it. The habitat would not be allowed to degrade, and the moon would be studied with the same avidness the terraforming process originally evoked. Hana knew it wouldn't be easy, but she believed it could happen. She had to because it was the only hope she had. It might never be the moon Hana remembered, but it could be a moon the future remembered. She'd try the sciences again, she'd come back if she had the slightest chance, and so would Jacinda and Reiko. The moon wouldn't be abandoned if she had anything to say about it.

Hana smiled. She patted the ground as if she petted an animal. It would be okay.

Entangled Web

By E.C. Myers

A wrapped box was on the kitchen table next to a platter of gleaming bacon. Yes, just one present, but I had asked for only one thing, what every sixteen-year-old wants this year: the first quantum smartphone, the Amplitude iQ6.

"Happy birthday, sweetie," Mom said. Dad pushed a plate of waffles shaped like the Death Star toward me.

I snagged a strip of bacon (crispy, almost charcoal, just the way I like it) and wiped my fingers clean before picking up the gift. I shredded the pink-heart paper (really, Mom?) to reveal the slim, black velvet case I'd been dreaming about.

Inside was a rectangle of translucent plastic engraved with my name. It glowed at my touch, the 3-D display informing me its name was Lex.

"Morning, Lex." I stroked the phone's cool surface, frowning at the laser-etched letters marring its sleek, simple perfection.

"Happy birthday, Erica." Lex's default voice was a sexy English lady, exactly what I would choose.

"How…?" Dad asked.

"Biometrics, dear," Mom said.

"I'm already in its quantum database. Other Ericas, same prints." I wiggled my fingers.

I started syncing my EveryMe account. No need to charge the phone even, because it drew power from the freaking *air*. Science FTW!

"—ignoring us. I already regret getting you that," Dad said.

"I'm listening." I scrolled through the transcript Lex had recorded of the conversation I'd fully missed.

Mom: We'll pay for six months of service, but then you're on your own.

Dad: A car would have been cheaper in the long run, and more useful. Helloooo? Oh, you're ignoring us.

"Six months is fully generous," I said. I'd need to pick up an extra couple shifts a week at the bowling alley to afford my new gadget. "Thanks, guys. I love you."

Aw. Group hug.

By the time I was dressed for school, my phone was ready.

I was ready.

The main reason everyone wants a quantum smartphone? To run its exclusive app: Tangle. I tapped the pulsing triangular icon, and my world expanded.

I snapped a picture of my bus as it arrived and uploaded it to Tangle. I climbed onboard, thumbing through identical photos of other buses.

No, not identical—*similar*. My school bus was classic yellow, but some were puke green or black and grey, or even a weird shape. In most pics Craig was in his usual seat, third from the front.

I didn't think too hard about the ones where he wasn't.

"You got it!" Craig said when I sat next to him. "Hippo birdie." He tapped his iQ6 against mine like a champagne toast. Our phones flared pink as Katie and Lex bonded. BPFs: Best Phones Forever!

"So?" Craig asked.

"Undecided. There's too much info coming at me."

My number of Tangle followers was increasing by the second.

"You're auto following. Here." Craig showed me how to limit my feed to the Ericas who were most like me, taking it to a manageable 430. And counting.

"Quick, check this." He tipped his phone toward me.

I—no, another Erica—grinned at the camera, holding up an iQ6. I snapped a pic of it on my phone before it disappeared forever.

The picture was reversed, creating an eerie mirror effect when I looked at it. Except other Erica was showing way more cleavage. Kinda hot. I tugged at my tank top.

"Don't upload that pic! Your account will be suspended. You aren't supposed to do that," Craig said.

"Oh. Oops." I deleted flirty Erica and uploaded a selfie. Not flirty.

The Ericas flashing by my screen all wore cuter outfits than me. They were having better hair days too. I had two zits on my chin.

Happy birthday, girl.

You're limited to following your other selves on Tangle, but there were more than enough of me out there in the whateverse to keep me busy swiping every chance I got, in the halls, during class, and yeah, on the toilet.

Oh, you do it too.

Soon I was quick at spotting all the differences in the allotted eight seconds. See enough pics, and you can even imagine what their lives are like. Some of us were obviously dating their Craig, which you know, I've considered, but he isn't *my* type.

A missing ping pong table in an Erica's basement made me wonder if her Dad hadn't survived the stroke a few years back. Some Ericas were smokers or drinkers—Untangle!—but most were into cinema like me.

There are even some guy versions. Erics? But they keep uploading pictures of their junk. *Boys.* Untangle!

I've been paying attention to one Erica in particular, even though that's against the terms of service too.

The fine print: Supposedly if you follow someone too closely on Tangle, you could start feeling what they feel. Thinking what they think.

But how could you tell?

Is that why I feel so sad all the time now?

It's hard seeing so many possibilities. Another you is always having more fun, looking shinier, getting better grades, having more sex. And some Ericas... They're *mean*.

Like, sure, I could be thinner.

Why *don't* I wear contacts?

Why don't I have a girlfriend?

Erica.2344 is going to kill herself. She posted a photo of sleeping pills, just like the bottle on my night table.

Erica.1111: Eh. What's one less Erica?

Erica.330: She's a waste of electrons.

Erica.Prime: Don't! Get help.

That's me, I'm Erica.Prime. But I bet we all think we are. I'm probably #9999. An unlimited edition. What do I matter?

Erica.2344 posts a photo of the open bottle.

I hold a handful of blue and gold pills.

She posts a selfie of her swallowing them.

I hesitate, counting the eight seconds until the photo disappears.

The message flashes: "User "Erica.2344" not found.

Hands shaking, pills slipping through my fingers like sand, I tap my screen.

Uninstall Tangle? Lex asks.

My thumb hovers over the green button.

Yes.

Blue Ribbon

By Marissa Lingen

I should have known when I didn't hear whooping and hollering and congratulations from Chornohora Station when I crossed the finish plane. My sister Luzia and I eked out a win over Scott and Ferenc Nagy in the maneuverability race even though Luz was just barely old enough to compete in the teen division. Usually that sort of thing calls for celebration, and Luz was not going to let it go without some.

"Wooo!" she hollered into the comms. "That's right, Pinheiros have beaten you *again*, even without Amilcar's help!"

Scott's voice sounded admiring and rueful: "Sneaky little demons. Next time, though…"

"Next time will have to wait awhile, with you guys in adult competition next year and us still in 4-H," I said. "You'd better spend that time trying to improve, maybe even looking at the throttle on that thing. Chornohora Station, I think we're ready for our victory lap, so go ahead and pop the champagne corks, we are coming in."

And…silence. Real silence, not just chatter unrelated to my obstacle-racing victory (teen division). I get that not everybody is thrilled with 4-H racing, especially not every adult. There are infinite varieties of 4-H contests, from chicken genetics to hydroponic tomato sauce competitions to straight-out speed races in the STL ships, and nobody can get excited about all of them, not even during the fair. But mostly the people manning the station comms during the race were racers themselves as kids and more than happy to give us feedback as needed.

"You getting anything from the station, guys?" I asked the Nagys.

"Negative," said Ferenc, the most he'd said all race.

"Not a word," Scott concurred.

"Us either." I tried switching frequencies. "Chornohora Station, hello?" Still nothing.

There were another couple of Muspel 670s hanging near the finish plane, nearly identical to ours in lines but painted wildly differently. They weren't from our race—those losers were still coming in and would be for quite some time, thanks—but I wasn't sure what they were from.

"Hailing the blue Muspel," I said over the comms. "This is the Pinheiro sisters, Luzia and Tereza. Do you require assistance?"

"I don't know," said a rather small voice. "This is Simon Chao-Cohen. I'm here with my in-cousin Huang Fu Chao-Cohen. We finished our race—"

Blue Ribbon | *Marissa Lingen*

"Which race?"

"Maneuvers preteen."

"Okay, sorry, go on."

"We finished our race, and nobody answered our hails. That was maybe two hours ago."

I frowned. Two hours was far too long for everyone to be busy with incoming ships, especially at this stage of the fair. We had been nearly the last ones in, and Luz and I had had to scramble into our Muspel and go in order to make our race registration cutoff—we hadn't even gotten to see the inside of the station yet. Nobody would be later than that for one of the year's three big fairs.

And *nobody* would leave a preteen division out there in radio silence for hours.

"Hang on a sec," I said. "My uncle taught me several miner emergency frequencies. I'll hail on those."

I tried the entire broad band to no effect. Another few Muspels straggled in from our race, and the little kids from the preteen course started to cluster theirs up with us, together, hanging in a constellation outside the station.

Finally I heard a voice, but it was not a response, or at least not the kind of response I wanted. "Attention, incoming ships. This is the Chornohora Station auto-response system. The Station customs and immigration personnel are unable to process your ship at this time. Please proceed to another station for your trade and leisure needs. Chornohora Station is closed for quarantine. Please proceed to another station for your trade and leisure needs. Chornohora Station is closed for quarantine. Please proceed…"

I punched the "accept" button so that it wouldn't keep playing us the same automated message. It would still let me know if the message changed.

Closed for quarantine.

None of the Oort Stations had ever been closed for quarantine. Ever. We learned about it in lessons because it had happened to one of the Jovians once, back before the Oort was even settled—the encephalitic measles, and that was horrible, five percent death toll. Now there was something on Chornohora that warranted a quarantine.

And our family was on the station.

"Tereza?" said the little voice I had come to identify as Simon Chao-Cohen. "What are we going to do? We can't go to another station like it says. Muspels don't have FTL, and all our parents' FTL ships are locked up to the station in the quarantine."

"I know, Simon," I said. "It'll be okay." Luz shot me an incredulous look, but I just kept talking. "You've got emergency rations in your Muspel, right?"

"…sort of?"

"Okay, we'll sort out 'sort of' when we've got everybody gathered. Meanwhile let's see who's here and go on to—hey, Scott, will you look for a good rock while I take attendance here?"

Blue Ribbon | *Marissa Lingen*

"Sure thing," he said. I might make comments about Scott and his in-cousin Ferenc when we were in the heat of the race, but it was all in good fun. They were some of my best friends, and I was glad to have them to count on in a crisis. Scott was going to marry my out-cousin Amilcar in another year, but they hadn't decided who would be the in-spouse and who the out-spouse. If Amilcar out-married, he and Scott would have more position on the Nagy ship, more seniority; with a single ship family like the Nagys (or like my own), it was much easier to make your voice heard, much less likely that you would be drowned out by still-living generations of ancestors, all of whom felt they knew more about mining, art, and life than you.

But if Amilcar in-married, Scott would have access to everything the Gouveia family had, which was a lot. Really a lot. A lot of ships, a lot of possessions, a lot of connections...anything at all that they wanted to do, anything their contract-children wanted to do, would be possible with the Gouveia family. My out-cousins were a pretty big deal.

It's part of why Dad out-married into the Pinheiros: he didn't like being just another Gouveia artist, without anyone who could keep track of what he did differently or why.

The point was: Scott was nearly family. So he ran the calculations while we took notes on who was who and who was where. We had four ships from the preteen division—it sounded like they'd lost, poor mites, and the winners had made it into the station before the quarantine shutdown. Which might have made them even unluckier. The rest of our division of teen maneuverability pilots was limping in a few at a time, and Luz and I hailed them and took stock of who they were, which families they were from.

Then I zapped the coordinates Scott had picked out to their ships, and we regrouped to an asteroid not far away: big enough to let us anchor our ships to it and power the artificial grav that way, but not far enough away that we wouldn't hear about it if in-system med ships came to Chornohora, or if the quarantine was lifted or like that. We formed a ring on the surface, able to pass things with waldoes if they were vacuum-safe but not actually connected by airlocks. Can't be too careful in quarantine.

Chornohora was one of the three big fairs of the year, so pretty much all my family was in that station except for Luz, even my out-cousins, except Amilcar's ship of them. I kept hoping we'd get the all-clear and laugh about it a little nervously with Mom and Dad and Grandpa and Grandma later. I started thinking about how to make them laugh, telling them about how we had to hang out in space sweaty and stinky from our victory. That many hours of obstacle-racing adds up; you get pretty rank together. But then the Chao-Cohens made it clear that they didn't have the regulation amount of emergency rations, and I got funny and serious stuff all in one package.

Blue Ribbon | *Marissa Lingen*

"What do you mean, you don't have the regulation amount? Come on, the Chao family practically founded Oort mining. You guys know better than this."

"Simon kept stashing things to eat and then coming back and eating them," said Huang Fu, speaking for the first time. He sounded, if anything, younger than Simon.

"Have you got *anything* to eat in there?"

"Oh yes!" chirped Simon. "I'm going to enter the preteen baking section for nuts." Of course. We were all 4Hers—that's who sponsored the racing, and in fact most events at the annual fairs. So Luzia and I wouldn't be the only one with our competition entries in our ships.

"Nuts? I bet," said a little girl's voice I recognized as one of his competitors, one of the Aafjes girls—either Grace or Anni, I couldn't tell yet which.

"It's got nuts *in* it, stupid! They're plum dumplings with ground walnuts, and they're really good, and just for that *you* can't have any."

"None of that," I said sharply. "No name calling, and absolutely *no* threats of food-hoarding, do you understand?"

"Yes ma'am," muttered Simon.

"We're entering the competition for novel flavors of lichen-based proteins," said the other Aafjes girl. I'm pretty sure that one was Anni. "We've got durian mac and cheese."

There was a general outcry on the comms.

"Not real durian!" Anni protested. "I know it's banned for the sake of the air vents. So we did our best to replicate durian flavors with lichens. It's really good!"

"We've got spruce beer," said Ferenc. Usually he lets Scott do the talking, so it must have been his spruce beer.

"Didn't *anybody* else do vacuum emergency kit competition this year?" I said plaintively. It transpired that the two little Van Haanrade boys, Liwei and Mikko, had, and also three of our contemporaries. In addition, we had my currant mustard, Luzia's dilly beans, and several more entries in the lichen competition. Everything had been canned except the dumplings.

"Okay, so, you keep the dumplings," I said to the Chao-Cohen boys. "We can't share those without risk."

"What do you mean, without risk?" asked Liwei Van Haanrade.

I took too long to answer. Luzia jumped in for me, and less delicately than I would have. "Look, there's some nasty disease on the station, right? Well, that means someone must have brought it, right? And the odds are pretty good that those of you who were on the station got exposed to it before you started your races. So we can't link life systems. We have to pass everything with the waldos and let the vacuum sterilize it."

"Will that work?" asked Scott.

"It's the best chance we've got," I said. "We can't let the Chao-Cohen kids starve, dumplings or no

Blue Ribbon | *Marissa Lingen*

dumplings. Everybody comm me what you've got for supplies, and we'll share them out evenly."

"Does this mean I won't win with the durian mac?" said Grace Aafjes.

"I think we've won all we're going to win today, Grace," I said.

"But we didn't win! We came in at least fifth, maybe sixth. The logs aren't auto-updating, so I can't see."

I did not feel like trying to explain to her that if we were dealing with plague protocols, just being alive and in a separate life-support system from the victims might be a win condition. So I just didn't argue. Instead, I did the calculations while Luzia manned the waldos, passing hardened vac-safe jars of preserves and lichens up and down the chain of ships on the tiny rock we'd found.

The sour smell in our Muspel was *not* going to get better any time soon.

We were chewing through our allotted mouthfuls of salt-and-pepper lichen (good) and washing them down with spruce beer (which is not alcoholic, for the record; being alcoholic might have helped the flavor, so: not good) when Luz issued a very dramatic sigh. "We're missing the Saloma concert."

Saloma is my sister's favorite singer. Mine too. We'd only ever been to her concert at the previous fair at Servaas Station. It was out of this ecliptic. I said, "We can put on one of our recordings."

"I guess," said Luz, "but we do that all the time. It's not the same."

"Luz...they might not even be *having* the concert."

"You think Saloma's sick?"

"I think anybody might be sick." Then I was glad I'd turned the comms off to the younger kids' ships, because Luzia started crying, loud and ragged and scared, and she didn't stop for quite awhile. I put my arms around her and muttered meaningless encouragement, and then when she got herself calmed down and curled up in one of the emergency blankets to listen to her favorite Saloma song, I had to go lock myself in the head so I could cry too.

Tear-streaked and stinking of old sweat, I picked up the inside of the Muspel as best I could. There was a comm indicator. "Tereza?" said a little voice. It was Mikko Van Haanrades. "They'll let us in tomorrow, right?"

"I sure hope so, Mikko," I said. "You guys look after each other in there, all right? Try to get some sleep."

I followed my own advice as best I could. I woke up with a crick in my neck and my hair stuck to my face. Luzia looked no better. The comm alert was going off. I pressed it, hoping for a station message.

"Tereza? They're still not answering," said Simon Chao-Cohen.

"It's awfully early, Simon," I said. "It looks like it's a real quarantine, not a drill, so we're probably stuck here until they get the med ships out from Ganymede."

Blue Ribbon | *Marissa Lingen*

"Shouldn't we…try to get somewhere else?" he said.

I sighed. It's really easy to forget how big the Oort is when you're always using FTL drives. Then get stuck in a Muspel 670 or something else with only STL, just a little mining vehicle, and see how big it feels. At top speed, we could probably make it to the next station in only four or five years, except that we'd run out of fuel and have nowhere to get more in less than a month. Food also. Earth people would probably compare it to trying to get from Oslo to Cape Town on a tractor. You'd be better off with a musk ox cart, because musk oxen can swim, or if you get too hungry, they're much tastier than a Muspel 670.

So I talked that through to the satisfaction of half a dozen ten-year-olds, all of whom were smart, all of whom were well-trained, all of whom just wanted their families. Nor could I blame them.

And failing their families, they wanted something to *do*, and I couldn't blame them for that, either. We all had movies and music and books downloaded to our Muspels for quiet moments of travel and letting the ship automate some of the less interesting mining functions, but that's not nearly enough when you're trying to distract yourself from a plague at your doorstep.

Luz set up a round-robin Go tournament, at which she soundly spanked all comers, and I taught the little ones to play cribbage through the ship computers. Squabbling and technical difficulties took care of most of a day, and we older ones got very few questions about where the med ships were and when we were going to get there.

We got to the end of a day-cycle out there in the dark and cold, and everybody was cranky and tired and getting smellier by the minute. So I did what I was taught to do: I tried to start a sing-along.

Other people are not very good at sing-alongs even when they're perfectly good at singing.

But oh, I did my best. I taught them "Rose, Rose" and "Sweet Deep Black" and "John Jacob Jingelheimer Schmidt", which is apparently a song about in-cousins whose mothers did not consult sufficiently about their names. Luzia tried to get everybody to sing Saloma's "Out-Cousin's Lullaby," which is a great song, but it's terrible for people who have less vocal range than Saloma, which is pretty much everybody, *especially* Luz. Ferenc unexpectedly saved the day then and jumped in to teach them "I Hate to Wake Up Sober on Europa" which under ordinary circumstances I would not teach to preteens, but what the hell, their parents could yell at me later.

If their parents were still alive.

I resolutely did not think of that, and I kept not thinking of it when he taught them the song about the seven old ladies and their misadventures in the head, and I was almost doing fine when he taught them the one about the miner and the chicken, which is dirty in at least two languages that I know of.

Blue Ribbon | *Marissa Lingen*

And then, very quietly, Liwei Van Haanrade said, "Tereza? I miss my auntie."

"We all miss our aunties, sweetie," I said. "We'll get to see them soon, when the med ships come."

But he continued, "Tereza, I don't feel good."

"He's all feverish," his brother Mikko reported, "and I think I'm a little feverish too."

"Probably too much of that yummy yummy durian-flavored lichen the Aafjes gave us," I said heartily. "Get some sleep."

"It was durian *mac and cheese*," said Grace Aafjes, and we all agreed that it was unforgettably that, that if she was going for durian mac and cheese, she had certainly achieved it. And then we went to regular comms for the night, and Luz said to me, "They're sick. The Van Haanrades. They've got whatever it is on the station."

"We don't know that," I said, but we had a pretty good guess at it.

Up until that point, we could almost convince ourselves that this was just another adventure, like a survivalist course under the domes or something. Like Earth people who go camping. None of us had ever been anything like camping, so—we read old Earther kids' books, and we could sort of half-convince ourselves it was similar.

But then I woke up in the night to Mikko comming me that Liwei had been throwing up blood. And there was honestly not a damn thing I could do except talk to them, sing to them, use my most soothing voice with them and be there through the comms. I had everybody inventory their emergency med supplies, but honestly I didn't expect much, and that's what I got. Muspels aren't meant to be far away from their parent ships for long. There are a few adhesive bandages and some mild painkillers, and that's about it.

And Liwei did not get better, and Mikko got worse, and even if I had been willing to expose myself to the plague—even if I'd been willing to throw precaution to the wind—there was literally *nothing I could do* except listen to these two little kids, brothers in their ship like Luz and I were sisters in ours, vomiting blood. Then shitting blood. And I'm not sure what-all happened toward the end there. It sounded bubbly and horrible.

I just know they died.

Early on I got Scott to handle the rest of the little kids, and I got him to tell everybody *not to comm* the Van Haanrades. If they'd had particular friends, I would have let them say goodbye, but we were just all Oorter kids who knew each other's families a little from fairs. There was no one who could be more comforting than I was, and what a sad state of affairs that was.

And the last thing I needed was more of the little ones to freak out.

That is, any more than was strictly necessary.

Which, frankly, was quite a lot. Luz and I held each other and cried and repeated reassurances about how we hadn't even been exposed to the station air. But that didn't help much.

Nobody took it well when I told them the Van Haanrade kids were dead. I didn't expect them to. The littler ones had started thinking of me as someone who was in charge, so I spent hours trying to explain to terrified, upset kids why I hadn't saved the others. They asked me the horrible questions, about whether I would let them die too. Because somewhere along the line, my 4-H pledge to the community had come to mean *them*, and they just could not wrap their brains around the idea that I couldn't fix it.

Scott tried to say something consoling over the comms, but he had to talk to Luz at that point, because I was not listening to anything but the white noise in my head.

The next morning, Simon Chao-Cohen commed me with a timid little voice saying, "Tereza?" And my heart went right back to my feet. I was just sure it would be another little kid vomiting blood.

In some ways it was harder than that.

"Tereza, our life system is malfunctioning. Help?"

"Oh shit," I said coherently. "Oh shit, oh shit, Simon, what have you got left?"

"Two hours. Can we come in with you?"

I looked at Luz. Luz looked at me. The Chao-Cohen kids had been on the station for days before the race, and we hadn't been there at all. Maybe we should try to shove them off on someone else. But the Muspels were small, and I *had* put myself in charge, so...

"Just a second," I said. I turned the comm off.

"We're taking them," said Luz. She sounded tired. No thirteen-year-old should ever have to sound like she's accepting her own death.

"We have to split them up. One each. A Muspel with four people in it would be completely unbearable, even if three of them are you and little bitty sprouts like those boys."

"But we're taking one. Scott and Ferenc can take the other—give them Huang Fu. He and Ferenc can be quiet together. Scott's used to it. But honestly, Tereza, which of our other competitors has shown the slightest bit of backbone? They can't take care of a little kid. And the Aafjes are just little kids themselves. And there's no way to sterilize the Van Haanrade vehicle thoroughly without losing most of the remaining life support anyway."

I forebore to mention that Luz was only one year out of the preteen division herself—that at this time last year, I'd been partnering with Amilcar for competitions like this one and watching Luz dazzle the single-digit set. I flipped the comms back on. "Okay, here's the plan," I said.

It sounds like Luzia and me, we were these amazing angels, so selfless and so wonderful, or alternately like we were just ordinary humans what you always hope ordinary humans would do. And maybe both of those were true.

Blue Ribbon | *Marissa Lingen*

What's also true is that the Chao family—all nine branches of it—are some of the most powerful people in the Oort. So...yeah, we were taking a pretty big risk. On the other hand, we could have the gratitude of an entire great clan if we succeeded.

Mostly, though, we took them in because if I was going to listen to another little boy cough and cry and die, I was going to do it where I could damn well rub his shoulders and stroke his hair and clean him up a little.

Maybe that makes me stupid. I don't know.

Simon cried for half an hour when he got into our ship and got his suit off, I think mostly with relief but also some with exhaustion. He had carefully brought his rations, good boy that he was. Once he finally stopped crying, Luz showed him cat's-cradle tricks and got him calmed down.

And then the med ships came.

We saw them approaching the station first and hailed them. One of them broke off from the main group and approached us immediately.

"We've lost two little boys in the third ship clockwise in the ring from me," I told them. "Do you know anything about what's going on there on Chornohora? We haven't been able to raise any kind of comms since the auto-signal went on."

"They have no spare personnel," said the Ganymedan medic. "I'm not sure how many are still alive, but certainly not enough to keep them out of emergency shutdown mode. It's pretty bad."

"What kind of bad?"

"We don't know, but it's hemorrhagic," he said grimly.

"Hemorrhagic" is one of those words you never, ever want to hear used near your loved ones. I had the urge to clap my hands over my sister's ears. But Luz had been coping with all of this just as I had, and when I turned to her, she had *her* hands over *Simon's* ears.

That's my girl.

The med ship personnel were using special suits to get in and out of Chornohora, and as long as nobody started running a fever, we were low priority. They passed us supplies through the airlock. It was a really bad sign that they were not sparing any of the Ganymedan personnel to keep our spirits up—they just took Liwei and Mikko's bodies and left us, and brought us rations from time to time.

It was another week before they actually towed the Muspels away to a big in-system med ship and let us out of them. They were going to separate me and Luzia to talk to me, but Luz wasn't going anywhere without me. She didn't actually threaten to bite anybody, but I think the implication was clear.

The in-system official waiting for us was not Ganymedan, as I'd expected from the med ships. She was Europan.

Which meant there were finances involved.

"Tereza Pinheiro," she said. "And Luzia Pinheiro, I presume, though you were not called for."

Blue Ribbon | *Marissa Lingen*

Luz jutted out her chin. "I came anyway."

"Well, girls." She looked at her handheld as if it carried new information, though I was sure she had loaded and read everything long before we'd walked in. "Looks like you could use a shower and a hot meal."

"And a beverage that isn't spruce beer or recycled water," I said fervently. "What—what's happening?"

"You have the gratitude of a grateful Chao family," she said. "So there's that for you. The seven branches want you to know that you can call on them at any time."

"Nine branches," said Luz, because in-system people don't always know.

The Europan glanced at her, and I saw that she was desperately trying to be kind. "No, honey. Seven."

I sat down in the ugly chair they'd provided and gripped the edge of the metal table for support. "Everyone's gone. Aren't they."

"I'm sorry. In addition to the gratitude of the Chao family, you have an offer for a new berth. Both of you. I'll send your accounts the details. Think it over. You don't have to rush." She looked at us both carefully, greasy and stinking and smudged. "It sounds like you did the lion's share of the work of keeping the other kids from completely panicking. If you play your cards right, that will serve you well in the future. Inasmuch as Chornohora has a hero, it's you."

She left us alone, left us to shower and eat and think and cry. We met up with Scott and Ferenc in the corridor, freshly scrubbed and stunned.

"Our offer is from the Gouveias," I told them all. "Our out-cousins say we can be in-cousins now."

"Then you'll be with us," said Scott. "I'm going to out-marry Amilcar—no reason not to, now—and we're making special arrangements to adopt Ferenc. He'll be my firstborn son, legally."

Ferenc tried to grin at that, but his mouth was only going through the motions.

"But we won't be Pinheiros any more," said Luz urgently. "We won't, will we, Tereza? They won't make an exception?"

"Honey, I don't think they can," I said.

"I don't want to be a Gouveia. I'm a Pinheiro, and you're a Pinheiro, and we were supposed to grow up and be Pinheiros together and do our own thing. I don't want to be a Gouveia!"

"I bet they'll call us 'those Pinheiro girls'," I said. Honestly I don't think Luzia had the least notion of how much worse things could be. We could keep the official legal name Pinheiro and get shipped in-system and not have it mean anything more than Argleblargle. Family names are like that in-system. They're noise.

"It's not the same," said Luz.

Scott bent down to talk to her, and I think he was the only one who could do it without Luz taking the opportunity to throttle him at that point. "Luzia, sweet, look. This way you and Tereza can be together, right? And you can be with me and Ferenc and Amilcar. And we'll be our own little unit inside the Gouveias.

And then when we make enough money—"

Bless Scott. Bless him, oh, bless him. "That's right, Luz, when we make enough money, we can get our own ship and be Pinheiro-Nagys. And neither of us will out-marry, we'll make any men we meet in-marry or gene-donate, and we'll have the babies for the new Pinheiro-Nagy ship."

Luzia's sobs slowed to sniffles. "You promise?"

"I promise, honey."

And Scott and Ferenc promised, too, and I expect they had time to go off and cry by themselves, as I did. But mostly we focused on taking care of Luz and each other, because that was the only way we could win now.

Bodies are the Strongest Conductors

By James Robert Herndon

Lumpy gave me a gift today.

"It's raining dinosaur piss out here," he said. "Let me in. Your mom went to work, I saw her get on the bus."

Mom would find out. She'd cry, which would make me cry, but I had to let him in. Lumpy was my only friend. We were only friends at recess even though he lived down the street, and now that Mom had pulled me out of school on doctor's orders, I felt lucky to be hearing from him at all.

"Open the door, Nicky," he said. "C'mon, man. Are you putting on makeup or something?"

"Yeah, lipstick." I laughed, too loudly. Mom always hid the deadbolt key in the same place: beneath a clay pot covering a vent from our building's laundry room. I grabbed the key with an oven mitt so it wouldn't leave a rash on my hand. The smell of brass made me gag as I unlocked the door.

Lumpy stomped in and dropped a wet cardboard box on the floor. He made no eye contact as he shook water from his hair like a pug, spraying metallic raindrops all over the walls. Two drops hit my neck and I hunched my shoulders to hide the marks. I was already being a wimp.

"Nicky, dude. You're wearing purple pajamas," he said.

"They're plum," I said. "I have to wear them as long as I'm, you know, grounded, because all my jeans have copper buttons." As if it were a common thing, as if he could possibly relate. "It's just for a while and then I can wear clothes like yours."

Lumpy was wearing the same unwashed flannel shirt and king-sized jeans he wore to school every day. The rainwater made his body smell stronger than usual, like runny eggs left on a plate all morning. He was also wearing an eye patch—a plastic lens from police sunglasses, pierced by a shoelace. The patch was stuck to his forehead because the shoelace had been tied too tight, too soon. I should have complimented the patch.

"You're gonna like this," he said, kicking the wet box. It had nearly come apart in the rain. "My dad is drinking Smirnoff Green Apple and watching *Monster's Ball* in the bathroom again, so I stole this from his closet for us." He wiped a glob of wax from his face with a sleeve. "You can go first."

Up close, the box smelled stronger than Lumpy's clothes. Like Mom had taught me to do with boxes we hadn't packed ourselves, I tried to pop open the flaps with the toe of my sneaker.

"Come on," Lumpy said. "Don't be a princess."

The words made my neck burn. At recess, Lumpy said "Don't be a princess" to kids who screamed when he stabbed them in the butt with a stick. He told me his dad said it when they wrestled and it was funny, wasn't it? It wasn't funny at all, but his real question was obvious. "Yeah, that's funny," I said, because if I had hugged him and said, "You're too amazing to feel ashamed of anything," he would have broken my nose.

"Stop ballet dancing with the box," he said slowly, "and I'll show you how to open it."

He pulled back a flap and removed a plastic container of boot polish. When he unscrewed the cap it smelled unsafe but good, as if the polish were meant to protect people and their things from the world, but could do the opposite if someone handled it wrong. It did have metal—the smell of petroleum is easy to pinpoint, that rock tar funk—but it was mostly wax and lanolin. Natural dyes, too. I never knew polish was fun for Lumpy, but from the way he sniffed it and crunched the container in his hand, maybe it wasn't.

"Does your dad use it a lot?" I asked.

"Why do you care?" he said.

"Just asking. You showed it to me."

"Watch this."

On the wall above our sofa, there's a graph that Mom drew on butcher paper. It charts the rising metal levels in my bloodstream, which she carefully measures every night. Lumpy began finger-painting on the graph with the polish, and he turned yesterday's spike into an adult penis. "That's awesome," I said, my stomach roiling as if he'd painted it on my skin. Whenever Mom looked at that graph, her entire jaw line was visible, from her retracted lips all the way back to her earlobes, like a bridle she wore on the inside. At least he wasn't asking me to join in. I would have drawn a boy who could touch and eat whatever he wanted, who had absorbed so much metal that he could use Earth's magnetic fields to fly. Lumpy would call it lame and be right.

"Hey, let's tell jokes," I said. Maybe he'd quit if I could distract him. "What's brown and sticky?"

"A stick," he said. "C'mon Nicky, that joke is from second grade." He threw the polish to me and laughed when I let it land on the floor. "Do you remember when I told the recess lady that Nicky was short for Nickel Humper and we laughed really hard?"

"My mom will get pissed if we mess up anything in here," I said. "She has it set up a certain way."

He looked around my apartment and frowned. "Dude," he said. "Your mom is gay for blue."

Blue dowel pins held our table together instead of screws. We had blue bookshelf pegs, blue kitchen chairs. Blue bandages were hiding the metal of every nailhead on the wood floor; blue streamers covered the cracks along the walls, across the saggy ceiling. Before

Mom decorated, she asked what my favorite color was. I'd been staring out the window at two kids kicking a bookbag around the sidewalk, no clouds in the sky.

"Actually, the cool thing about all the blue stuff," I said, clutching my belly, "is when you sit upside-down on the couch for a long time and then jump up, you get the spins and it looks like the room is erupting in laundry detergent."

Lumpy raised an eyebrow at me. As he should have.

"I wish you had brought sticks over," I said. "Then we could sword fight."

"The stuff in my dad's box is cooler than sticks," he said. "Look."

I touched the box with my fingers. No pain, but it felt like wet fruit in my hands. When I peeled back the lid, two dark eyes were staring back at me. A raccoon teddy.

Lumpy scratched a blob of red skin on his throat. "Go ahead, pick it up," he said.

Touching the raccoon teddy's fur, I realized it wasn't a teddy at all but a real raccoon. It was as light as a kickball, but as hard as a kickball made from skulls. Bumpy skulls with lots of gashes. The dirty salt and pepper fur looked like it had been gripped too tightly by sweaty hands during the stuffing process and was now matted in clumps all over the raccoon's body. Little naked paws were as boney as my own, the fingers so slender at the base, but fattening into cartoon exclamation points as they moved out to the nails. The raccoon's dark lips were swollen and had been mushed into a smile. I was forcing a smile too. The snout was crooked and had clearly been cut off and glued back on at a bad angle. Fake black eyes smelled like boot polish and Lumpy.

"Cool, huh?" Lumpy said. "My dad made this."

Maybe if something was sensual but hard to justify, Lumpy's dad kept it in a box. How Lumpy could be proud of the raccoon, I had no idea. "What did he stuff it with?" I asked.

"Whatever he wants," Lumpy said. "We don't have to worry about toxic stuff."

This was a lie. Once, at the end of a fun recess together, he told me that sometimes during flu season he had to stay at home all day in his underwear. His dad cleaned him with a yellow sponge. It sounded weird, but I felt happy to hear about it because it meant Lumpy trusted me, and that he had body problems just like I did. I said this to Lumpy and he got really quiet. When I asked if he wanted to play superheroes after school he ignored me. He ignored me for the rest of the week.

"Everyone has to worry about toxic stuff," I said.

He yanked the raccoon out of my hands and held it up in front of his face. "Nicky!" he squealed in a high voice. "I am your mother! Go to your room!"

He wanted me to laugh at my mom so he could forget about his dad. Why did I have to do all the work? "You do a really good impression of a girl," I said.

"The world is dirty!" he squealed, more insistently this time. "Stay inside or I'll claw your face off!"

"My mom only does what the doctors tell her to do," I said. "I'm the one with all the metal in my blood. Everything wrong with my body is basically my fault."

Lumpy frowned, not liking this idea at all. He put the raccoon down and reached into the box for something else. "Here, this will make you feel better," he said.

He handed me a wrinkled magazine. *Split* was written across the top in swollen pink letters, and a woman was sitting on a man's lap. She looked as if she were falling asleep and waking up at the same time.

"I don't get it," I asked.

"It's a magazine. Look at it."

Women with no clothes were squatting at funny angles over marble desks, clawfoot tubs, and aluminum kitchen chairs. I felt a water balloon pop inside me and spill confusion and heat all over my organs. All of their legs were far apart, so you could see the places where their skin grew darker and disappeared inside them. Their wrists, earlobes, and necks held silver jewelry, and even though the jewelry was big, none of it left a rash on their skin. Every single woman stared back at me with a happy boredom on her face. Lumpy pointed to a man inserting a spoon between the legs of a strawberry blond schoolteacher who was making a face like the spoon had drugged her.

"This magazine is weird," I said.

When Lumpy scowled, the rain outside grew louder. "You're weird if you think this magazine is weird."

"They look like they're trying to get rid of their own bodies," I said, not wanting to relate. I closed the magazine and handed it back. "Hey, do you know how to thumb wrestle?"

"Are you gay?" he asked.

It would have been simpler to lie and say yes, or say no and kick him in the stomach like a normal boy. To have a friend, I'd simplify anything. But I wanted more than friendship from Lumpy: I wanted to be Lumpy. I wanted to be stronger, louder, and tougher in front of the world than I was in my skin. I wanted that superpower. Lumpy could turn shame into electricity, giving him not only confidence, but power over other people. If you had this, you didn't have to be exposed all the time. You did what felt good, what made you come alive. If Lumpy could say anything that made him feel important, anything that made him feel as if he were in charge of something, why couldn't I?

"You stole secret stuff from your dad's closet," I said, "and now you're playing with it. You're looking at his naked people magazines and you want me to look too. That's way gayer. You and your dad."

The natural light in Lumpy's eyes dimmed. A wind seemed to blow through him and take him out of my apartment, and when it brought him back, it put him in his body backwards. My chest fizzed with new and unfamiliar energy.

Lumpy reached deep into the box. He pulled out a heavy and twirl-tied floral pillowcase, and I could smell the pennies inside it without him showing me.

"Don't," I said.

He raised the sack up over his head. When he dropped it from as high as he could hold it up, the smash made my nostrils buzz. There were teeth inside my teeth and they were having a tantrum and making my gums upset. Every breath I took pulled in more penny smells, coating the inside of my nose and the back of my throat. For a second I thought the coins were already inside me.

"Okay, enough," I said. "You can stop."

He untied the pillowcase. That smell. It felt as if a penny-scented bathroom freshener had been sprayed in my face.

"You're afraid," Lumpy said. "Admit it."

I felt my bellybutton telescoping inward with nausea. "No, I'm not. I feel bad for you. You're excited about pennies."

He scooped up a handful of pennies and brought them to his nose as if they were fresh coffee beans and he were an old man on TV. Mom had gotten rid of our TV—too metallic—and I missed it. TV could be muted.

"If you don't want to play anymore, I'm leaving," he said.

If I mashed my tongue against the roof of my mouth, I could usually stop myself from crying. A vein behind my front teeth was throbbing gently and I pressed it with my tongue as hard as I could. When he pretended to throw a penny at me, I flinched like a first-grader. "Stop," I said.

"Settle down," he said. "Why do you squirm so much?"

He dropped a handful of pennies on the floor and I felt a horrible ache in my spine. The sides of my face started to hurt because my jaw was too tight.

"I'll get you a tissue," he said, reaching for the magazine.

I yanked the pillowcase out of his hands. It was a sloppy show of muscle, and gallons of pennies crashed all over the floor. We watched them clatter across the room until they spun to a flat stop, or disappeared under the couch.

I braced myself for a beating. But the beating never came. Lumpy looked at me as if I were durable. No one, not once in my life, had ever done this.

"Watch," he said, and stuffed a handful of pennies into his mouth.

When Mom's teeth banged against her fork during dinner, my nerves were more awake than any other time we were together, more awake then when she gave me a hug before bed and in the morning. Every nerve in my body was aware of Lumpy's teeth crunching against pennies. His jaw sounded like a chain being kicked.

"I dare you to swallow," I said.

He spat out the pennies.

"I will if you will," he said.

The pennies felt hot against my fingers. A long time ago, I had a little book about a man who shoveled coal into an oven on a train. The oven's belly got so hot it turned the color of a heart.

"On three," Lumpy said.

I didn't want to die.

"Two," he said.

I didn't want to be alone.

"One."

Both of us lifted pennies above our heads and let the metal rain come down on us. I kept my mouth and eyes shut and let the pennies stick to my sockets and bounce off my face. My body shivered in the wrong direction, starting with my skin and moving down into my bones. If I opened my mouth, the pennies would probably taste as familiar as morning breath. I could tell from the wet sounds I was hearing that Lumpy was really doing it. Pennies were going down the hole in his mouth. At first I thought he'd faked it but I heard a far-away sloshing, as if his stomach were trying to hide its contents. I wanted to barf because Lumpy wasn't barfing. His oily cheeks were fatter and redder than ever. Maybe it was a magic trick. No, it wasn't—Lumpy stuck out his tongue and burped. A single leftover coin fell to the floor.

His face looked like it was going to slide off his head. Whatever lived inside his skull and steered him around and made him swallow pennies was about to expose itself, and prove it was realer and meaner than me.

"Swallow," he said.

Once the pee starts dribbling out it's really hard to fake bravery. "I can't," I said.

Lumpy picked up a new handful and stood close to my face. His penny breath made my eyes sting.

"You have to do it," he said.

I clenched all my teeth and pulled back my lips so he could see every last tooth. With one hand he grabbed my neck. When I finally gasped for air he was able to shove a single penny inside, but I dug my fingernails into his strangling hand as if it were crusty bread. When his hand unclenched I spat the penny in his face.

"I'll do it myself," I said.

He smiled. I leaned down as if to grab a fistful of coins, but instead I grabbed the raccoon. I was done.

Lumpy cocked his head in confusion right before I whacked him above the eye. The raccoon popped with a crunch and some of the thick yellow foam his dad had sprayed down its throat came back up and out. Lumpy fell with a bang on top of the box.

Nothing was ever under control. "You deserve it," I said.

Lumpy was still blinking way too hard. He was dizzy and wanted to get up.

"If this is how you treat a friend then you deserve it."

He looked as if he had been paused.

"If I ever meet your dad, I'm going to tell him you deserve it."

Faster than he'd fallen down, he was up and running at me, but I was already out the front door.

From the porch I tugged on the knob as hard as I could, trying to hold him inside. There was so much rain coming down I couldn't see the street. I wanted to barf like a change machine at an arcade after someone shoved a million dollar bill inside me. Lumpy was pulling from the other side of the door as if his life were the one at risk. When I started to lose the tug-o-war, Lumpy slipped his hand around the side of the door so he could pull with more force. I spat on his knuckles. This weakened his grip for a half second, and I slammed the door as hard as I could on his fingers.

Lumpy screamed and fell back into the apartment. Through the door I heard books thrown against the wall. A shelf was pulled down, slapping like a giant's hand against the floor. Couch cushions were ripped open. All of these sounds might have been Lumpy's screaming. My clothes were soaked all the way through and the skin on my chest was humming as if it had been plugged in.

Mom said that breathing deeply can help us accept what's happening. I was breathing deeply to resist it. Soon my legs were shaking too much and I had to lay down on the doormat. When I took my thumb in my mouth it tasted like a spoon. I bit the bottom of the nail as hard as I could, and a tiny lake of blood bloomed beneath the nail. It wasn't silver, it was ordinary, red and dark, and whatever was wrong with it couldn't be seen. No one could say that about Lumpy.

I blacked out.

Someone was dragging me back into the apartment by my arms. The tape covering each nailhead on the floor brushed against my back until I came to a stop and heard someone crying.

It wasn't Mom.

"Don't leave," he said.

He would not let go.

Some gifts might be impossible to receive. But I did not imagine this. The acceptance streaming out of his hands, reversing directions and then coming back to me again, over and over. This felt realer than the world.

If I kept my eyes closed, he would say it again.

"Please. Don't leave."

Pineapple Head

By Joel Enos

Carl's school dated back to the turn of the last century. While much of it had been updated in the last decade, the east wing was a sad mix of misguided seventies facelifts over moldy mid-century modern over basically ancient broken useless things.

The keys to the mythical bathroom in the mostly unused teachers' lounge were a coveted prize for a student. For years, Carl had heard tell of this far removed room with clean stalls and walls and no waiting in lines. Now that he was a senior and a teacher's assistant for Mr. Walcott's Advanced Placement History class, he had the keys in his hand at last.

Because there was only one teacher's assistant allowed per period, the bathroom was all Carl's this morning, the first day of the new semester of his last year of high school. And he was going to enjoy it.

So Carl was surprised that someone was already inside the first door when he clicked it open with the old key.

The boy lounging in one of the threadbare chairs wore ill-fitting clothes. Not in an "I don't care" way. But in a carefully slouchy, calculated, oversized fit way. The canvas jacket was an ill-advised shade of not-quite-olive that sloped off the boy's already slender shoulders so much that the seams were almost to his elbows. The rolled sleeves at the wrist gave the impression that his forearms were strangely truncated. On his arms were a mishmash of black rubber rings, leather straps, and what looked like shoelaces tied amongst copper, silver and cheap imitation gold bracelets. The boy's hands were covered in rings, including one with some kind of Celtic knot, and one with an oversized blue stone that was probably plastic.

The t-shirt the boy wore under his jacket was black, faded, and loose at the neck because it was probably at least three sizes too big. His pants were a clashing shade of not-quite-green with seams sewn into them vertically, adding fabric to create a ballooning effect that again dwarfed his already slight shape. The only thing form fitting on him were the bottoms of his pants, which were tightly bunched and rolled to show a bit of leg over enormous yellow socks that were sticking out of surprisingly small black boots. The overall effect made the boy look like some kind of overgrown wraith-like elf.

And then there was the haircut, closely shaved all the way round the sides and back, but leaving the top an unkempt stalk of sandy brown weed-like hair.

That ridiculous haircut was why Carl eventually found himself calling the boy, who never did tell Carl his real name even after all that happened, "Pineapple Head." Facetiously at first, as a comment on the boy's unfortunate style choices. And then, as things progressed, affectionately and without irony or malice.

But that first time, the day they met, all he could muster was, "Hey."

"Hey," the boy said without looking up at Carl.

"Um, are you a teacher's assistant?" Carl asked, eyeing that important next door, which led to the fabled bathroom stalls.

"Not anymore," the boy said.

"Uh, ok." Carl walked past the boy to the next door, the one to the actual bathroom, and clicked it open. The bathroom was all he could have wanted and more. Small and spare, but clean and best of all, pretty much unused by the unwashed masses of the student body or even the teachers.

He was going to get to go to the bathroom in clean serene peace for an entire semester. It would be the best thing about high school.

Only it wasn't. Though that lounge did bring about what was...

Pineapple Head wasn't in the lounge when Carl came out of the bathroom. The dilapidated velvet chair was empty, though it did show an indentation where Pineapple Head and countless other teacher's assistants had killed time before going back to their paper grading and coffee getting and pencil sharpening for exams. Carl almost sat in the chair himself, but he didn't. Not that first time, anyway. Not alone.

A full week passed before Carl saw Pineapple Head again. The fact that he was wearing exactly the same clothes as before was not as strange as their conversation. Carl had not been able to stop thinking about the odd boy all week. But though he had gone to the hidden room a few times, he'd never run into him again. Until today.

"Right on time," said Pineapple Head.

"For what?" asked Carl.

"Conversation with a lost soul."

"Oh." Carl had thought about what to say to this kid for a week, but now that the opportunity arose, he was at a loss.

"I'm not a Goth," the boy said before Carl could say anything or walk away. And for the first time, the boy raised his eyes to lock onto Carl's. "I'm not. It's not a thing for me."

"I wasn't going to…" Carl's voice trailed off.

"I'm not though. In fact, I didn't even know what that was when I got dressed that morning, or any morning. It wasn't a thing at all." The boy was adamant.

"I guess with your haircut I'd say you were more alternative anyway than just Goth, if you want to label yourself," Carl said helpfully.

"Alternative's not a thing for me either. Or Industrial. Or Progressive. Or Indie. Or Emo. None of it." Adamant again.

"What's Industrial?" Carl asked.

"What year is this?" The boy looked a little worried.

Carl started to worry too. Maybe this kid was on something. Could he be dangerous? "Uh, I have to pee and get back to Mr. Walcott's room."

"Go," Pineapple Head said, looking away. Carl hadn't realized how intent their locked gaze had been. When the boy finally looked away, Carl let out the breath he'd not even realized he'd been holding, seeing stars. "We'll get to this another time."

So Carl went. And this time it was almost three weeks before he saw Pineapple Head again.

And, yes, Pineapple Head was wearing the same clothes again. But this time he opened the conversation with a new topic.

"There are other people who dress like me, you know."

"I didn't…" Carl started. Man, this guy was hung up on labels.

"I didn't make this up. I copied it," said the boy. "It's what different people dress like. I'm different. I'm not like the other people here. I'm not like you. You're a normal. Right?" Again with the eye-locking.

Carl was suddenly intently aware of what he thought of as his 'uniform', his easy to match jeans and t-shirt and hoodie combo that worked well with either the white Adidas or the black Adidas, depending on which he grabbed.

"It's how I show people I'm different, you know," said Pineapple Head, staring hard.

"I get it," Carl said. He really did have to pee. And this talk was really not making a whole lot of sense.

"Do you, Carl?" Pineapple Head asked.

It wasn't till after Carl had gone to the bathroom and made his way back to Mr. Walcott's room that he realized he'd never actually told Pineapple Head his name. And that it was rather odd that, even though there were hundreds of students in Carl's graduating class, he'd never seen Pineapple Head before. Not even once. And with that haircut, he'd have remembered.

The next day, Pineapple Head was in the lounge. No waiting time between appearances this week.

"How do you know my name?" Carl asked.

"You told me the first time you came here," Pineapple Head said.

"I really didn't," said Carl.

"Didn't you?" Another gaze from Pineapple Head. But this time Carl didn't look away.

"You're not a teacher's assistant. And you're not as mysterious as you try to be."

"I'm not trying to be mysterious," Pineapple Head said. "I'm being careful."

"About what?"

"About you and what you'll do if I tell you certain things."

"Well, since you seem to be magic and know my name, why don't you just *see* how I'll act and don't be so weird."

"It doesn't work like that." Pineapple Head paused. "You think I'm weird?"

"No. But you think you're weird. So there's that." Carl turned to leave.

"Don't you have to go to the bathroom?" Pineapple Head asked.

Carl turned back around. "No, I came here to talk to you, but I think I'm done for now."

"Whatever." Pineapple Head was staring at the rings on his hands.

Pineapple Head wasn't in the lounge for a whole month.

When Pineapple Head showed up the next time, Carl just said it. He figured he had to.

"You know I'm gay too, right?"

Pineapple Head just stared at him.

Carl went into the bathroom, did what he needed to do, and when he came back into the lounge, almost jumped.

Pineapple Head was still there sitting in the chair. He'd never still been there when Carl came out of the bathroom before.

"You're brave to just say stuff like that," Pineapple Head said. "What if I freaked out and got all weird?"

"Uh, I'd tell Mr. Walcott an asshole was in the teachers' lounge and he'd make you leave so you didn't bother me," Carl said.

"You'd tell your teacher you like guys?" Pineapple Head asked.

"I mean, yeah, I guess, but I mean…they just know by now. I've gone to school here for three years," Carl said.

"You…" Pineapple Head seemed unable to get out the words. "You just, like… You just tell people?"

"Well," Carl said. "I don't, like, wear a sign or anything, but I'm on the mentor committee for the group home and I liked Adam Lambert more than the rest of America, apparently."

"Is he a politician?" asked Pineapple Head.

"Who?"

"What if your teachers tell your parents?" Pineapple Head ignored Carl's confusion.

"Tell them what?"

"About you…"

"Well," Carl said slowly. "They are my parents. So they kind of know me better than my teachers do."

Pineapple Head looked scared and fascinated.

"Are they hippies?"

"No, but my grandparents probably were," said Carl. "But to be honest, they are weirder about it than my parents. My mom is actually a teacher, but at an elementary school. And my dad works at a tech company. He's kind of a nerd. My mom's much cooler. Or she used to be. She doesn't wear her nose ring anymore, but she still has some tattoos. Though it's kind of embarrassing. I think she used to be in a band, but they never really got famous. She still goes out with her friends once in a while. I call it old lady dancing, but not to her face. She's alright. They are alright."

"Your parents sound cooler than any parents I've ever heard of. Are they young?"

"I don't know, like 55?" That sounded old enough to Carl so it was probably about right.

"Wow," Pineapple Head said.

"Yeah, not young." Carl shrugged.

"That's not really what I meant." Pineapple Head looked a little confused. Carl wasn't sure what he meant, but Mr. Walcott had a lot for him to do today so he needed to get back.

"I have to go," Carl said. "But if you're around tomorrow I can come earlier and we can keep talking."

"It's got to be the right time," Pineapple Head told him. "I mean, I can stay later though, if you want to talk more. But you have to come at the right time. To start…"

"Okay…" Carl said. Whatever. The kid enjoyed being mysterious. It was definitely a thing.

So Carl came at the right time, over and over and over, and that's how he started to get to know Pineapple Head. And to realize that he never saw him outside of the lounge, or if he was a little late for their meetings. It wasn't long before Carl developed a very crazy theory about Pineapple Head, who seemed out of time, trapped forever in the lounge where he had hidden from other kids, from his parents, his teachers, his fears and most of all himself.

Pineapple Head was fascinated by how much things had changed since he was in high school. But Carl would also point out how much certain things had stayed the same. And how while people weren't allowed to be as outright hostile as they were when Pineapple Head wandered the halls of this place, that didn't mean people still weren't cruel. And there were methods now of being anonymously cruel in a very personal way… which made no real sense to Pineapple Head in theory, but as a practice, he understood it far too well.

Pineapple Head asked Carl one morning, theoretically, if he thought it was actually less acceptable now to tell people he was spending his mornings with a ghost than living his life truthfully.

Carl told him that it probably was.

And then he said, "It'd be even weirder if I told them I was in love with one."

"One what?" Pineapple Head wasn't the best at following trains of thought.

"A ghost," Carl said, staring straight at him to see what he'd do.

Pineapple Head looked concerned.

"You can't do that, Carl," he said very seriously. "Because it doesn't turn out well. I've heard about this."

"You talk to other ghosts?" Carl asked.

"It's not a term we use amongst ourselves," Pineapple Head said.

"What, 'ghost'? Or 'talk'?"

"Either, really," said Pineapple Head. "But that's not what's important. What's important is that I'm in love with you too…and we can't do that."

Carl's heart hurt.

"Whatever." He turned to leave.

"We can't, Carl," Pineapple Head said again. "It ends us both when it's over. And you're alive. You're alive in a world I can't imagine. With a future that's brighter than I could have thought."

Carl turned back around to face him. Pineapple Head had tears running down his face.

"This could be your world," Carl said, voice shaking. "You killed yourself, didn't you? You ended your interesting, beautiful, weird, stupid haircut life because of what other people thought of you."

"I would not have grown up in your time, Carl," Pineapple Head said. "I came to terms with my decision a long time ago. I've had a lot of time to think, to regret, to understand, and to find calm."

"Is it that simple?" Carl asked.

"It's not simple," Pineapple Head said. "But it *is*. And you *are*. And we're *this*."

"But maybe this is okay," Carl dared take a step closer to Pineapple Head.

"It's not okay, Carl," said Pineapple Head. "But you are. I never was. I never was. Please know that. I wouldn't be now either. But the brightness that you see ahead of you is real. I am not that brightness, Carl."

"I don't really care."

305

"You will, Carl." Pineapple Head gave him that gaze. "You've taught me so much and now I'm able to do something I couldn't do before."

"What's that?" Carl asked.

"I can come to terms with what's going to happen next."

Carl had never watched Pineapple Head leave the lounge. Usually he just left first and when he returned later Pineapple Head would be gone. Or he'd go in and use the bathroom and come out and the chair would be empty. But this time was different.

Pineapple Head didn't shimmer or glow, or, god forbid, sparkle. He just seemed to get dimmer...till he wasn't there anymore.

Carl stifled a sudden sob, but he didn't actually cry. He just walked over to Pineapple Head's beaten up chair and, for the first time, sat down. It was not warm like he'd expect after a person had been sitting in it. But it was, well, the only way to describe it was this: happy. With just a hint of hopeful.

Carl sat there for a long time. Just feeling. And then he got up and walked out of the lounge. He never went back. He knew Pineapple Head wasn't going to be there. And he knew that Pineapple Head was right. The world was out there, waiting for Carl. And it was going to be so much more mysterious, and strange and frightening and beautiful, than sitting in a dark old teachers' lounge with an interesting ghost.

Grass Girl

By Caroline M. Yoachim

The other girls are made of driftwood, but I'm made of bamboo that whistles in the wind. My bamboo makes a hollow thud when the other girls kick pebbles at my legs on our way to school.

"Bamboo isn't wood, it's grass," Sylvia says. She isn't kicking pebbles, and I can't tell if her statement is meant to be an insult or an observation.

Sylvia is the most popular and prettiest of all the girls. She's made of smooth driftwood with smoky quartz eyes. The other girls hang on her every word, and after she mentions my bamboo, they mock me.

"Do you fall over when the wind blows, grass girl?"

"Solid beats hollow."

"Hey grass girl, the monkeys look hungry."

I ignore their taunts. The monkeys only eat fresh shoots and leaves, not the thick woody stems of bamboo that I am made of. Sometimes they nibble at my seaweed hair, but that's no big loss since I have to redo it with fresh seaweed every couple days anyway.

When we get to school, the other girls leave me alone. They don't want to get in trouble. The teachers dismantle girls who misbehave, usually only for a couple hours but one time for an entire week.

I'm supposed to learn the species name for every variety of willow tree, but instead I daydream about replacing my bamboo with driftwood.

At night, I comb the beach. Eventually I find a nice flat piece to replace my left foot, and swap out the old for the new. I hurl my unwanted bamboo foot into the ocean. It makes an eerie whistle as it flies through the air—a wail of loss, as if the small segments of bamboo are sad that they're no longer part of me.

It's hard to walk with one foot wood and one bamboo. I practice on the beach until the moon sets, checking my footprints in the sand to see how badly I'm dragging my heavy new foot. When I go to bed, I'm exhausted.

The next morning I catch up with all the other girls on the path that winds through the bamboo grove and up the hill to our school. Despite my practice last night, I'm limping.

"Nice foot, grass girl," Sylvia says. She's looking at my foot with a thoughtful expression on her face, and I think she maybe means it as a compliment. The other girls are not as kind.

"Hey grass girl, your feet don't match."

"One good foot isn't going to make up for the rest."

"Too weak to walk, grass girl?"

The words sting. I'm supposed to go learn about botanical history, but instead I go back to the beach to look for more driftwood. I find a few small pieces that will make good fingers, and a curved piece for my jawbone. I leave my old bamboo body parts in the sand. When the tide comes up, the waves will wash them all away.

I notice a nice piece of seaweed, the shiny dark-green kind that makes the nicest hair. I've always thought my hair was one of my better features, for all that I have to replace it every couple nights. None of the other girls have seaweed hair. They all have shells or bones that don't need to be redone as often.

I pick up the seaweed and bring it home.

"Mom, why didn't you make me more like everyone else?"

"Because you're you," Mom answers. "You're special."

She helps me weave my seaweed into my scalp, and the wind blows across her bamboo fingers in a low whistle. Three of her fingers are split, and she'll need to replace them soon. I suggest that we go out together to look for new fingers, thinking that maybe I can convince her to switch over to driftwood too.

I'm disappointed when she insists on going to the bamboo grove instead of the beach. After she finds her new fingers, she points out some other nice stems, and mentions that lighter feet are easier to walk with. I refuse to take the hint. Solid beats hollow.

When I'm about half wood, the other girls stop calling me grass girl and mostly leave me alone. But the girl whose approval I really want is gone. Sylvia hasn't been coming to school, and nobody knows where she went. Or nobody will tell me, anyway.

I wander through the bamboo grove on my way to the beach, whacking the tall poles of bamboo with my hand and listening to the hollow sound. When I tap my arm, I hear the satisfying clack of wood on wood. I am becoming sturdy and strong. I don't whistle in the wind.

I go farther down the beach than I've ever walked before—all the way to the stony cliffs. I'm determined to find as much wood as possible. When I get to the end of the sand, I find a girl reclined against the cliffs, her body made entirely of stone. The tide is high and warm ocean waves wash up onto her feet, but she doesn't move.

If wood is unchanging, solid and good, stone must be even better. The stone girl is beautiful, gray and still, serene despite the waves that crash over her feet. Indestructible. Her eyes are smoky quartz. "Sylvia?"

She doesn't answer at first. When she eventually speaks, her voice is raspy like crashing waves. "Please help me. I remade myself in stone, but now I'm too tired to move."

Grass Girl | *Caroline M. Yoachim*

I tried to figure out what to do. Of all the girls, she's always been the least mean, even though she's the most popular. I don't see any driftwood nearby. Someone must have stolen the pieces of her old body, or maybe the waves have reclaimed it for the ocean.

She's too heavy to lift; I need something to replace the stones. I run to the bamboo grove, and the trip takes longer than it should—my driftwood body is so much heavier than my bamboo was. I gather up an armful of bamboo and run back to the cliffs.

The bamboo in my arms whistles as I run.

I replace Sylvia's stone arms with bamboo and bind her together with seaweed. When only her legs are stone, I'm able to help her to her feet.

We walk slowly up the beach because her stone legs make it hard for her to move. On our way to the bamboo grove, we meet a girl made of the smooth driftwood that had once belonged to Sylvia. They are the same pieces, but somehow this new girl doesn't wear them as well. She lacks Sylvia's grace. The new girl sneers at Sylvia's bamboo, then looks down at her legs.

"Sylvia?" she asks. "I thought you'd gone all the way to stone."

"I did. I changed my mind." She shrugs like it was no big deal, and I marvel at her confidence, to not care that another girl is seeing her while she's half stone and half grass, and honestly looking like a complete mess.

I glance down at my own body, with its patchwork of driftwood pieces, mixed together with my last remaining scraps of bamboo. It's better than the body Sylvia has, but she's proud and I'm ashamed. Why do I want to be all solid and unchanging, anyway? Who says the solid clack of wood is better than the hollow whistle of bamboo?

I sit in the sand by the bamboo grove and rebuild myself as I had been before, a girl of grass, with gorgeous seaweed hair. Sylvia sits with me and replaces the stone in her legs with bamboo so that she can be a grass girl, too. The ocean wind blows through our fingers, and the music it makes is beautiful.

The Birds of Azalea Street

By Nova Ren Suma

When the police questioned me—same as they questioned Paisley and Katie-Marie—they didn't want to hear about the birds. They weren't paying attention. None of the adults around here ever did. Even when the body bag was carted out, on wheels, and the wheels got caught in a gopher hole in the lawn, and the stretcher knocked into the tree, and the sudden motion caused a whole host of birds to burst out of the branches, exploding into the blue over our subdivision, and I looked up after them, and the EMTs guiding the stretcher stopped and looked up, and all my neighbors who'd gathered to see what the commotion was about looked up, heavenward, into the sky, even then they thought it meant nothing. "So that's where the birds have been hiding," one of my neighbors said. Not one adult could connect it to the fact that Leonard was now dead.

I knew the birds were no longer hungry—they'd feasted and had their fill, and now they took off, every last one of them, satisfied. But the adults of Azalea Street, curious about the murder, seeing as it was the first since our subdivision was founded, gathered in knots on our landscaped sidewalk corners to talk. They were hungry for information and gory details. They should have looked out of their windows sooner. They should have been watching. We were.

Truth is, we'd been watching out for our neighbor Leonard for years. Since we hit puberty, and for some of us, that was way early. Since forever and always, it felt like. Before we saw him bring that girl home in the dead of night, all we knew was that he'd been trying to get his hands on us.

My house on Azalea Street was next door to his house, so I'd say I got the worst of it, what with my parents always feeling sorry for him and inviting him for dinner on Sundays. The three of them would sip watery pre-dinner drinks out back by the bug zapper, and somehow my parents would miss how, when he apologized for his stomach growling, the object he had his eyes hooked on wasn't the cheese plate. It was me.

He said things to me sometimes, in the hallway while heading for the guest bathroom. Did I have a boyfriend yet? Did I ever happen to try the kind of kissing that used tongue? Then he'd shuffle away, fast, making me question what I'd heard. When I caught him looking at me later, over the pear tart he'd brought from next door, or over the sugar-dusted strudel, I saw his round black glasses go dim with sweat and fog.

Other girls had run-ins with him too. Some of our fathers and stepfathers used to work with Leonard at the plant, before he got downsized and they got to keep their jobs, so they said we had to be civil. Even kind. Our mothers and stepmothers appreciated how he'd bring something fresh-baked for potlucks and fund-raisers, like a Bundt cake or a still-warm pie. None of our parents saw what we could see, which had us decide that growing up into adulthood must mean going blind.

Teenage girls know more than we're given credit for. We sense danger even when everyone's telling us it's fine, he's a perfectly nice man, an upstanding member of our community, have you *tasted* his sugar-cream pie?

When Leonard's gaudy lawn came into view, we knew it was time to cross the street. Ever since he lost his job, he liked to feed the birds, and he hung lots of birdhouses, spilled lots of seed.

It seemed innocent from the outside, maybe. But out back, from over the white picket fence that separated Leonard's house from mine, I could swear I heard the shots. Little pops in the air. I was never sure of it, never positive. But one time there was a squawk and a feathered eruption as a bird went down.

I can't prove he shot it, but I did see him hunching over it, kicking it with his enormous shoe. Other times I suspected he used poison in the feeders. This was slower and left them stiff, so when they fell from their

315

perches they dropped to the ground like rocks. I found one over the fence on our side of the lawn once—red-bellied and dark-feathered, its beak open mid-bite—and I buried it in an orange shoebox, the most cheerful I could find, near where we made the cairn for Buster.

When the birds stopped coming—not just to Leonard's house, but to my house and to the Willards' house across the street, to Aggie's house a few doors down, to any house I passed on the way to the bus stop and back, all our trees birdless, all our patches of sky clean—I guess he turned to other hobbies. That must have been when he bought the camera.

We'd catch him standing on his porch, fancy long-lensed camera trained outward like he was waiting for a finch or a woodpecker. But with all feathery creatures avoiding his feeders, he couldn't have been aiming for the birds. His telephoto lens was as long as an arm and seemed suspiciously trained at the sidewalk. When Katie-Marie went past in her field hockey skirt, on the way to my house from her house so my mom could drive us to practice, she swore she could hear his camera snapping. She took off in a run.

The last time one of us was alone with him, it was Paisley. She said he cornered her in his kitchen and forced her to bake bread. Her mom had sent her on an errand, wanting one of Leonard's recipes, and when Paisley knocked on his back door, she found him elbow-deep in flour, prepping sticky coils of corpse-pale dough.

"Why, hello there," he said in his deep baritone. His lips were pink and plushy and we didn't like to look at them when he shaped words.

Paisley told us she could sense the hunger coming off of him, like she was plump and roasting and he hadn't eaten for a week.

She heard a faint titter behind her, a lone bird that had lost its way in the treetops over our subdivision and drifted to the wrong set of branches over the wrong house. Or maybe it wasn't lost and that was a warning call. Maybe it knew what was about to be set in motion.

Paisley stepped inside his house.

"What're you doing?" Paisley had said. I would have asked for the recipe without going in, I would have told my mom to just get Leonard to e-mail it, but Paisley pressed her whole body into his kitchen and let the door shut behind her. She leaned forward on the counter, letting her long hair fall and her split ends dance. She took a finger. With it, she traced a word in the flour dusting on the counter for him to see. It said *hi*. She was testing him. She was testing herself.

Leonard lit up. We imagined it wasn't often a teenage girl started a conversation with him voluntarily. He was pink in the face usually, but at that point he was bright red.

He began talking. He kind of couldn't shut up. He was explaining his method for baking braided bread, and then it became very important, essential even,

317

to teach Paisley how to properly knead the dough in order to do it herself. She had to put effort into it, use all her strength and not hold back. It's just that she had such small hands.

On the windowsill, while this was going on, the bird was perched, black-eyed and unblinking. Paisley only thought it was weird later. Leonard was behind Paisley, very close, so close, she couldn't back up and get around him. She felt the bird watching. She smelled Leonard's yeasty breath.

We know our parents wouldn't believe us if we told them. Leonard was only *instructing* her. He was only being a *kind neighbor,* which in these times was a dying breed. That's what they would have said. They wanted us to have skills beyond phone-scrolling and one-finger texting, like knowing how to bake edible food in the oven and feed ourselves if they suddenly were dead.

But we believed Paisley right away. We knew he was too close. We knew how he pressed his front up against her to adjust her technique and how he breathed heavy, shaggy breaths against the nape of her neck. We knew how much he was enjoying this.

"Knead," he told her in a low, careful voice. "Go on, yes, like that. Knead."

He meant the slick mush in her hands, but Paisley had had enough. Out of all of us, she was the strongest, and that went far beyond her arm-wrestling skills against her brothers and the thick runner's muscles in her legs. She told us she'd only wanted to prove he was a perv, prove it once and for all so there was no longer any question, and with this little bakery demonstration, she had won.

She elbowed him in the stomach and whipped a braid of wet dough at his rosy, stubbly face. She dodged him and was heading for the door before the dough was even on the baking sheet, before the baking sheet was even in the blazing oven, before the bread had risen, before it had browned. She was breathing fast. The bird outside the window flapped its wings in a frantic slap and took off.

Behind Paisley, there was a strange sound. A faint, high-pitched whimper. In a moment of weakness, Paisley paused and turned back.

He was talking, but his voice was different now. Smaller in his throat. Pathetic.

He only wanted to teach somebody something, he called after her. He was sorry, he said, he didn't mean to scare her, it's just that he led such a lonely life.

The door was open. The sky bare and blank.

Paisley held still in the entryway. She was questioning herself, having a peculiar moment of compassion. Sometimes she could be so very live-and-let-live.

"Maybe…" Paisley started.

Leonard pinkened—or else he was standing in direct range of the oven light.

"Maybe you should get a dog," she said at last. "So you're not so lonely."

He looked down the length of his giant legs to his giant feet. No dogs, he said. Animals didn't like him for some reason. He shrugged.

Paisley smirked. She had a dark streak. "Then you should buy a blow-up doll online and make her your wife," she said. "I can send you a link." At this, his mouth gaping open, his cheeks full of flames, she took off. She'd gotten what she came for: Leonard's sugar-cream pie recipe for her mother was already secured in hand.

But so was the thought of Leonard getting himself a girl.

It was Paisley, we've agreed, who gave him the idea. He couldn't have her, and he couldn't have any of the rest of us, but his hunger was still there, eating at him.

It was days later when we heard his car pull into his driveway in the middle of the night. His house was one of the smaller designs in our subdivision and didn't have a garage, so we could see everything from my bedroom window. There was nowhere he could hide.

Usually his car held only him and sometimes a tripod or some grocery bags. That night we noted the questionable shadow in his passenger seat. It was taller than usual. It had a distinctly human-size head.

Had he listened to Paisley and bought himself a make-believe companion? No. Our illusion was shattered when he circled the car to open the passenger-side door, and the shadow moved on its own and stepped out.

What he came home with that night couldn't be brought to life with a tire pump. She was already alive and breathing. We would have sworn she was real.

She wore a dark hood, and around it was a haze of fur, like she'd just landed in our subdivision from the North Pole and didn't realize that, down here, it was spring.

The problem with the hood was that it hid her face. And her puffy coat hid the rest of her, though it did stop at her hips, and her legs could be made out beneath it. Even from my bedroom window next door, with a picket fence between us and the dark having fallen and the motion sensors not responding to the motion as she walked past where we swore they were. Even with all that, I could see her legs. Her legs were in black stockings, the kind with seams. At the end of her legs were little pointed blades that took to the pavement like ice picks. When she touched grass, her heels sunk in and she stopped and the light from the car door showed us one leg bent to retrieve the shoe. I wanted a leg like that. I wanted to grow up and look like that and have two.

Paisley was sleeping over. So was Katie-Marie.

"Leonard has a new friend," Paisley announced. "A *lady* friend. Did you know about this, Tasha? You knew, and didn't tell us?"

I shook my head, unable to keep my eyes off the lady in the night. She'd retrieved her shoe, slipped it back on. She was now standing still on the lawn while he was closing the car door. The fur lining on her coat rippled in the wind like a layer of black feathers. Her legs didn't fidget or pace or shake, showing no hint of nerves. Leonard was right there. He was *right there*, and she didn't run.

"I've never seen her before," I said. I would have remembered.

But there was something about the way she moved. She didn't seem surprised by the clutter of ugly, vacant dollhouses meant to entice the nonexistent birds. She wove around the maze-like lawn as if she'd been here before.

"Is she tied up in the trunk?" Katie-Marie called out from across the room. "Is she bound and gagged?"

Katie-Marie couldn't see the scene outside. She was lying on my bed, an arm draped over her eyes. Before we heard Leonard's car, we'd been trying to psychically impress boys we liked into becoming our boyfriends by thinking about them with pointed intention and hoping, somehow, across the airwaves, they heard. Paisley had long given up on Georges, and I only halfheartedly tried to psychically seduce Takeshi because I was pretty sure he liked me already and I figured I didn't have to try so hard. But Katie-Marie really wanted Mike, and her forehead was all scrunched up with effort.

The power of the mind was something we experimented with on Friday night sleepovers. Also light-as-a-feather-stiff-as-a-board, and the Ouija, before Katie-Marie's dad burned it in her backyard.

We also tried texting boys alluring emoticons and, on one brave night, posted photos of our faceless boobs to a message board, but then took them down fast when the comments got scary and promised among us that we'd never show the photos to anyone, not even Georges or Takeshi or Mike.

After Paisley's visit to Leonard's house, we had wished harm on him and tried out our psychic impressions to make that happen. We realized it would be easiest if he just went away, so we wished him gone, like to Florida. Then he showed up for Sunday dinner like always, my father sharing a cigar with him in the garage, where he thought we couldn't smell the stink, and I had to admit our magical thinking wasn't making any magic. Leonard was still here.

All that seemed so juvenile now. Leonard had real live company, and we couldn't see who it was.

"Leonard's friend is walking on her own two feet," I narrated for Katie-Marie. "Leonard's friend's nails are painted"—I waited for it as she reached up to touch one of his gaudy hanging birdhouses, then recoiled like it stung—"ooh, black."

"No," Paisley corrected me. "Purple."

She was right. His lady friend had dark, deep-purple-painted nails, and they were long and curling, almost like claws. The hand seemed to lift up and out. It seemed to face us, to be motioning our way, like it was...waving. Then the sleeve dropped and hid her hand from view.

I blinked.

"She has very nice legs," Paisley said.

Katie-Marie finally opened her eyes and crawled over to join us by the window. "I hope he doesn't bake her in his oven like he tried to do with you, Pais," she whispered.

Paisley nodded solemnly.

We lost the will to make jokes or even talk. We watched as Leonard unlocked the front door and his friend entered his house. We knew the layout because there were only five different kinds of architecturally approved homes for the subdivision, and his was the one with the front porch and the sunken living room and the two bedrooms that had windows like eyes on the second floor. She must have gone down to the living room, because we didn't see a light come on.

Leonard came out once more and headed for the trunk. He seemed so eager. We watched him lift something out, and at first we assumed it must have been a suitcase, but then we noticed the odd, bulky shape and the way he had to circle it with his long arms. The bird cage was round and empty, as far as we could tell from this distance, and it had a latched and gated entrance that flapped in the wind. He carried it toward the house and didn't return for more luggage.

Her legs had told us one thing. Her lack of suitcase another. But it was the quivering smile on Leonard's face when he walked under the porch light that told us so much more.

*

The first night there were no birds, as usual. The first night was dark and quiet. The first night was long.

The second night, Paisley and Katie-Marie stayed at my place again, even though Katie-Marie's house had satellite TV and all the premium channels, and we perched at my Leonard-facing windows. We'd skipped dinner. We were worried for his lady friend and had lost our appetites. She hadn't come outside all day, which meant we hadn't seen her leave. We discussed ways of sending over a warning, like slipped in the mail slot, or left on the welcome mat to tell her she should not feel so welcome, but we knew he'd see it before she did. We tried looking up his number and couldn't find it, so we couldn't call and feign wrong number if he picked up. We were deep in discussion when she appeared at the window across the way.

The light came on, a bright spot in the darkness, and we ran to the window, huddling under the sill. One by one, we popped a head up.

Paisley said she was prettier than she thought she'd be—a high nine to Leonard's withering two—but to me, her face was exactly how I'd pictured it, as if I'd selected her from a catalog. Or conjured her up from the *Vogue*-glossy pages of my imagination and sent her here. In a way it felt like I had.

She was all mystery. She had dark, low-lidded eyes and a small, subtle mouth that did not seem capable

325

of making a smile. Her cheekbones reflected stabs of light. Her hair was purple-black, much like her nails. It was wild, ragged, coasting into her eyes. I wanted to get close enough to see her eyes.

"Do you think she goes to our school?" Katie-Marie said.

We were getting bothered by how young she looked. She wasn't so much a lady as a girl like we were. The age difference couldn't have been much. Chop off a couple, and she could have been us.

"No," I said. "No way she goes to our school." She didn't look like she lived around here—she didn't look like any girl we knew.

"We should go in there," Paisley said. "Tasha, your parents made you water his plants when he was away on vacation that one time, didn't they? We need a key to his house."

I knew where the hide-a-key was kept—it looked like a rock under the fifth shrub. But should we break in right then, in the middle of the night? Should we barge in, guns blazing? The only weapons we had were a field hockey stick and a bottle of slick, sticky leave-in conditioner to aim at the eyes.

"We can't go in there!" Katie-Marie said. "We have to talk to her from here."

I nodded.

She was in the bathroom window, at the sink. We could tell by the way she bent down, and how when she came up, her face was dripping wet. Cleaned of makeup, she looked even younger. She didn't see us through the curtain at first, but then our waving must have gotten her attention. She parted his ugly curtains and she put her pretty face to the screen. It pressed against her skin and waffle-ironed her cheeks.

She was watching us as we'd spent the weekend watching her.

"Tell her to run," Katie-Marie said. "Tell her to get out of the house right now."

"We can't yell that," Paisley said. "He'll hear."

"Tell her she can come over here," Katie-Marie said. "You have that extra sleeping bag, Tasha. Tell her."

I hesitated.

"We can just yell fire?" Katie-Marie suggested. "Then she'll know it's an emergency and come out?"

"They both will then," Paisley said. "And Tasha's parents and brother will wake up too. And they'll be like, Where's the fire? And we'll have to say there isn't one."

"Let's write her a note," I said.

We started off with a simple message. I used my special notepad with the lavender paper and the pink lines, so she wouldn't be scared, and used marker to write in the biggest letters that could fit on the page so she could see from across the way.

WHO, I wrote, *ARE YOU?*

She cocked her head in the frame of the window, eyeing our words. She made no reply.

I held my arms as far out the window as I could, waving our sign, but still…nothing.

"Do you think she doesn't speak English maybe?" Katie-Marie asked. "Do you think she's from another country?"

"Oh, *everyone* speaks English," Paisley said. "Tell her our names. She's probably just shy."

PAISLEY, I wrote, with an arrow, and held the sign under the face of Paisley. *KATIE-MARIE*, for Katie-Marie. Then I shoved my body out of my window and showed her: *TASHA, I LIVE NEXT DOOR, HELLO.*

No change in expression. She bent down once more and came up with a wet face again. She dried her face with a towel. She barely blinked.

We offered her my cell number. We asked if she was in danger. We said, *Do you need help? Should we call 911?*

There wasn't any hint she understood.

We stopped, frustrated.

Then she made a movement. Sudden, like time skipping. There'd been a screen in the window, but she must have popped it out. Her bare arm, purple-taloned and catching the moonlight, came thrusting out into the open air. In her fist was something white and balled-up, like a hunk of tissues, but when she opened her hand, the white thing cascaded into one long, light expanse and caught the wind and fluttered down and down. I thought for a moment that she was performing a trick—a gasp of supernatural, like that time our few fingers lifted Paisley's body a whole inch above the carpet and when we removed our fingers, she stayed aloft from our concentrated energy alone. At least it felt like she did.

But no. The girl in the window had only thrown something white-colored out through the frame and it landed in a heap over the fence and on my side of the lawn.

A bedsheet? No, not a sheet from a bed. A veil.

The kind a bride would wear on her big day. Why was she showing this to us? Was this some kind of clue?

The veil drifted languidly in the faint wind, and understanding came over me.

"That's his wife," I said. The word turned my stomach. "He found some girl to marry him and he brought her home."

"No," Paisley said in horror.

The girl in the window watched us watching her. She did not scream. She didn't have to.

"Oh my freaking god," Katie-Marie said, and the dread in her voice made our hearts seize and our fear spike. "Do you think he made her marry him? Do you think he stole her passport? Do you think her parents know where she is? Do you think she's a prisoner?"

What did we know? Only that we had suspicions. We had to assume she was here on false pretenses, because who would marry Leonard by actual choice? We suspected we were the only ones alive who were aware she was here on Azalea Street, inside that house. He could have gotten her from anywhere. Maybe he found her in a parking lot. Maybe he picked her up on the side of the road and offered her a ride. Maybe he bought her off the Internet, like Paisley had innocently suggested. Maybe the girl came from nowhere we could name, and would fly off to nowhere we could pinpoint on a map, and maybe, ever after, we would remember her and think about where she could have ended up.

She replaced the screen in the window and turned off the light. We couldn't see where she went in the darkness, but we felt her there, right next door. Our subdivision vibrated with the sense of her, this stranger among us, this caged girl.

We didn't suspect then that she had come as if we'd called for her, as if our magical thinking on the night Paisley still smelled like yeasty-wet dough had come to fruition, rising up like the browned loaf of bread before it turned charcoal and burned.

"We have to help her," I said.

We tried to stay up all night, making plans that became all the more impossible, until Katie-Marie crashed on one side of my bed and Paisley crashed on the other and there was no room for me to sandwich in between, so I had to take the sleeping bag on the floor.

I curled up on the carpet, near the window. Just as I was about to drift to sleep, I sensed stirring over the fence. Something pulled on me, forced me to sit up.

I rubbed the sleep from my eyes. I was right: she'd come outside. I spied the girl through the window. There she was, his new bride, in the backyard of his house. His lawn actually touched our lawn—the same grass grew—but the white wooden fence stood between. Still, seeing her bare feet in the dewy-green blades of grass, mashing her toes in, like she wanted to wake the ants and gather up all the mud, it felt like she was walking *my* patch of green grass, wandering my backyard.

Where was Leonard? Sleeping. The light in his bedroom was off.

The girl was out there alone, in her fur-lined coat. Nothing on her feet and nothing holding back her hair. Without the makeup and the stockings, she looked smaller than before. She looked skinned.

She turned her face up, and then up some more, and at first I thought she was counting the stars above our subdivision, seeing if the stars here were the same ones she remembered from there, wherever she came from.

All this I could see through the window of my bedroom.

Then I noticed the sag in her cheeks and the shift-shaping of her mouth and realized she wasn't doing what I thought she was. She wasn't stargazing. She was searching the tree branches. I don't know why. Each one she came to was empty.

She reached the farthest tree. She put one hand, palm out, onto the rough bark and pressed it in, like she wanted the ridges imprinted on her skin. Then she pressed her other hand into a nearby spot. Then she pressed her face, the whole side of her face, cheek and chin and eye-bone and nose bridge and nostril, into the bark of the tree and stayed that way for some time.

The sounds of the neighborhood filtered through. I could hear them faintly: Mrs. Abernathy had her car alarm set too sensitive again and the acorns dropping kept setting it off. The Willards across the street were up way too late watching a sports game of some kind, I could tell by the cheers. A dog barked—the Ruiz dog. Another dog barked—that mini screechy one that belonged to the McCoys. A car pulled up, quiet, and a door opened, a giggle emerged, and then so silently like it was lined with cotton, the door closed. That was Aggie home from the party with her boyfriend; her mom would kill her if she knew she'd stayed out till three.

All around, the usual things were going on, and down there in Leonard's yard was the girl we thought could be his child bride, hugging a gnarly tree instead of sleeping in bed with him. It was the saddest thing I'd seen all year, even worse than the time Miranda from school showed us her suicide notes and asked us to pick the best-written one so she could impress her dad.

The girl stood still. She looked up in her dark coat

at the branches. The clouds moved to cover the stars and not even an owl hooted, but far away, down the street, Mrs. Abernathy's car alarm sounded again like a sudden, lonely song.

I closed my eyes. I told myself to get up, get to my feet, put on some jeans, they didn't have to be clean jeans, go outside. Go help that girl.

When I opened my eyes, the sky was filled with them. It was night, and they never came out at night, but there they were, a ferocious fog of winged creatures, covering her coat and coating her hair and seeming to beat all around her, to drone a cyclone around her body, to buzz. The birds had come back.

I couldn't have said for how long this went on. A few minutes at least, maybe more. I really had to pee, so it seemed much longer.

Then the flock of birds lifted, and the black sky was full of static like a dream had already been long going, and I was asleep and didn't come to again until sunrise.

We decided to knock on Leonard's door in the morning. We couldn't wait. We'd considered calling the police and leaving an anonymous tip to check his house for a missing girl, but then Paisley said we should see her in person first. How many times had we said Leonard squicked us out and our parents responded by saying we were exaggerating, making fun of the poor man, being cruel? If we saw the girl in daylight—better yet, if we could speak to her, face-to-face, if we could introduce ourselves and say a proper hello—then we'd know for sure if she needed saving.

It was Paisley's idea to bring the empty bag of sugar and ask if we could borrow some (we dumped it out in the garbage so it would look like it needed filling), and it was Katie-Marie's idea to invent a baking project we were doing to raise money for field hockey. We'd noticed how he paid extra careful attention to us whenever we wore the plaid uniform skirts.

We did look for it in the grass, walking all up and down the white picket fence trying to find it, but it wasn't there. The bridal veil. The wind must have blown it away in the night, or else the birds must have snatched it.

When we entered his yard through the fence divider, that's when we noticed them. Birds on the branches above us. Birds all along the bushes and on every shrub. Birds clamoring at his feeders and lining the sloping arc of his roof. Birds on the gutters. Birds perched on the roof of his car. There were so many. Silent. Pointy beaks aimed down on us, following our path to the back door, beady eyes on our every move.

Paisley knocked.

When he came to the door, he didn't open it all the way. Through the crack, the Sunday sunlight showed us his pink-tinged face, and his mouth, so fat, it looked swollen.

I held up the empty sugar bag but swallowed my words too fast. Katie-Marie grabbed on to my shirt from behind, pulling the neck tight and practically strangling me.

"Hi, Leonard. Good afternoon. I mean good morning. Um. We were hoping we could borrow some sugar?" Paisley said, taking over. She talked fast. Bakesale, she was saying. To raise money for the team. He didn't need to know that the season was over or that not all of us were on the team.

"What are you making?" he asked, and his words jolted us, because we'd forgotten to determine what it was we were pretending to make before we walked over.

"Cookies," Katie-Marie said from behind me while at the same time I said, "Cupcakes," and Paisley said, "Cake pops."

We shot glances at one another, alarmed.

"You'll need a lot of sugar, then," Leonard said. "It's early, so I'm not decent yet. Wait here."

He closed the screen and then the door behind it. Paisley had her body pressed up against the screen, and it practically scraped off the tip of her nose. She rested an ear to it, trying hard to listen. But she shook her head: nothing. We strained our ears in case the girl was crying for help, and we wondered from where she'd be calling—from the basement? From the broom closet beneath the stairs? The windows were shuttered. The walls were warm.

"We need to go in there," Katie-Marie said.

My hand reached out and there was this brave bolt of energy in my body that made me turn the knob. The screen door came open and then there was one more door to open and in seconds we were inside.

Leonard was in a pair of boxer shorts and a stretched-out V-neck shirt that horrified us with its display of chest hair. He held a large ceramic container that said SUGAR on one side. His glasses were crooked on his nose. "I told you to stay outside," he said. What—who—was he hiding?

"It's cold, we were cold," Katie-Marie started, but Paisley had had it with the lies.

"Where is she?" she said.

"Who?" Leonard said. He was holding the sugar container in front of his crotch, but believe us, we were already averting our eyes.

"The girl. The girl with the purple hair. The girl with the fur coat. The girl we saw you bring inside. Where's the girl!"

He set the sugar down. Outside a bird shrieked. Another followed, and another. The room was very hot, and his oven wasn't even on.

Katie-Marie was so shaken, she'd begun to cry. Paisley was on alert, hands in fists. I held the empty bag up like a weapon and a few kernels of sugar rattled inside. We were not prepared.

"What girl?" Leonard said. We watched his pink lips. How carefully he said it, how slow and with drawl, like he believed that because we were girls ourselves we could be fooled.

"We *saw* her, Leonard," Paisley said. "We saw her come in."

"There isn't any girl," Leonard said. "Apart from you three."

Once he said that, it happened. The sound of rustling from another room.

His neck snapped toward the noise, knowing he was caught, then trying to hide it. But he couldn't hide her.

"What's that!" Paisley shrieked, pointing wildly, vindicated and foaming at the mouth practically, and we kicked open the door and converged on the next room. We expected to find her there, cowering. The girl. She'd be in her coat, pulled up to hide her face. "It's us," we'd tell her. "It's us." At first she wouldn't know we'd come to rescue her.

But when we landed in the room, it was a room with no other doors out and only the way we'd come in. It was a room with shuttered windows, hiding the view of the neighbors' houses and all trace of sun. It was a room meant to be the dining room, maybe, but the table was covered with papers, so no one could eat a meal on it, and up above the table, like a centerpiece, was an object hung from a hook in the ceiling, swinging ever so slightly like someone had been here to give it a push. It was a cage built for a bird, the same one he'd carried out of the trunk. The cage was empty.

The room was empty too, except for the girls. There were girls everywhere. Girls on every surface. Girls splayed out on the table and girls spilled over the chairs. Girls pinned up against the walls and girls pasted to the back of the closet door. Girls propped up against the shuttered windows. Girls on the floor, some facedown and some face-up staring blankly at the ceiling. As we stood shocked in the doorway, a few girls skittered through the air as if from the sky itself, like a burst of bad weather, and Katie-Marie startled and stepped on one.

We were the girls. These were our photographs. It had been Leonard's hobby these past months to take pictures of us, from his porch or from his bedroom window, and he must have spent hours printing them all out to collect them—to collect *us*—together in this room.

There was Katie-Marie, bent over on the sidewalk picking up something she'd dropped. The camera focused on what was under her skirt. There was Paisley, in the hammock in my backyard, legs stretched out. The camera looked down her shirt and centered in on her crotch. There were girls I knew from down the street, and girls I knew from across the way, and the girl in the house behind mine, Aggie, slipping a bare leg out of a car in the dark night.

There were also photos of me, a great many—as if of all his targets, I was most wanted, I was the star. In some, I was sleeping. In others, I was on my lawn, or on my porch, or in my bedroom, getting undressed. Sometimes I was looking out my window, like he was looking into mine.

Leonard's photography hobby was worse than we'd guessed. What would he do now that he had us all inside his house, in real life?

We backed away and got jostled in panic. Paisley bumped into me, and I knocked into Katie-Marie. When we untangled and shot out of the room, Leonard was there, blocking the way through the hallway. None of us wanted to get near enough to touch him.

"The three of you," he said, in wonder. Like we'd fallen from the heavens into his cupped and waiting hand.

There were three of us, and one of him. We outnumbered him. We had strong legs from field hockey and track. We had sharp fingernails, painted in bright colors. We had knees and elbows and teeth.

But something held us back. It was all too real, all of a sudden. We'd suspected. We'd told tales. We'd heightened our stories into gross and grandiose lies. And even with all of that, we never really thought we were in danger.

The slithery smile on his face sent us into a tailspin. Until we looked past him. Until we saw what was there. Who was.

She was behind him. The black-eyed girl. Right there drinking at his ear, and somehow he didn't sense her hovering.

Then he must have caught something on our faces because he turned. How innocently he turned around to look.

She was strong. She grabbed his neck and dragged him back into the kitchen, and we followed the blur.

It was hard to keep focus. She was purple-black and without hard edges, like a cloud of static, a mass of feathered fury and fright. She didn't voice anything to us in any human language, but we heard it all the same. A high-pitched shriek. Something terrible and terribly right.

Paisley was shaking—since she'd seen the photographs, she hadn't stopped. But Katie-Marie was animated. "Get him!" she was crying, drowning out the wails. "Get him, get him!" We were surrounding him on the linoleum, but all we had to do was watch. Leonard had dropped the sugar container and there was white powder everywhere, covering him but also sifting into the air so it got in our eyes, our noses, our mouths, studding our tongues. How sweet it was.

She came at him, it looked like with her mouth. The sounds in the room were squishy and made of wet smacks. She was stabbing him, but she didn't have a weapon, not that we could see. Still, something was leaving punctures. Something was bulleting him with small holes.

Then quiet through the white haze. Dead calm.

Katie-Marie lifted her head. Paisley hiccupped uncontrollably, breaking the silence. We looked down and down. He was quite tall, and his legs took up a lot of space on the floor, so I had to step over him to get a view from a better angle.

It seemed like he'd been pecked to death, like from the knife beaks of a horde of birds. None of us could look at where his face had been. None of us wanted to remember his plushy lips, or his certain kind of smile.

"I—" Katie-Marie started, and said nothing else. Paisley was hiccupping and shaking.

The girl in the black-furred coat seemed fine, though. Black hides blood, so she looked clean, she looked calm.

"She—" Katie-Marie tried to say, and said nothing.

Through hiccups, Paisley spoke for all of us. "You," she told the girl. "Killed him." The way she said the words, it was almost a question.

"You have to go," I said to the girl. She stared me down and made no move. "Can you understand what I'm saying? You have to get yourself out of here. Do you get that?"

She only wrapped the coat tighter around herself. Her legs were bare underneath, and she didn't have shoes.

I turned to Paisley, I turned to Katie-Marie. "We have to get her out of here. She has to go."

"How?" Paisley said, and her voice was the smallest I'd heard it. "None of us can drive."

Katie-Marie was holding her nose and trying not to retch in the sink. Then she did retch, and I turned to the girl. Her eyes were perfectly black, swallowed by pupils. She didn't blink. "Who are you?" I said. That had been our first question.

She cocked her head to one side, like she was saying didn't I know already? Hadn't I known all along?

Katie-Marie was hunched over the sink, and Paisley was stunned into an un-Paisley-like silence as if she'd bitten off her own tongue. Only the hiccups shook her. I was the single coherent one left. I led a path through the red-spattered sugar. The back door was open. We'd forgotten to close it when we came in.

"Go," I said.

The girl stared at me, black eyes unblinking. Her mouth was covered in blood.

"Run," I said.

She must have heard me. But she didn't run. She didn't have to.

There was a point when she was still in the kitchen with us, the air heavy and sickly sweet with what she'd done to him, and then there was the point when her feet were lifted in the air and her legs, her beautiful legs, shrunk in and shifted. Her coat became a part of her body, or maybe it always was. Her arms—what was left of them—opened wide. A dark streak took off from the back steps and the sky caught it and it was a bird, it was always a bird, she was, and the bird soared up into the clouds, a rapid retreat of wings, until it was a speck, a small seed, a dot, a blink, a memory.

I wanted to give her a head start, so I waited a good while before calling my mother to say we'd come over to borrow some sugar and found Leonard stabbed to death on his kitchen floor. I said "stabbed" because we didn't know what else to call it. My mother was the one who called 911.

When the police questioned me—same as they questioned Paisley and Katie-Marie—they wanted to know only certain things. Their questions were so ordinary. Why did we knock on our neighbor's door so early on a Sunday morning? Where exactly did we find his body? What did we do next, after Paisley froze and started hiccupping and Katie-Marie puked in the sink?

They didn't mention the photographs, and we weren't sure if they were protecting us because they thought we couldn't handle it, or if they were waiting for us to say it first.

I didn't say, and Katie-Marie didn't say. Paisley didn't say either. We didn't want to give ourselves any motive, now that the girl was long gone. We'd all agreed on that ahead of time.

Besides, they couldn't pin anything on us. No witnesses, no fingerprints that matched ours on the body. No connection, except my house was right next door and my sugar bag was covered in blood on the floor. It was all I could do not to wave my arm up at the blank blue sky and tell them to search there for answers. Except that would have given her away.

Then the police had one last question, and it was here that I sat up straight and felt the heart in the cage of my chest pounding.

Could I describe the girl who was in his house the night before?

I didn't know who let that piece of information loose, Paisley or Katie-Marie, but to me this question had only one answer. "What girl?"

It was easy to deny her. Even as I remembered the blacks of her eyes, and the painted points on the ends of her fingers. That was only my mind making her into what I thought she should be.

"So there wasn't ever any girl," the police said, they made me say, they made me write in some kind of official statement and sign while my parents watched, and I had to do it. I don't know what Paisley said, and I don't know what Katie-Marie said. But I said we were mistaken. It's what we owed her. We thought we saw a girl, but it was dark. It was dark outside and confusing and we were wrong.

"So you're sure?" they said.

"I'm sure," I told them. "I never saw any girl."

Because, could a girl be so terrible? Could a girl tear a man's face out and could a girl litter his body with holes from the sharpest parts of her red mouth? Could a girl do something so perfect, and then vanish into the clouds?

Could a girl come at the exact moment we needed her? Could she come only to protect other girls?

I wasn't lying when I said that to the police. In the end, she wasn't even anymore a girl.

For Leonard's wake—closed-casket; no one would have been able to stomach it otherwise—my mother made me help her bake his signature sugar-cream pie. His murder would be unsolved for some weeks, and then I guess it fell off the police's radar, because summer was coming, and the softball tournament was approaching, and we were fund-raising for the dying oak trees now, and at some point our parents said it was safe to canvass the neighborhood and knock on every door.

Before his house sold, I ducked under the crime-scene tape and went onto his lawn. I swiped one of his bird feeders and put it on our side of the picket fence, and robins and little swallows started to flock to it. I fed them seeds from my trail-mix packs and sometimes bits of sugar-coated breakfast crunch. Sometimes I'd go outside under the bright beautiful blue and all I'd hear were these little titters, like the birds were trying to tell me something in a language I couldn't understand.

I tried to tell them I knew. I tried to say thanks. I spent a lot of time in the backyard, searching the sky.

About the authors

Chesya Burke has written and published nearly a hundred fiction pieces and articles within the genres of science fiction, fantasy, noir and horror. Her story collection, *Let's Play White*, is being taught in universities around the country. In addition, Burke wrote several articles for the *African American National Biography* in 2008, and Burke's novel, *The Strange Crimes of Little Africa*, debuts later this fall. Poet Nikki Giovanni compared her writing to that of Octavia Butler and Toni Morrison.

Burke's thesis was on the comic book character Storm from the X-MEN, and her comic, *Shiv*, is scheduled to debut in 2016.

Burke is currently pursuing her PhD in English at University of Florida. She's Co-Chair of the Board of Directors of Charis Books and More, one of the oldest feminist book stores in the country.

Leah Cypess wrote her first short story—in which the narrator was an ice cream cone—at the age of six, and sold her first piece of fiction while in high school. She has degrees in biology, journalism, and law, and has traveled to Iceland, Israel, Jordan, and Costa Rica, among other places. She now lives with her family near Washington, D.C. She is the author of four young adult fantasy novels: *Mistwood, Nightspell, Death Sworn*, and *Death Marked*. You can find out more about her and her writing at www.leahcypess.com.

Tamlyn Dreaver grew up in rural Western Australia and now lives in Melbourne. She's never had a secret basement or a dragon nesting in the backyard or anything nearly as interesting, so she makes up stories about them instead.

She can be found on Twitter at @tamlyn_dreaver, though she doesn't really say much, and also on the web at www.tamlyndreaver.com.

Joel Enos is a writer and editor who has written comics (*Sonic the Hedgehog*) and graphic novels (*Ben 10 Omniverse*) and published short fiction in *Whispers from the Abyss, Visibility* and *Flapperhouse*. His comics adaptation of Anais Nin's short story, "Under a Glass Bell," with artist Fiona Meng was published in *A Café in Space*. He's also edited projects for Image Comics and worked on best-selling manga for VIZ Media. You can keep up with his work at joelenos. com or follow him on Twitter at @joelenos.

Felix Gilman is the author of five novels, including *The Half Made World, The Rise Of Ransom City*, and most recently *The Revolutions*. He lives in New York.

Cat Hellisen is the South African-born writer of the fantasy novels *When the Sea is Rising Red* and *House of Sand and Secrets*. She has had short stories included in *Apex, Shimmer, Fantasy & Science Fiction*, and

Tor.com, and in 2015 took the Short Story Day Africa prize with *The Worme Bridge*. Her latest novel is a folktale for the loveless, *Beastkeeper*.

James Robert Herndon is a graduate of Clarion West and the Warren Wilson MFA Program for Writers. His stories have appeared in *Strange Horizons*, *Halfway Down the Stairs*, and other publications. His short story "Mammals" was selected by Jeff VanderMeer as the winner of the Omnidawn fiction contest, and is now available as a chapbook. He lives with his wife in Atlanta, where he works in the field of digital accessibility and is a dog transporter for a local animal shelter. His website is jamesrobertherndon.com.

Sylvia Anna Hivén was born and raised in Sweden but lives and writes in Atlanta, Georgia. Her fiction has appeared in *Beneath Ceaseless Skies, Daily Science Fiction*, and others.

Marissa Lingen lives in the Minneapolis suburbs with her family. She is the author of more than one hundred fantasy and science fiction short stories, including one in last year's volume of this series. She likes her chocolate bitter, her snow at least knee-deep, and her dogs in all sizes.

Heather Morris is a cyborg librarian living in North Carolina. Her fiction and poetry have appeared in

Strange Horizons, Apex Magazine, and *Daily Science Fiction,* among other publications. You can find her on Twitter @NotThatHeatherM.

E.C. Myers was assembled in the U.S. from Korean and German parts and raised by a single mother and the public library in Yonkers, New York. He is the author of numerous short stories and three young adult books: the Andre Norton Award-winning *Fair Coin*; *Quantum Coin*; and *The Silence of Six.* His next novel, *Against All Silence,* a thriller about teenage hacktivists investigating a vast conspiracy, was published in July 2016 from Adaptive Books. E.C. currently lives with his wife, son, and three doofy pets in Pennsylvania. You can find traces of him all over the internet, but especially at http://ecmyers.net and on Twitter: @ecmyers.

Daniel José Older is the author of the Bone Street Rumba urban fantasy series from Penguin's Roc Books and the Young Adult novel *Shadowshaper* (Scholastic, 2015), a *New York Times* Notable Book of 2015, which was shortlisted for the Kirkus Prize in Young Readers' Literature and named one of *Esquire*'s 80 Books Every Person Should Read. He co-edited the Locus and World Fantasy nominated anthology *Long Hidden: Speculative Fiction from the Margins of History.* His short stories and essays have appeared in the *Guardian, NPR, Tor.com, Salon, BuzzFeed,*

Fireside Fiction, the New Haven Review, PANK, Apex and *Strange Horizons* and the anthologies *Subversion* and *Mothership: Tales Of Afrofuturism And Beyond.* You can find his thoughts on writing, read dispatches from his decade-long career as an NYC paramedic and hear his music at http://danieljoseolder.net/, on YouTube and @ djolder on Twitter.

Sarah Pinsker is the author of the 2015 Nebula Award winning novelette "Our Lady of the Open Road." Her novelette "In Joy, Knowing the Abyss Behind" was the 2014 Sturgeon Award winner and a 2013 Nebula finalist. Her fiction has been published in magazines including *Asimov's, Strange Horizons, Lightspeed, Fantasy & Science Fiction,* and *Uncanny,* among others, and in anthologies including *Accessing the Future: A Disability Themed Anthology of Speculative Fiction* and *Long Hidden.* This is her second appearance in the *YA Year's Best.* She is also a singer/songwriter with three albums on various independent labels and a fourth forthcoming. She lives in Baltimore, Maryland with her wife and dog. She can be found online at sarahpinsker.comand twitter.com/sarahpinsker.

Rivqa Rafael is a writer and editor based in Sydney. She started writing speculative fiction well before earning degrees in science and writing, although they have probably helped. Her previous gig as subeditor and reviews editor for *Cosmos* magazine likewise fueled her imagination. "Function A" was her first published short story; she has since been published in *The Never Never Land* (CSFG Publishing) and *Defying Doomsday* (Twelfth Planet Press). She can be found at rivqa.net and on Twitter as @enoughsnark.

Erica L. Satifka's fiction has appeared in *Clarkesworld*, *Shimmer*, *Queers Destroy Science Fiction*, and various other places. Her debut novel *Stay Crazy* will be released by Apex Publications in August 2016. She lives in Portland, Oregon, with her spouse Rob and three needy cats. Visit her online at ericasatifka.com or on Twitter @ericasatifka.

Nova Ren Suma is the author of four novels, including the YA novels *Imaginary Girls*, *17 & Gone*, and *The Walls Around Us*, which was named the #1 Kids' Indie Next Pick for Spring 2015 and a Best Book of 2015 by *The Boston Globe*, NPR, *School Library Journal*, the Chicago Public Library, and *The Horn Book*. Her short story "The Birds of Azalea Street" appeared in the YA horror anthology *Slasher Girls & Monster Boys*. She has an MFA in fiction from Columbia University and a BA in writing & photography from Antioch College and has been a fellow in fiction with the New York Foundation for the Arts, the MacDowell Colony, and Yaddo. She teaches in the MFA program in Writing for Children & Young Adults at Vermont College of Fine Arts and has taught YA novel writing at Columbia University, the Djerassi Resident Artists Program, the Highlights Foundation, and elsewhere. She is from various small towns across the Hudson Valley and now lives in New York City. Visit her online at novaren.com.

Shveta Thakrar is a writer of South Asian–flavored fantasy, social justice activist, and part-time nagini. Her work has appeared or is forthcoming in *Interfictions Online*, *Clockwork Phoenix 5*, *Mythic Delirium*, *Uncanny*, *Faerie*, *Strange Horizons*, *Kaleidoscope: Diverse YA Science Fiction and Fantasy Stories*, and *Steam-Powered 2: More Lesbian Steampunk Stories*. When not spinning stories about spider silk and shadows, magic and marauders, and courageous girls illuminated by dancing rainbow flames, Shveta crafts, devours books, daydreams, draws, travels, bakes, and occasionally even plays her harp.

Genevieve Valentine's (www.genevievevalentine. com) first novel, *Mechanique: A Tale of the Circus Tresaulti*, won the 2012 Crawford Award. Her second, *The Girls of the Kingfisher Club*, appeared in 2014 to acclaim. *Persona* appeared in 2015 and sequel *Icon* is due later this year. Her short fiction has appeared in *Clarkesworld*, *Strange Horizons*, *Journal of Mythic Arts*, *Tor.com*, and others; several have been reprinted in Best of the Year anthologies. Her nonfiction has appeared at *NPR.org, the AV Club,* and *The New York Times.* She has written *Catwoman for DC,* and is currently writing *Xena: Warrior Princess* for Dynamite! Her appetite for bad movies is insatiable.

Sabrina Vourvoulias is the author of *Ink* (Crossed Genres, 2012), a speculative novel that draws on her memories of Guatemala's armed internal conflict, and of the Latinx experience in the United States. It was named to Latinidad's Best Books of 2012. Her stories have appeared at *Tor.com, Strange Horizons, Crossed Genres* and in a number of anthologies, including *Long Hidden: Speculative Fiction from the Margins of History* (Crossed Genres, 2014), and forthcoming in *Latino/a Rising* (Wings Press, 2017). She is the executive editor of *aldianews.com* in Philadelphia, and was the editor of Al Día's book *200 Years of Latino History in Philadelphia* (Temple University Press, 2012). She lives in Pennsylvania with her husband and daughter. Follow her on Twitter @followthelede.

Sean Williams is an award-winning, #1 *New York Times* bestselling author of over forty books and one hundred short stories, plus the odd odd poem for readers of all ages. He has been called many things in his time, including 'the premier Australian speculative fiction writer of the age' *(Aurealis),* the 'emperor of sci-fi' *(Adelaide Advertiser),* and the 'king of chameleons' *(Australian Book Review)* for the diversity of his writing. As well as his original fiction, he has occasionally worked in universes created by other people, such as *Star Wars* and *Doctor Who*. He also enjoys collaborating, most recently with Garth Nix on their Troubletwisters series. His latest novel is *Fall,* the concluding volume of the Twinmaker series, in which universe "Noah No-one and the Infinity Machine" is set. He lives in the dry, flat lands of South Australia, just up the road from a chocolate factory, with his wife and family and pet plastic fish.

Caroline M. Yoachim lives in Seattle and loves cold cloudy weather. She is the author of dozens of short stories, appearing in *Fantasy & Science Fiction, Clarkesworld, Asimov's,* and *Lightspeed,* among other places. Her debut short story collection, *Seven Wonders of a Once and Future World & Other Stories,* is coming out with Fairwood Press in August 2016. For more about Caroline, check out her website at http://carolineyoachim.

Honourable Mentions for 2015

The following is a list of stories we found worthy, but didn't include in our final selection. Some of them were discounted due to being more middle grade or adult than YA according to our definition of YA, or due to not having enough of a speculative element. Others were very good but didn't end up in our final list for various reasons including having chosen a similar story already or wanting to select stories from a wide variety of fiction venues. The honourable mentions list is in alphabetical order according to author's last name.

Acks, Rachael, "Superhero with Crooked Nails", *Protectors 2: Heroes: Stories to Benefit PROTECT*

Bigelow, Susan Jane, "Traffic Circles of Old Connecticut", *Luna Station Quarterly*

Bowles, David, "Ancient Hunger, Silent Wings", *Devilfish Review Quarterly*

Choksi, Roshani, "The Star Maiden", *Shimmer*

Choksi, Roshani, "The Vishakanya's Choice", *Book Smugglers*

Clitheroe, Heather, "Wild Things Got to Go Free", *Beneath Ceaseless Skies*

Connolly, Tina, "That seriously obnoxious time I was stuck at the witch Rimelda's hundredth birthday party", *Tor.com*

Cornell, Paul, "Find a Way Home", *Uncanny*

Dawson, Delilah S., "Catcall", *Uncanny*

Doyle, Aidan, "Naoko's Dragons", *Orbit Magazine*

Enos, Angela, "Shallow Living", *Visibility Fiction*

Forrest, Amanda, "Of Apricots and Dying", *Asimov's*

Gaal, Kim, "In Sheep's Clothing", *Andromeda Spaceways Inflight Magazine*

Hall, Kate, "The Snow Globe", *Flash Fiction Online*

Hans, Sarah, "FawnGirl14", *Not Our Kind*

Heartfield, Kate, "Limestone, Lye, and the Buzzing of Flies", *Strange Horizons*

Holl-Jensen, Carlea, "The Lady's Maid", *Queers Destroy Fantasy*

Huang, S. L., "By Degrees and Dilatory Time", *Strange Horizons*

Im, Christina, "They Held Starlight", *YARN*

Kabza, K. J., "Steady on Her Feet", *Beneath Ceaseless Skies*

Kemp, Adrik, "Drought", *The Never Never Land*

Kiste, Gwendolyn, "Things to Know About the Ten Questions", *Nightmare Magazine*

Lane, Verity, "The Springwood Shelter for Genetically Modified Animals", *Crossed Genres*

Lingen, Marissa, "It Brought Us All Together", *Strange Horizons*

Lingen, Marissa, "Ten Stamps Viewed Under Water", *Fantasy & Science Fiction*

Liow, Robert, "Spider Here", *The SEA is Ours*

Liu, Ken, "The Gods Have Not Died in Vain", *The End Has Come*

McCullough, Kelly, "The Totally Secret Origin of Foxman", *Tor.com*

McFarland Kyle, Rebecca, "Cross the River", *Lost Trails: Forgotten Tales of the Weird West*

McGuire, Seanan, "In Skeleton Leaves", *Operation Arcana*

Meadows, Foz, "Bright Moon", *Cranky Ladies of History*

Mehentee, J., "The Salt Mosquito's Bite and the Goddess' Sting", *Strange Horizons*

Mehrota, Rati, "Charaid Dreams", *Apex*

Mok, D. K., "The Heart of the Labyrinth", *In Memory: A Tribute to Terry Pratchett*

Mudge, Faith, "Blueblood", *Hear Me Roar*

Muir, Tamsyn, "The Deepwater Bride", *Fantasy & Science Fiction*

Norton, K. C., "The Kiss", *Flash Fiction Online*

Nuallak, Pear, "The Insects and Women Sing Together", *The SEA is Ours*

Pinsker, Sarah, "Remembery Day", *Apex*

Reed, Gabby, "Glaciers Made You", *Strange Horizons*

Rich, Samantha, "Screens", *Accessing the Future*

Roberts, Adam, "Zayinim", *Jews Vs. Zombies*

Rodriguez, Jason, "Try Looking Ahead", *Try Looking Ahead*

Rustad, A. Merc, "Where Monsters Dance", *Inscription*

Seiberg, Effie, "Redchip Bluechip", *Crossed Genres*

Sparks, Cat, "Dragon Girl", *The Never Never Land*

Sparks, Cat, "Veteran's Day", *Hear Me Roar*

Vibbert, Marie, "Butterflies on a Barbed Wire", *Analog*

Ward, Marlee Jane, "The Walking Thing", *Interfictions*

Wilde, Fran, "Bent the Wing, Dark the Cloud", *Beneath Ceaseless Skies*

Winters, Ben, "Heaven Come Down", *The End Has Come*

Yap, Isabel, "Find Me", *Apex*

Yap, Isabel, "Good Girls", *Shimmer*

Yoachim, Caroline, "Ninety-Five Percent Safe", *Asimovs*

Year's Best YA Speculative Fiction

edited by Julia Rios and Alisa Krasnostein
2013 — ISBN: 9781922101273
2014 — ISBN: 9781922101358

Our goal is to uncover the best young adult short fiction of the year published in the anthologies dedicated to the form, the occasional special edition of a magazine, and individual pieces appearing in otherwise "adult" anthologies and magazines, and bring them together in one accessible collection.

Fans of *Kaleidoscope* will find more tales of wonder, adventure, diversity, and variety in this collection devoted to stories with teen protagonists.

Teaching notes are available.

Kaleidoscope: Diverse YA Science Fiction and Fantasy Stories

edited by Julia Rios and Alisa Krasnostein
ISBN: 9781922101112

Kaleidoscope collects fun, edgy, meditative, and hopeful YA science fiction and fantasy with diverse leads.

These twenty original stories tell of scary futures, magical adventures, and the joys and heartbreaks of teenage life.

Featuring New York Times bestselling and award winning authors along with newer voices:

Garth Nix, Sofia Samatar, William Alexander, Karen Healey, E.C. Myers, Tansy Rayner Roberts, Ken Liu, Vylar Kaftan, Sean Williams, Amal El-Mohtar, Jim C. Hines, Faith Mudge, John Chu, Alena McNamara, Tim Susman, Gabriela Lee, Dirk Flinthart, Holly Kench, Sean Eads, and Shveta Thakrar.

Defying Doomsday

edited by Tsana Dolichna and Holly Kench

ISBN: 9781922101402

Teens form an all-girl band in the face of an impending comet.
A woman faces giant spiders to collect silk and protect her family.
New friends take their radio show on the road in search of
plague survivors.
A man seeks love in a fading world.
How would you survive the apocalypse?

Defying Doomsday is an anthology of apocalypse fiction featuring disabled and chronically ill protagonists, proving it's not always the "fittest" who survive—it's the most tenacious, stubborn, enduring and innovative characters who have the best chance of adapting when everything is lost.

In stories of fear, hope and survival, this anthology gives new perspectives on the end of the world, from:

Corinne Duyvis, Janet Edwards, Seanan McGuire, Tansy Rayner Roberts, Stephanie Gunn, Elinor Caiman Sands, Rivqa Rafael, Bogi Takács, John Chu, Maree Kimberley, Octavia Cade, Lauren E Mitchell, Thoraiya Dyer, Samantha Rich, and K Evangelista.